Praise

Bridges between Our Hearts *is a beautiful exploration of what it means to be a family, navigating the joyful and agonizing territories of love, loss, and deep soul connection. Jennifer Collins uses the metaphor of bridges to help us fully feel the thread of love that doesn't die when we lose someone, including how we traverse the bridges of faith, hope, independence, and interdependence.*

> —Sharon Rosen, Mindfulness Coach, Intuitive Guide, and author of *Crazy World, Peaceful Heart*

A bridge analogy is perfect for this heartwarming story of a family's love, loss, and building bridges between generations to come back together. The sacrifices, devotion, and love so evident in this family saga will pull at your heartstrings and leave you satisfied.

> —Laurie Gifford Adams, author of *Attic Letters: Secrets of Love and War*

Collins skillfully weaves a poignant narrative exploring the redefining of purpose and meaning while grieving loss amidst the little bumps and big potholes of life. Journey with her on the winding path to find signs of connection, hope, and love that add a rich depth to the narrative.

> —Teresa Q. Bitner, author of *Soul Love: How A Dog Taught Me to Breathe Again* and founder of Bold Fulfilled Coaching

This author seems to excel in two aspects of novel writing—first, her ability to offer the reader strong, interesting characters to get to know and to root for. Her protagonist, Larissa, is particularly memorable, a woman who's suffered a lot in her life but is determined to find a better life for herself. The second aspect is the "spiritual" element, through which the author successfully uses her characters to explore love and loss....

So, if you happen to be on the hunt for a cleverly plotted drama populated with characters who enjoy exploring life, the afterlife, and all things spiritual, this book is for you. However, I would recommend reading the first two novels first; it'll help you to get to know Larissa and what she's been through.

—Wishing Shelf Book Review, 4-star rating

Also by Jennifer Collins

Comfort in the Wings
Book One in the "Love That Does Not Die" Trilogy

With striking clarity of prose and a feeling for surprising human connections, Collins, in her debut, reveals the inner life of a woman facing grief, uncertainty, and the possibility of restoring severed relationships.... From the first page, Collins demonstrates rare acuity and precision in pinning down Larissa's complex, shifting emotions.... This detailed, immersive novel of a woman facing grief offers wisdom and surprise connections. —BookLife Reviews

Wonders in the Waves
Book Two in the "Love That Does Not Die" Trilogy

In this outstanding tale of love, loss, and redemption ... Collins grabs readers by the heartstrings and doesn't let go until the final page is turned.... [Her] lyrical prose and touching insights are as comforting as waves hitting the shore, even as the story takes readers places they might not expect, such as a surprisingly cathartic visit to a tattoo parlor. Well-drawn characters reveal surprising, but ultimately believable plot twists.... Beautifully written and heartbreakingly real, this is a first-rate novel women's fiction lovers will quickly devour. —*BookLife Reviews* "Editor's Pick"

Bridges between Our Hearts

Book Three in the
"Love That Does Not Die" Trilogy

Jennifer Collins

Words in the Wings Press, Inc.
New York

Published by: Words in the Wings Press, Inc.
2366 Turk Hill Rd.
Victor, NY 14564
wordsinthewingspress2021@gmail.com

978-1-7376766-7-6 Hardcover

978-1-7376766-8-3 Softcover

978-1-7376766-9-0 Electronic Book

Library of Congress Control Number: 2023924061

Publisher's Cataloging-in-Publication data

Names: Collins, Jennifer E., author.
Title: Bridges between our hearts / Jennifer Collins.
Description: Victor, NY: Words in the Wings Press, Inc., 2024.
Identifiers: LCCN: 2023924061 | ISBN: 978-1-7376766-7-6 (hardcover) | 978-1-7376766-8-3 (paperback) | 978-1-7376766-9-0 (ebook)
Subjects: LCSH Family--Fiction. | Adoption--Fiction. | Parent and child--Fiction. | Women--Fiction. | BISAC FICTION / General | FICTION / Family life / General | FICTION / Sagas | FICTION / Women
Classification: LCC PS3603.O454255 B75 2024 | DDC 813.6--dc23

Author photos, back cover and interior: Photography by Anna

Cover design by Sarah Maxwell

Interior design by MediaNeighbours.com

First Edition

Printed in the USA

Although portions of the content of this book, including but not limited to events, people, or entities, were inspired by real life encounters, they have been adjusted or woven together in entirely new ways to create a story that is fiction. Please—if you think you might know someone—forget it and allow yourself to enter the lives and journeys of the characters within these pages.

To Andrew
I'm honored to be your business partner,
Happy to be your neighbor,
And blessed beyond measure to be your mother.
May the bridges between our hearts last forever —
illuminated by the presence of
loved ones here and afar.

1

Fall, 2019

Memory is the diary that we all carry about with us.
OSCAR WILDE

Dear Diary:
Haven't done this in awhile! I wrote diaries for years—
total stream of consciousness stuff, dumping my emotions out
on paper gave me a chance to get it out and then move on.

Until it didn't. Until moving on felt insurmountable. When
the shit hit the fan two-and-a-half years ago, my old ways of
coping were useless.

Now, I want to try again. Try to get some thoughts down
on paper every now and then. Not sure why this moment? Not
sure if I'm writing for myself, to my family/future family, or just
putting it out into the universe. No matter, actually. It's the writing
that brings me some solace, some clarity.

If some great-grandchild happens to stumble upon this
diary someday, I'm putting down my current cast of characters
in the front cover of this diary. I remember as a little girl, finding

a diary of my great-grandmother's and being totally fascinated by her list of children we never knew she had (two died shortly after birth, another as a toddler after drinking poison) and a sister who had run away never to be seen again. The twists and turns in my configuration of family and friends might cause a poor reader's head to spin without a list.

So, here goes—in chronological order (or some semblance of that sequence, anyway!):

Maggie and Tom Whitcomb: My parents; passed away five and seven years ago . . . oh, how I miss them. My kids called them Gamma and Pops.

Jeff Whitcomb: My sweet, younger brother; also passed—damn cancer!

Emery Everett Lewis: My firstborn child, b. 1982—my mother orchestrated an adoption because I was only sixteen. Never thought I'd see him again, but old letters of my mother's, all kinds of searches, DNA, and ultimately, his adoptive mother, Harriett, reunited us last year—2018. The year I finally knew all three of my children.

Steven Parsons: First husband, such a good person. I left him after a miscarriage, but always kept in touch. Accepted a consulting gig from him two years ago and we realized, by putting time lines and DNA data together, that he is actually Eric's father. Long story, but we're good friends again.

Eric: My son, b. 1993, with Steven. Ran away when the going was tough with his baby sister. Since he's been back, he's become my rock, my anchor. We're as close as can be.

Roger: Second husband; arrogant son of a gun. The only good from our marriage is Emma.

Emma: My sweet daughter, b. 1997; smart, kind, carried the weight of the world on her shoulders. Gone far too soon, d. 2017.

Renee: Dear friend; feisty, passionate, with me through thick and thin.

Isabel: Another dear friend; kind, reflective, a steadying force. Single mom, two kids—Lisa (sorta named after a shortened version of my name—she's like a little adult) and Bobby.

Marie: Not family, but the only counselor (after many!) who has ever helped me navigate the chaos. I'm guessing my written musings might, at times, include her words of wisdom.

Hilary: Became Eric's wife last year—delightful young woman. She lost a brother, David, around the same time that Emma passed. She and her father, Paul, quickly became integral parts of our lives.

Nina: Steven's daughter. Until Steven's DNA was out in the databases to verify our hunch of him being Eric's father, he never knew he'd fathered another child.

Beth Lewis: Everett's daughter, b. 2013; my granddaughter—only met her a little over a year ago when reunited with Everett (see above), already a shining star in my life.

Monica: A friend of Emma's that Eric met when he was missing in 2017. She's come into our lives again.

And, it's anyone's guess who will be next.
I'll keep you posted,

Larissa

2

How do I do this without you?
How does anyone continue in a story
that ended before it was supposed to?
LIZ NEWMAN

An ivy-covered stone archway welcomes me into the green haven of the park closest to home. My pace quickens as I spot the next curve in the path, leading to my favorite bench nestled in colorful perennial gardens. Catching sight of the blue-green pond serves to quiet my breathing. My mind wanders to the first time I felt the presence of Emma here. When the butterfly landed on my knee, then lingered longer than I could hold my breath; it was clear she was connecting with me. Whenever I return, so does that feeling, and sensing her around me is calming. For that, I seek out this place. To relish in the certainty that although she is not here in physical form, she is with me in spirit. The bustle around me disappears and time stands still.

Just as I decide to turn around and head home, my phone is ringing. Figuring it's some kind of annoying sales call, I start to press the decline button, then see that it's Eric. Middle of the day? *Hmm—not typical.*

"Mom, where are you, what are you doing?"

I smile and think, *At least he's consistent. Direct, demanding.*

"I'm out walking. Aren't you at work?"

"I'm on lunch break. Are you almost home? I really need to talk to you."

"You are talking to me."

"No, I mean in person—need to tell you something. I should have told you a long time ago. Don't go into panic mode, everything's fine, but this just can't wait any longer."

"Okay, okay, I'll be home in ten minutes. Are you sick? Is something going on with Hilary?" I've come to love Eric's wife like another of my own.

"No, she's fine, nothing like that. I got another email from someone who once knew Emma, and well--"

"What do you mean, another? Why didn't you--"

"Long story—just head home and I'll meet you there."

As I come to my driveway, I see Eric's car turning onto the street. I think back to how many times over the years I could breathe a little easier as soon as I saw his car, or Emma's, a block away from home. No matter the circumstance, once they were in my sight, we'd deal with it together. That same sense of connection comes over me as we find ourselves in the kitchen—the quintessential gathering place.

"Shall I put on some coffee for us, Eric? I could use some after my walk."

"Yeah, sure, whatever. Can you come sit down?" He's rubbing his hands together—he used to do that as a little kid when he was nervous to tell me something.

"Do you remember when I told you about Monica? The woman who I came upon while on a trail out West?"

How could I forget? It takes focus and control not to start replaying that whole string of events when Eric left home while Emma was struggling. Slammed the door and didn't return for months. *Don't let your mind wander, Larissa, just answer his question.*

"Yes—the one who seemed to come out of nowhere, pointed to a monarch and said she could see Emma hovering around you?"

He nods his head and rubs his hands more urgently.

"You told me that whole story when you first got back. You told me about Monica after I told you I connected with Emma by seeing a psychic medium. Remember?"

"I didn't forget—not at all, not ever. I left something out, though. At the time, you and I were trying desperately to catch up after those lousy months apart. I didn't think it was important to share right then—thought it could wait till things calmed down. But then--"

"But what, Eric? This has to do with an email? I'm confused."

"Let me back up. When Monica came walking down that trail, I told you it was amazing. She had this presence—she was ethereal, yet earthy. Then, she told me about being able to see people who've transitioned to the spirit world, and being sure the monarch butterflies were a sign, a message from Emma. She was pretty damn convincing. I didn't want to believe Emma had died, refused to believe it. Until I had no choice. But here's the part I left out when I told you before, Mom. She knew her, Monica knew Emma. She claimed that Emma was the one who sent her to me."

"What do you mean? How could this young woman in the middle of—where were you then, Wyoming? Colorado? Wherever? How could she know Emma? I never met her, never even heard her name. How did she find you?"

"She met Emma at the rehab center. Monica was a counselor there; I think she said an arts therapist. And, well, they got pretty close. Monica told me they both liked similar music and talked about song lyrics and the meaning of particular songs, that kinda stuff."

The mention of lyrics sparks a memory. "Wow, this just came back to me: Emma asked me to mail her songbook while she was in rehabilitation. She said staff usually limited the reading materials residents could have, but thought if I wrote a letter about how important this particular songbook was, one that included lyrics, they might let her have it. Never gave it another thought—till now. Maybe your Monica was who I wrote to. How did she end up in Colorado with you?"

"It makes no sense, Mom, unless you believe in these unexpected connections, or signs, or whatever, that keep happening since Emma's been gone. I guess Emma gave her my contact info at some point. Monica said she was led to me. I don't know how to explain it, except she came along, helped me, then made me see it was time to get back home. And, well, she asked me to keep in touch. Once I made it back here, I sent her word that I was back home safe, and thanked her."

"So, then, she sent you an email? Or two? What's she doing now? Why is she still in touch?"

"Here's the part I should have told you: when I got the first email, I just didn't know if it would actually amount to anything. Monica, well, she wrote a song. A song about Emma. And now, she's going to record it. She thought I, uh, we, should know."

A song about Emma? Someone I don't know, didn't even realize was connected enough to Emma to write about her, is recording music inspired by her? Can someone just do that? I guess so. I can't formulate any words right now about how I feel.

Except for one thing, one thing for certain. "I want to hear it." I add, "And I want to talk to Monica, like yesterday."

Shortly after Eric told me the story, he forwarded Monica's contact information to me. I've left her two messages already. Ever since Eric and I talked about Monica and her song, I can't get the idea out of my head. And now I can't get Emma out of my head. The jumbled-up mix of feelings about Emma hadn't monopolized my thoughts quite as much in recent months. So much has been happening in my life. Finding Everett, the son I'd been forced to give away as a baby, has turned my world upside down, in a good way. And getting to know his little girl, Beth— my granddaughter—has brought a new kind of love into my life, along with hope for our future.

Guilt settles in. The guilt around being the mom who let her slip away from this world, instead of protecting her. For months, now years, I thought about Emma constantly. *Could I be forgetting her? I'm a lousy mom to let the gut-wrenching loss of my daughter move out of the forefront of my mind.*

Thinking back to my counseling session with Marie yesterday helps me halt this negative cycle. She says this type of self-talk— that I didn't do as much as possible for Emma or that I deserted Everett—is the worst form of cruelty. Cruelty to oneself has no purpose. The world is brutal enough without me piling more on. And one of the things she asked me was, "Why would you ever push yourself back down into a dark hole when you've worked so hard to emerge into the light, to do good in Emma's name, and to shine brightness on others who are stumbling in the dark?" Backsliding is too easy. Staying the course takes effort.

Determined to do something positive, I'll put the effort into something that makes a difference. Sitting around waiting for Monica to call back accomplishes nothing, so I log in to my work email and plod through the last two days of correspondence.

Three hours into that virtual abyss, an email pops up on my screen from someone I don't recognize. Clicking on it, I can't even focus on the words strung into sentences because my eyes leap to an attachment at the bottom. An attachment titled "Smiles from Her Heart." My own heart begins to race immediately. *Is this the song?*

My cursor hovers over the title. I finally click on it and am immediately furious at my laptop, at Monica, at the irritating instruction to choose which program should be used to open the file. *How should I know what program to use? For God's sake, there's a song sitting out there in the digital universe dedicated to my child and I can't get the blasted thing to open and play. This is some kind of sick game to play with my heart.*

Dropping my head onto the desk, I start pounding the surface in front of me. "Come on, will you, just open!"

"All right, geez—cool down, I didn't hear you answer me right away." Sounds like Renee's voice. She must have been knocking at the door. Did she hear me pounding and screaming at the damn computer to open?

"I'm in here—I didn't know you were at the door. I'm so frustrated. Come see if you can help me before I smash something, will you?"

Only a long-time friend can breeze into the room, almost floating on air, after my half-crazed outburst. She looks puzzled, but far too calm for my liking.

"I know technology supposedly makes our lives easy, but not when I can't make it work. I need to open this damn attachment. Can you do it?"

Renee smiles and says, "Well, I'll do my best. Want to tell me what has you so freakin' frazzled?"

"Not if it's going to slow you down. Please just open it. I'll explain after. It's another story I didn't expect to--"

Music emanates from the computer's speaker and immediately surrounds me. I catch words like *smiles, heart, too soon,* and *Emma*, all connected by a beat that is both pounding and soothing at the same time. My heart is now racing even faster. I want to stop the music, no I don't. What do I want? As the echoing refrain of the name "Emma" slowly quiets, I drop my head again. Now, there's nothing but heavy silence and my sniffling attempt to hold back tears. From melody to silence. From frustration to tears. From not knowing what the song would sound like, to knowing. Three minutes and thirty-something seconds, according to the timer on the attachment. How things have changed.

No clue how much later, because there is no timer on Renee and me, she whispers as if she's in a trance and doesn't want to break the spell. "Uh, wow. What is this? What did I just open? What did I hear?"

Equally entranced, I try to find the words. All that comes out is, "It's about Emma. Someone wrote a song about Emma. For Emma. I just found out."

"I don't know what to say. It's beautiful—haunting and beautiful. But how did you get this? Who is this from?" She's scrolling back on my computer to see where it came from.

I try to tell her the gist of this whole thing, get sidetracked reminding her of the story of Monica and Eric meeting up out West, then just can't continue. "Renee, play it again, will you? I need to hear it again."

We listen to it at least three more times. I hit pause to tell her a little bit of the story, then hit play again. Then I stop it because the words flood me with emotion. Too much, then not enough. I need more, then I don't.

"Larissa, let's take a break and go for a walk. This is exhausting."

She's right. A walk is exactly what I need.

In silent agreement, we start down the street toward the park. A quiet place to process. Process whatever just happened with that song, the way the universe takes away precious people then gives memories to sustain us, the constant roller coaster of emotions that occupy every single day.

Renee offers up, "See—that's why I can't be a mom. I can't take it. I can't watch your pain at losing Emma and even think about how that would feel. Nope, not me. It's been what—almost three years since your daughter was here with us? And look at us after hearing that song. To love a child that much and then lose that human? I can't fathom that whole thing."

Renee vacillates between thinking she should adopt a child before she's too old, and then proclaiming it's the last thing she'd ever consider doing. There's so much I want to say to Renee, but choose to tread softly. "Oh, damn, Renee. It does hurt. But, really—do you want to live life not doing things because they might hurt at some point? Just because my sweet Emma isn't with us here anymore, do you think I, for one second, regret having her? Bringing her into this world? Being her mom? No, nope, never. She's a gift, being her mom's a privilege. I'm not telling you what to do one way or the other. No one can. I just want to be clear that the joy of being in her presence for twenty years is so very precious. I may regret some of my actions or the times she was in pain, but not that she was here."

"I didn't mean to switch the subject away from the song, Larissa. Forget I brought up me. The song is amazing. Give me the details. What's going to happen with it?"

I pick up where I'd left off back at the house and add in what I'd read in Monica's email. "I guess Monica told Eric about this quite some time ago. He wasn't sure whether to believe she was really writing a song, so didn't tell me. She finally got back to him and asked if he thought I'd like to hear it before it gets released—she's hoping for some time toward the end of the year. She asked Eric if she could surprise me with it around Christmas. Can you imagine if she'd tried to surprise me? If I heard that without any advance warning?"

"No, I can't imagine. She clearly doesn't know you." Renee's face breaks into the wide grin that makes her so endearing.

"Thankfully, he let her know it was better not to wait and then told me about it. I contacted her right away. I haven't been able to think of anything else, can't concentrate, praying to hear from her. You came over just as it popped up on my screen. I should probably get home and respond to her. I want more info. Like, what if she really records it? I'm scared to have something so personal out in the world. Can I stop her? Do I want to?"

The ping of my phone grabs my attention. It's Eric asking if I'd received the email. I answer with emojis—thumbs up, heart, crying. That kind of says it all—at least all that I'm capable of right now. His response is a heart and "Later." There are times, like these, when those quick responses really serve a purpose. Times when more, more words, are just not necessary, and take too much emotional energy. Catching up later is fitting for how I feel now.

3

*Love is the honoring of others in a way
that grants them the grace of their autonomy.*
ANNE TRUITT

Feet up, cushions plumped just perfectly behind my back, wine glass in hand, I tilt my head back to stare at the countless, pinpoint-sized lights beaming softly through the black sky. Contemplating whether my dear Emma is up there somewhere watching my every move, I'm startled by a boisterous greeting from inside the house, "Ma! Madre! Where are you?"

Never could teach that guy anything about an "inside voice." Before I answer, Eric bolts out the back door onto the porch. Hilary is two steps behind trying, ineffectively, to shush him. "Calm down, she's right there. Hi, Larissa, uh, Mom, trying to enjoy the peaceful night?" She's not too comfortable with the "Mom" thing yet, but I gotta hand it to her for trying.

"There you are—geez—you didn't answer, Mom. What're you doing out here all alone?"

Amused at his thinly veiled concern for my whereabouts and what I'm doing, I reply, "Hilary's right. Just out here contemplating all these amazing points of light—stars everywhere. What are you guys up to? Good to see you both." I stand up and get one in each arm, pulling them in for a much-needed hug. Eric's long arms encircle me protectively; Hilary leans in, taking and giving support in equal amounts.

Hilary reaches into a large tote bag, saying, "Hope it's okay we came over without calling, just wanted to share--"

Eric cuts her off, "We got the photos back in an album for you, Mom. They're awesome. You're gonna love them!"

Realizing he means the photos from their wedding, I'm tempted to snatch it from her hands, but slow myself down, "Why don't we go in the house and you can show me? The lanterns out here aren't really bright enough to see them."

Slowly turning the pages, we're all transported back to their special day a few months ago. The palm tree landscape is spectacular, the smiling faces endearing.

"Mom, it's so cool that you got us the houses to stay in. Best wedding ever. So happy we decided to go back to Hutchinson Island. I know, I know, I might be biased, but come on, wasn't it great?"

There is something about that island—a picturesque oasis between ocean and lagoon. Bridges connecting to the mainland for the rare times you need to leave the peaceful haven. A safe harbor that helped Eric and me reconnect to so many people now integral to our lives. A spur-of-the-moment yearning to find the place my parents loved to vacation led us to a retreat, a sanctuary, and ultimately, to Everett and his adoptive family. What better place for Eric and Hilary to begin their own lifelong connection with one another?

Hilary points to a stunning silhouette on the next page. Everett and Beth are out on the porch. The Indian River Lagoon ripples in the background and he's braiding her hair for the wedding. The lighting, just before sunset, provides an orange-pink glow that outlines her profile. "Oh my gosh, Hilary, that *is* beautiful. We need to get that one framed for Everett as well. And look at this—you and Nina standing in the little secret garden before the ceremony." The quiet place on the side of the house, full of flowers and little figures—garden gnomes, birds, and butterflies adorning a small fountain, bench, and stepping stones. My secret hideaway during our first getaway at the rental house became a serene backdrop for photos.

The three of us flip through dozens more poses. All the combinations of people important to us, gathered to honor Eric and Hilary, are laid out in the album. Parents of the bride and groom first—there's Hilary with her father, Paul; then Steven and me with Eric. Eric with his half-sister, Nina, who we all met and got to know while in Florida; and many more of Everett and Beth. Connections that have made their way into our lives since Emma died. And, yes, on the last page of the album, there's a photo of the memory table. Hilary and Eric dedicated a candlelit table of photos to the memory of their siblings. They each lost a sibling, then found their way to one another. Losing and finding—such a contrast.

I must have zoned out. I hear Eric from the kitchen asking, "Hey, Mom, come out here and join us. I want to talk to you. Come have a toast with us."

A toast? To what? As I walk in, I hear Hilary whispering to Eric, then holding one finger up to her mouth to quiet him. Something to talk to me about? I thought they just came over to show me the album. Are they? *Just stop, Larissa—no jumping ahead.*

"Mom, what's that weird look on your face? Just want to make a toast to my fabulous wife and my awesome mom. Thank you both for everything you do for me. I'm a freaking lucky guy."

"Oh, Eric, thank you, honey. It's hard to believe that we went through all those months of you being away. Once you were back and we needed to plod through life *without* Emma, and then initiate a life, a relationship *with* your father. I'm grateful you think I'm awesome; some days I'm not so sure." It was thoughtful of him to acknowledge his feelings of contentment. I was jumping the gun and thinking there was something else he was going to say, some kind of news.

Hilary chimes in, "We're sure. It's been a strange ride, but I'm glad to be on this train with you both. My dad is grateful, too, you know. He was so worried about traveling for work and leaving me alone after David died. I miss David like crazy, but you guys make it bearable—mostly." She looks down and I grab her hand. No matter how happy she is with Eric, she'll always miss her brother, just like Eric will always miss Emma. You can make space in your heart for new loves, but the empty holes left by others remain.

Characteristically jumping to another topic, Eric asks me, "Hey, Mom, have you heard from Everett?"

I tell him about our conversation the other night, describe a cute art project of Beth's, then ask him, "Have you heard from him? I don't know, sometimes he seems hesitant to talk to me. Does he seem that way to you?"

"Mm . . . not really. But I keep it simple, you know? Nothing serious. Like how's work? Been fishing lately? That's his comfort zone, Mom. He does talk to me some about Beth, says he worries that work keeps him away from her too much."

"Right—so then I offer to go to New York to help take care of Beth, and he reminds me that I need to work, too. Like I can't figure out my own work schedule after twenty plus years of training others in how to best use our medical equipment? Does he just not want me around?"

Eric shakes his head and says, "Chill out, Mom. You read into things. He's not used to getting help from you, or anyone else. He's still working at the single-dad thing, and I think, maybe, too proud to accept help."

"It's not easy to raise kids on your own; I should know. And, a dad with a little girl? He's got some hurdles to get over."

"But they're his hurdles, Mom. Try something else—like invite them for Christmas and offer for her to stay the whole break. It might be a really hard time for him to get help with her when he only gets a short time off. Just sayin' . . ."

I'm not so sure when my son became an armchair psychologist/counselor, but he has a point. "I've never known you to think that far ahead, Eric, but that's not a bad idea. It's a way off, but it'd be something to look forward to and maybe ease his mind about the holidays."

"Glad to be of help. Maybe you should pay me instead of that counselor lady—what's her name again?"

A few days later, I'm at Marie's office. In spite of Eric's new-found, or maybe, newly noticed guidance, there are things better spoken to someone more objective.

Marie asks, "What about Everett? How's he doing?"

"He's fine, I guess. We talk every so often. When it comes to him, I catch myself wanting more from him, more time with Beth. Maybe more than he's ready for. But Eric actually had a great idea. Everett and Beth are going to come visit at holiday time. He can only get a couple of days off, so Beth is going to stay with me the rest of the break. It helps Everett with his childcare dilemma over the break, and I get some special time with Beth. She seemed excited about it when we told her."

"That's going to be the first time for Beth to stay alone with you, right? How does that feel?"

"I'm excited, I'll tell you that. Always loved this age with Emma . . ." I hear my own voice trail off, and I picture Emma at seven or so playing with dolls one minute and acting twice her age the next.

"Larissa, have you thought about how that will be? Just you and Beth? Holiday time? Any concerns?"

I let out a long, slow breath. "No, not till, uh, now." I hesitate, then continue with assurance, "It'll be good for both of us. Not saying there won't be bumps in the road, but it'll be good."

"I'm sure it will. Just give her space, too. Holidays might be just as tough for her as they are for you. She lost her mother early on, and you miss Emma. Memories and emotions are unpredictable, right?"

*Gratitude helps us to see what is there
instead of what isn't.*
ANNETTE BRIDGES

Thanksgiving is just Eric, Hilary, Renee, and me. Fewer people, yet the heat of the oven going for hours and the unmistakable aromatic mix of sage combined with pumpkin spices deliver the holiday warmth. We've learned to tolerate the once-occupied, now-empty chairs at our gathering and put our focus on being thankful for the people and things that bring us happiness.

Even with only a few of us, we keep the tradition of each expressing something for which we are grateful. Renee goes first and proclaims she is grateful to always be included in our family gatherings. Sweetly, Eric and Hilary each give a romantic sentence or two about how grateful they are to have found one another.

Eric turns to me and says, "Mom, I know I sorta said this before, but I'm so damn grateful that when Steven told you that he thought he was my dad, that you didn't shut him down. I'm grateful you guys figured it out. Couldn't have been easy after all that time. But it's so good having both of you in my life.

Especially, well, it was hard with Emma gone, so lonely. It's been good to have him."

He stops to collect himself, then looks upset. "I didn't mean Steven, or anyone, could replace Emma, Mom, really. Guess I messed that up."

"No, no you didn't. I'm happy too, that we figured out Steven is your dad. We all miss Emma, and are happy to have Everett, Beth, and your sister Nina in our lives. It's a choice to find things to be happy and grateful about. A choice I make every day."

Then I continue with what I'd been ready to say before Eric shared his feelings. "I'm immensely grateful that Monica's song has given us a new way to honor Emma. This expression of love is a creative tribute I never expected. Who knows where it will go, or who will hear it? This whole thing scares me, yet knowing that someone cared enough to write about Emma is magical. 'Smiles from Her Heart' brings a smile to my heart."

There are nods of agreement and Renee asks, "So, Eric, has Monica told you what's next? I don't know a thing about recording or promoting music; it seems so complicated."

"Yeah, I'm not super familiar, either, but she says it'll be available on all the different streaming options for music in a couple of weeks—before Christmas, anyway."

Thinking out loud, I try to articulate what has been on my mind. "It's crazy to think about that song being available to anyone, pretty much anywhere in the world. I wonder what people will think. Obviously, it's special to us because of our connection. But everyone else?"

It strikes me that I have a kind of love/hate relationship with the whole idea that's tough to put into words. Do I want others to hear it? Does it even matter if they like it? Why do I set any expectations? Isn't the existence of the song enough? So many questions, so few answers. Maybe I should take my questions to another place, get another perspective.

"I've been thinking about going to a psychic medium again. My other visits brought answers to lingering questions. If I have the chance to connect with Emma in spirit and find out her reaction to this song, some clarity might come to me. Just an idea swirling around in my head."

Eric hunches his shoulders, indicating he has no opinion. Renee speaks up and offers, "If you decide to do that, I'll go with you again. It was an amazing experience last time. I mean, if you want me to."

Yup, she was right by my side when I took the leap and visited a psychic after Emma died. I had no desire to hear about the future, I just wanted to find some assurance my daughter was at peace. Renee's right—it was amazing and so much more.

As the food gets passed around, there's more speculation from the others about the song, marketing, and the remote possibility of it becoming a hit. What would Emma think of all this?

Letting the idea of the psychic go for now, I respond to their speculation, "I wonder how much Monica knows about any of these things. When I searched her production company, it seems legit. They've released other songs that have gained popularity. Only the future will tell us more."

Eventually, the conversation switches to Christmas.

With an unmistakably teasing tone to his voice, Eric asks, "So, what do you have planned, Mom? Is every minute accounted for yet?" Renee and Hilary giggle a bit and wait to hear my response.

"Well, you already know how excited I am that Everett and Beth are coming. He jumped right on your idea, Eric. Suggesting that Beth stay for her whole school break took a load off his plate. No need to try to patch together childcare. Needless to say, I can't wait! Did you talk to your father yet about coming?" It's only been since Eric returned three years ago from his self-imposed exile, that we knew Steven as his father. I left Steven not knowing I was pregnant. Years later, we put the pieces together and we're still finding our way as his parents.

"Yes, I talked to Dad earlier this week. He said he'd call you to be sure it's okay with you."

"Of course it's okay with me. And I hope he invites Nina. Your sister is always welcome too. Anyway, back to your question. I don't know about every minute, smart guy, but meals are planned—actually, Hilary volunteered for you two to make Christmas breakfast. Renee and Isabel are helping me with dinner. I'm thinking we make Christmas Eve something simple, like soup. Everett and Beth arrive at the airport around noon, they'll need time to get settled, and before we know it, we'll all need to get ready for Santa to come, right?" Memories of so many Christmases when the kids were little start rushing through my mind. It felt like a myriad of details to attend to back then, but in reality, it was such uncomplicated stuff. Easy and so much fun.

Eric breaks into my wandering thoughts with, "Mom, do you even know if Beth believes in Santa? Or what they've done for Christmas other years? Might not want to dive into making things the way you always did for Emma and me. Did you check in with Everett on all that?"

A little deflated, I reply, "Yeah, well, hadn't really thought of that. Guess I shouldn't assume, didn't even consider whether she believes in Santa. I'll call Everett this week." *One more topic I need to broach carefully—I don't want to rock the boat with him the first time we're doing holidays together—I don't want it to be our last.* "Thanks, Eric. It's no secret I want this to be a special Christmas. I want them to come back other years; I want this to become a tradition."

Renee adds to Eric's cautionary comments, "Of course, you do, Larissa, but maybe slow down. Enjoy time together this year. Not sure you want to let the need to make it a tradition take over. As the adage goes, 'one step at a time.' Cherish the moments and let the future work itself out."

When I reach Everett to talk about Christmas, the wise counsel of Eric and Renee help me sail pretty smoothly through the planning conversations with Everett about Beth and the upcoming holiday.

He offers, "Hmm . . . well, on the Santa thing, she's somewhere in the middle, I'd say. She came right out and asked me last year if Santa really wears a red suit and travels from the North Pole to the whole world. She's way too smart for me to try to lie my way through those questions. So we talked about Santa being the spirit of doing nice things for people and giving gifts to your loved ones. I told her the stories about Santa are to help little children understand the meaning of Christmas. We agreed that because she's a 'big girl' and she now understands, she can help tell the story to others. I told her I'd probably never stop signing her gift tags as being from Santa because it's a beautiful story and she'll always be my little girl. She seemed happy with that. That's the long answer to your question, but I think you can talk about Santa or not and just follow her lead. She likes to be part of adult conversations. I guess it's because she's around adults most of the time, other than when she's at school."

"Sounds like you dealt with her questions perfectly. I'm excited about seeing you both and, then, about my time with her during her school break. I'll try my very best to do whatever you want me to that week. I respect--"

Using the endearing name that Beth came up with, Everett cuts me off. "Lissa, I feel like you somehow got the impression I don't trust you or something. That's not the case—far from it. If I've sounded reluctant, it's because I've hardly ever left her alone. Haven't been away from her for more than two days, except that one time when my mom, uh, Harriett, was sick. I'm worried I'll miss her so much that I'll drive you both crazy checking in. I won't be checking up on you—I'll be just wanting to hear her voice. It's sweet music."

Huh, Eric's right again. I've been reading into Everett's hesitancy way too much. And the feeling that your child's voice is sweet music—oh, how well I know. I owe so much to his adoptive mother. Harriett made sure she found me for him before she passed away. Since then, Everett's voice has become as sweet to me as Eric's and Emma's were for their whole lives. I still hear Emma's in my sleep sometimes. When I do, it's a sound I adore and dread the waking up to reality.

"We'll be available to talk or video chat as often as you want to—my total pleasure. Sounds like we're all set. Travel safely and I can't wait to see you both soon."

"Thanks, Lissa. I think this holiday plan is going to be a blessing for Beth and me. I'm glad we're making it happen, and sorry it's taken us this long to do it."

What an unexpectedly wonderful end to a call I was fearful to make. After hanging up, I sit to take stock of my blessings. Focusing on blessings after tragic loss isn't easy. I'm tested several times a day. Different strategies work at different times. Sometimes it's looking back at photo albums and being grateful for all the times I traveled with Emma and Eric, yet sometimes those photos scratch open the wounds of loss. Sometimes it's more reassuring to turn my attention to the offerings of nature and embrace the beauty of my surroundings, reminding myself that I am one miniscule part of this huge universe. Right now, it's being grateful for reuniting with Everett, meeting Beth, and

Eric living close by with Hilary. Do I wish my parents, brother, and daughter were also having Christmas dinner with us? Yes, but they're here. I feel it. Somehow, some way, they are nearby.

Two days before Everett and Beth are due to arrive, a news alert says the northeast is going to get a substantial snowstorm—something they're calling a "bomb cyclone." Sounds awful! Disruptions in holiday travel are likely. I feel a sinking in my gut.

As I pick up my phone to call Everett, there's a text from him. He'd written last night after I'd turned on the do-not-disturb feature. It says he's heard about the storm and is trying to get out of JFK before it hits. He's hoping I'm okay with the possibility of them arriving early.

Okay does not begin to describe how my sinking feeling vanishes and my mood immediately improves. I quickly text him saying I'd love nothing more than for them to get to Atlanta ahead of the storm and be safely under this roof. I can see the small letters that the text has been read, but no response. Maybe he's still trying to reach the airline?

A call from Eric comes in. "Hey, Mom, are you up? Did you hear from Everett? He called me late last night—guess you didn't answer. He heard a bad forecast, changed their flight, and he's getting into the airport in an hour. I'm going to pick them up. Want to come along or stay home and get stuff ready?"

Add Everett's quick response after news of the storm to my list of blessings. "I'd love to go, but I'll run to the grocery store and be here when you guys get back from the airport. Thanks for calling. Love you!"

When Beth walks in the door a few hours later, dragging her little, purple rollaboard, my heart nearly explodes with joy. Any worries about safe travel or how the next few days would unfold vanish and are replaced with a calmness that envelops all of us.

The camaraderie that's been slowly developing since I first met her and my son is becoming so much more. It's come full circle into a love of one another. A family, perhaps not so traditional, that has morphed into something very special. What better way to honor this than Christmas?

Over a dinner of pizza and chicken wings, I ask Beth about the airplane and whether she likes to travel.

"It was good, Lissa. I like watching the movie and having snacks the most."

"Yup, that is fun. I used to travel all the time, but haven't as much in a long time. I think I'm ready to enjoy planning trips again. The travel bug has bitten me once more."

"What's a travel bug? Bugs are yucky. You enjoy them?"

I smile as I begin to answer her question, but Eric beats me to it. "Oh, Beth. She more than enjoys it. *Travel bug* means wanting to travel all over. Like when you get bitten by a bug and there's an itch—the only way to stop the itch is to plan another trip. And for your grandmother, that literally meant trips all over the world. She used to want to travel all the time—took me and Auntie Emma with her everywhere. Said we needed to see the world while we could. Emma and I teased her that she was trying to find herself. There used to be a game when we were little called "Where's Waldo?" We thought it should be named "Where's Our Mom?" I finally got old enough to say when I wanted to go or not, but she always took Emma along."

I can't help but laugh at Eric's summary of my penchant for travel and the comparison to the Waldo character. When Eric was about seventeen, he posted a cartoon of Waldo sitting in a yoga pose with a caption about finding oneself—he added my name to the caption, thinking it was the funniest thing ever.

His response is entertaining, but I want her to hear my version of why travel is an essential part of life for me. "Beth, he doesn't really get why I liked to travel so much. I wanted to learn about people around the world and how they live. I wanted the kids to do that too. The more you spend time with people that we think are different from us, the more we learn about how we're actually all the same. Does that make any sense? I stopped doing it for awhile, but I'd like to do it again. You talking about your plane ride made me think about more trips."

"Like where did you go? To, um, what's it called, Mexico or someplace?"

"Yup, that's one place. But also to countries across the big oceans, the Atlantic and Pacific. Countries like Italy, Spain, Japan, and India. And all over our own country. The U.S. has so many fun places to see. I have photos of all the trips. Maybe we can look at them together sometime."

Eric playfully claps his hand to his forehead. "Oh boy, Beth, get ready. She has lots of pictures and lots of stories. Not tonight, though. I have a movie for us all to watch. Let's clean up this mess, make popcorn, and go watch. What do you say?"

5

*Music is the divine way to tell beautiful,
poetic things to the heart.*
PABLO CASALS

*B*efore I know it, Christmas Eve and morning have flown by in a flurry of shiny wrapping paper and tangles of ribbon. Isabel is helping me with the finishing touches for dinner. My sweet friend misses her kids today; it's the alternate year when they spend holidays with their father. I counted and recounted the number of people needing place settings, but since I never came up with the same number twice, we decide to serve it all buffet style and just put out a huge stack of plates and utensils.

Shortly before everyone else is expected to arrive, I'm startled to hear the now familiar beat, then notes, of "Smiles from Her Heart" wafting from upstairs. I tell Isabel I'll be right back and go upstairs to investigate who's playing it. The melody is coming from the room I've given Beth for her stay. She and Eric are bent over his phone, intent on the music.

A little surprised he would play that for Beth, I make questioning eye contact with him. "What's going on, you guys? What're you listening to?"

"It's a song about Auntie. Uncle Eric came running in to tell Daddy about it, but Daddy's in the shower. I wanted to know what was so exciting. He let me listen. I like it." She stands up and starts wriggling her little hips in synchrony with the beat, evidently to show me her admiration for the tune. Not sure why I initially thought it wouldn't be appropriate for her to hear, I'm touched at her genuinely enthusiastic response. Who knew it would appeal to a seven-year-old?

"Yeah, Mom. Monica definitely followed through. Her song to Emma has been listened to over ten thousand times on this music app. And it was only made available a few days ago."

Everett walks into the room, toweling his hair dry and asks, "What was just made available?"

"An Auntie Emma song, Daddy. Listen."

Now it's Everett with a questioning look on his face.

I make my exit to let Eric explain. I hadn't had a chance to tell him about the song or find out what he thinks of the idea. We've never really even talked about what he thinks of how Eric and I include Emma in our everyday lives. Oh well, it was Eric's idea to share with Everett, and now Beth, in the first place. "I need to get back to helping Isabel. Beth, you can come down and help us whenever you're ready, honey."

As I stroll back into the kitchen, Isabel asks, "What was the quick exit about?"

She knew about the song, but at least to my knowledge, hadn't heard it yet.

"I heard the song about Emma playing and was confused about where it was coming from," explaining my reaction as best

I can. "Turns out, Eric was playing it for Beth. He said it's already had ten thousand listens on just one of the music apps. It's really happening. I wasn't sure how I'd feel about it. On one hand, it's so personal to me. On the other hand, it's Monica's artistry, right? Artists create from people and things in their environment all the time without approval from anyone. I'm getting more and more used to the idea. And Isabel, Beth stood up and danced to the song. I made a quick departure—didn't want them all to see me crying over that. So precious, though."

"It's amazing there's been so many listens. What a tribute. You know, Larissa, you and Eric might want to think about playing it for everyone later—after dinner or something? It could be our own tribute to Emma. A way to include her in our holiday this year."

"Nice idea, Isabel. And if we're going to share it, I want to hear it on a good speaker. I'll ask Eric when he comes down."

The day progresses with doorbell rings, hugs, red and green packages galore, all peppered with the squeaky tones of Beth's animated voice as she greets everyone who comes in the door. As the only child here among so many adults, she's the center of attention. The smile hasn't left Everett's face—he seems more comfortable than I've ever seen him with this crowd.

I'm able to corner Eric and ask about playing the song for everyone as a surprise tribute to Emma. His answer is a bit cryptic. "Yeah, sure. I have a surprise planned for you but--whatever. We'll make it work."

During coffee and dessert, the doorbell rings once again. I'm kind of confused, because I wasn't expecting anyone else. Eric jumps up and rushes to the door. Instead of excited greetings, what I hear is more like loud whispers, yet indiscernible. Must be one of his friends, maybe Arnie?

Nina, Eric's adorable half-sister, Hilary, and I are in the kitchen, almost done cleaning up, when Eric starts clapping to get everyone's attention and calls, "Come out into the four-season room, everyone. I've got a surprise."

My lack of movement away from the sink causes Hilary and Nina to beckon in unison, "Come on, Larissa. Let's see what's going on."

A woman I don't know is standing in the center of the room, with chairs in a u-shape around her. I see a microphone and speaker at the same time I hear her say, "This is for you and your family, Larissa. It's my pleasure to bring you 'Smiles from Her Heart.' To Emma, from me."

The melody, which has now wound its way around my heart and into every vein in my body, begins. Monica's voice is even more beautiful in person. The presentation with only her guitar rather than a whole band behind her is mesmerizing. I'm awe-struck. Within thirty seconds, Beth is dancing again. Another thirty, and pretty much everyone in the room has joined her. I sense a hand reaching for mine, and Steven is there inviting me to dance with my family, with Monica's song, for Emma.

When Monica's voice sings "Emma" one final time, the silence is as inspiring as the notes had been just a few moments ago. Monica puts down the microphone and comes toward me. We're drawn together like magnets, a tie between us woven of the threads of Emma's life. Monica touched different threads than I had, but they were all part of Emma, nonetheless. It's as if we've always known one another, always shared a love of the beautiful girl in the song. Her arms wrap around me, and for just a moment, Emma is in the middle of this hug, here with us, just as present as everyone else in the room.

He waits patiently, but soon Eric can't contain himself any longer. "Surprise, Mom! Monica and I arranged this a few weeks ago, and I thought we were actually going to be able to pull off the surprise. Then you come up with the idea for me to play the song for everyone. You totally took me off guard with that one. But looks like it worked out anyway, Monica. Thank you so much for coming! Come get some food and something to drink. You've been traveling all day. Glad you were coming from the opposite part of the country than the damn storm."

Taking in the small crowd around her, Monica bows her head forward for a moment then looks directly at me. "It would have taken more than a storm to keep me from getting here. This song has been part of me for so long. When I met Emma, she was obviously not in the best place. Her enigmatic smile captivated me, though. She was struggling, she was sad, lonesome for her family. In spite of that, when she smiled, her whole being smiled. When she spoke of her family, somehow that smile became even warmer and deeper. The expression 'wearing her heart on her sleeve' did not begin to describe it. Emma's heart was the root of her smile and she won me over, her cabin mates, and everyone else at the center without doing much at all. Just by being herself, listening to others, and radiating her warmth. It was an honor to know her, and I'm grateful I've found a deserving way to let the world know Emma. Thank you for sharing her. Thank you all for dancing along. I couldn't ask for anything more."

Everyone is at a loss for words. No words, and a fountain of tears. All I can do is reach for her hand and whisper, "Thank you. Thank you for an amazing Christmas. There may have been an empty chair at our table, but the whole house is full of Emma."

6

Rainbows remind us that even after the darkest clouds
and fiercest winds, there is still beauty.
KATRINA MAYER

Beth is still sleeping. I'm sipping my coffee and flipping through my collection of photos. Preserving memories and trips in the form of photos has changed so much since phones became our portable cameras. It was great to discover a way to upload them to a website and make a book. Now I have stacks of photo books—one for each trip, others for family holidays.

The day after Christmas, when Beth and I were making a list of everything we wanted to do in our time together, she piped up, "I want to see the pictures of your trips. I want to get a travel bug like you." I couldn't help but laugh and assured her we'd do that. But going to the zoo and hiking got checked off the list first. Although it's fairly warm for December, today has started off drizzly, so I'm thinking art projects and looking at photos are the best choices. There are so many, I need to pick a few to start. If I don't preselect, I'll get caught up reminiscing and the whole day will vanish.

A wee voice calls out, "Lissa, can you come up here?"

I enter her room with a smile that only widens when she says, "Can you lay down here with me? My mama used to lay in my bed with me sometimes and talk. I liked that."

I'm touched. She doesn't mention her mother very often.

"I'd love to, thank you for inviting me. What do you want to talk about?"

"Can you tell me a story about Aunt Emma and Uncle Eric? About when they were little?"

I tell her about our visit to California to see an old friend of mine. "Her kids and mine were around the same age. We had so much fun. We rented bikes, cycled around town and down to the beach. Her son and Uncle Eric went surfing while her daughters helped Emma put on makeup for the first time. At night, we made a fire on the beach. Cooked hot dogs and s'mores and sang songs."

"That sounds nice. I wish my daddy coulda been there, too."

Oh boy, what do I say to that? "Yes, honey, me too. But Daddy was with Grandma Harriett and Aunt Kristy. He was growing up with them and having fun by the beach in Florida. It wasn't our time to be all together back then. I'm glad we're together now, though."

"Yeah, I guess. But we're not really all together. Auntie Emma's not here, my mama's not here. I think it would've been fun. And you know that nice house you had in Hutchinson Island? We could have gotten an even bigger one with enough rooms for everyone to be all together all at the same time."

Ah, wise words from the child. "Yup, I agree. It would have been fun. Sometimes I do feel like Auntie Emma is in the room with me. Or when I see a butterfly, it reminds me so much of her that I'll even talk with the butterfly and call her *Emma*. Do you ever feel like your mama is nearby?" Not sure if Everett would approve of me asking that, but too late now. It just slipped out.

"Uh-huh. Almost every day when I start to wake up, I think I hear Mama say 'good morning, honey-bunny, sunshine girl,' just like she always used to. And when I say good morning back, it feels so good. I don't tell Daddy, though. He cries when I talk about Mama. I don't want to make him cry, Lissa."

"That's nice of you to worry about your daddy. But, you know, crying isn't always a bad thing. I usually feel better after I cry. Someone once told me crying gets all the sad out, and maybe Daddy needs to get the sad out once in awhile. I don't know—we all think about it differently. You are a sunshine girl, Beth. That's a good name for you."

It must be that's all she has to talk about this morning, because she shifts quickly to, "Can I have hot chocolate for breakfast now? It's my favorite. With marshmallows? That s'more story made me think of marshmallows."

"Absolutely. I'll go get it started while you brush your teeth. See you in a jiffy!"

"What's a jiffy?"

"Wow, guess no one says that anymore, huh? It means just a little bit of time. And sometimes I even say "jiff"—that's even quicker, right?" We both start giggling. Such innocent silliness. She is certainly sunshine for me.

Sipping the hot chocolate, we agree that an art project sounds like fun.

I suggest, "The weather app says that it's supposed to stop raining and clear up in a little while. How about if we go to the park and gather smooth, flat stones? I have paints. We can paint pretty things on them and nice words, words that make people happy. Sometimes people leave them scattered around for others to find. I saw it online as *kindness rocks*—what do you think?"

"Can you show me, Lissa?"

I start scrolling to show her photos and she jumps up, "Yes, let's do it. I want to make kindness rocks. When we talk to Daddy tonight, let's surprise him."

"I know the perfect place. How about I pack us lunch, or at least a snack? Picking up rocks might get our appetites revved up. If the sun does come out, we'll have a picnic. Bring your jacket just in case, little sunshine girl."

Beth smiles, runs to get her jacket, and is back downstairs in no time. She's carrying a canvas bag with her initials on it. She holds it out proudly to show me and says, "My other grammy, Mamma's mamma, made this for me. She left it on our front stoop, with a Christmas card, the day before we came here. I don't see her too much, either."

Hmm. If I lived only a few minutes' drive away, I'd want to see this little one every day.

Kristy told me once that Everett's mother-in-law never really liked him very much. Kristy's theory? It was because he's white and the mother-in-law thought that would be tough for her daughter and her grandchild. Everett's never shared any of that with me himself, so I don't know it to be fact, and a little touchy to bring up.

"Is that hard? Do you want to see her more?" I don't want to assume and need to respect whatever the relationship is.

"Kinda. When she sees me, I think she looks at me funny. Daddy says it's cuz I remind her of my mama, her daughter. I don't know if she wants to see us. But, I like this bag, don't you?"

I'm not going to pry any further; just take my cues from her. "Sure do—the colors are pretty. I guess she must like crafts, too. We can send her a picture of the rocks later if you feel like it."

With that, we're out the door.

"Lissa, I think the clouds are going away. Oh, look!"

Her squeal startles me, so I pull over to the side of the road. The little finger is pointing at a rainbow; its colors gradually becoming brighter, more vivid.

"That's beautiful, Beth. I think rainbows are magical." I think of all the rainbows I saw in the first year after Emma died. They always seemed to come when I needed a little magic to get me through a rough moment. A message from heaven, a way to connect with my daughter, my parents, my brother.

Beth nods her head, then points again.

"Look, there are two!"

"A double—that is super special. Rainbows mean there is sunshine after the rain, happiness after sadness, don't you think?"

Her smile broadens. "Yup, I do. What about the pot of gold? Isn't that magic, too?"

"I think the pot of gold is just like the sunshine—something good when the clouds clear up. We're going in the same direction as the rainbow, let's see how long we can follow it. Maybe we will find something special when it ends."

Of course, like most magical moments, the rainbow doesn't last long, but the sun emerges to give us a golden guide for our rock hunt.

We arrive at my favorite spot in the park and start off for a place to settle and search. It doesn't take long before rocks in that canvas bag are making it a struggle to carry. There's a grassy area encircled by trees that cut the wind. Those protective trees and the sun make it ideal for picnicking, in spite of it being late December.

"I like picnics, Lissa. Sometimes Daddy and I take the subway to Central Park and have a picnic. Not so much in the wintertime, though. It's not really like winter here!"

"And where your daddy grew up, he could picnic any time of year. He must miss it sometimes. I miss Hutchinson Island, and I didn't even grow up there."

"I think he does miss it. And he sure misses Auntie Kristy—he talks to her on the phone a lot. Maybe we can make kindness rocks for her, too. One with a fish on it to remind Daddy of his home and one with a flower on it for Aunt Kristy. Can we eat our lunch and go back to do our painting?"

Beth helps me spread a blanket for us to sit on.

"It's kinda bumpy under the blanket here, Lissa. Oh, wait, I see what's making it bumpy. There's three pennies under this corner. Look!"

"Let's see, Beth. I love finding pennies and dimes. They always make me think of people I love who are not living on this earth anymore." That just popped out. Not sure how much I should share about "pennies from heaven," but I know I'm not the only one who thinks that.

"My friend's mommy told me about that. She said her grandma sent them, that the pennies come from heaven. Who sends yours? Auntie Emma?"

Phew—at least she's heard it before. "Never know, honey. Let's look at the date—sometimes the year gives me a hint who might have sent it. Can you read the numbers?"

"Yes—this one is 1-9-8-2. Is that a hint?"

"Hmm . . . let me think." *As if I could ever forget.* "That's a very special year, Beth. That's when your daddy was born!"

"So, do you think it's from heaven? Daddy's not gone."

"He's sure not! Let's see what the others are and try to figure it out."

"This one's kinda worn down, but I think it's 1-9-9-7."

Of course, it is. Emma's birth year. Smiling, I tell her, "That's when Auntie Emma was born. Maybe we're getting a message from Auntie. What do you think?" I'm thinking it has to be Eric's birth year. Three pennies, my three children.

She's already on to the next. "This one is my birthday-year, Lissa! I'm not gone, either. Why?" Her eyes scrunch together, wrinkling her usually smooth forehead into a V-shape of puzzlement.

Struggling a moment to figure it out myself, I pull Beth into my lap and hold her hands. "You know, messages from heaven are not always clear, but maybe this means that Auntie Emma is happy that I found you and your daddy, that she feels she's with you two. Does that make any sense to you?"

"I like that. But, where's Uncle Eric?"

Good question. Not sure how to come up with an answer that makes any sense to a little girl, but I try anyway, "Maybe we need to keep our eyes open and we'll find more. Maybe later today, maybe another time."

"All right, I'll watch. Can I keep these?"

"Of course! Finders keepers!"

She giggles, stuffs the pennies in her pocket, and rummages through the picnic basket, inspecting each little, carefully wrapped morsel as if she hadn't eaten in a month.

After a quick picnic, the ride home, and a full afternoon of coming up with ideas and painting rocks, Beth and I stop to take a break. I'm thinking tea and cookies would be fun, but I'm not sure what she will think of that.

"Beth, does Daddy let you drink tea? I always used to have tea in the afternoon with my grandma. We'd stop whatever we were doing and read the sayings on the little paper tags on the tea bags."

"I'd like that. Daddy says I can only have drinks that don't have caffeine. Does tea?"

"Well, I happen to have some peppermint tea that's really yummy and no caffeine. Shall we?"

As we settle into the places at the table we've each been using since she got here, she looks at the tag and proudly announces,

"I can read mine first. It says, 'Always stop to smell the roses.' I like the smell of roses, Lissa. Do you have them in your garden?"

"Oh, I definitely have roses. And you know what that saying is trying to teach us? It's a really important lesson, I think. It means that sometimes if we hurry too much, we forget how pretty the smell of roses can be and pass them right by. Or, if we think of a bigger idea than the roses, it means when we hurry, we can miss a lot of beautiful things."

"So, it's a fancy way to say slow down and look at things, right? Like, if we hadn't stopped and looked at those penny dates, we might have missed a special message? What does your tag say?"

"Hmm . . . it got a little soggy. Let me see. 'If you enjoy the fragrance of a rose, you must accept its thorns as well.' I guess it's a day for sayings about roses. What do you think of that one, Beth?"

I can almost see the wheels turning in her head as she ponders this one.

"Well, roses are pretty but they have sharp prickers. I don't really like the prickers. Maybe it means that I have to like the whole rose, not just the pretty smell."

"I think you've got it. Maybe the saying wants us to remember that almost everything has some good parts and some bad parts. If we're going to enjoy something, we have to take the good and the bad. You know, sometimes I have to remind myself of that with people and with feelings. I love my friends Miss Renee and Miss Isabel, but sometimes they do something I don't like. Doesn't mean I stop loving them, you know? Or when we were talking about crying and you said your daddy doesn't like to cry? I said that sometimes crying makes me feel better. The good and the bad can't always be separate."

"Yup, me too. Like where Daddy and I live. I like the park and my school, but the loud noises—cars beeping their horns and stuff—not so much. It's kinda cool that we both got messages about roses, but really about more. Hey, are those your photo albums Uncle Eric told me about? Can we look at them?"

Trying not to laugh at how quickly she switches gears, I tell her, "Sure. It would be fun to show you pictures of our trips. Spread them out and see what one is calling your name!"

She looks at me very seriously at first, then giggles. "Oh, I get it—another funny way to say something. Albums can't talk, but you mean I should pick one that looks good to me. How 'bout this one? Who is this with a big snake around her neck? Is that a poisonous one?"

"That album is a trip to India, and that's Auntie Emma with a python snake—no, it's not poisonous. At the center where they were teaching us about snakes--"

I guess my explanation is not too exciting because she's flipping ahead and finds another photo, "Wow, is that her again riding an elephant?"

"Sure is—she always wanted to ride one and she got to do it in India."

Beth has gotten to the end of that book and picks up another.

"Where is this one? Oh, I know from school. Is it the Grand Canyon? Now she and a boy are riding a donkey. Who's that?"

"That's Uncle Eric, and we were riding mules down to the bottom of the canyon."

It continues like this for at least an hour. Mexico, Italy, Hawaii, Niagara Falls, and more national parks. I offer a few comments, but mostly she loves spotting all the different animals and finding both Emma and Eric.

As she closes the last one, she says, "I think I want to have a travel bug, like you, Lissa. These are really cool. And all the animals. Daddy and I go to the zoo sometimes, but to really ride them? I want to do that someday. When are we going to have dinner, anyway?"

She cracks me up again at the quick transition from traveling and riding animals to the dinner schedule, and reply, "I'll get right on it. Come help me make a salad, Little Miss Travel Bug."

After dinner and the bedtime routine, Beth falls asleep after just one story in bed. I put up my feet and think about the day. She has seemingly boundless energy and is always so ready to get on to do the next thing. Yet, I could have sat on that grassy knoll and pondered picnics and rocks with Beth all day. And talking about the tea bag messages was precious; I didn't want to stop. Wait a minute—it's another example of stopping to smell the roses. No need to jump to the next thing. Today was a gift—wouldn't change a thing.

7

While we try to teach our children all about life,
our children teach us what life is all about.
Angela Schwindt

"The days are going way too fast, Isabel. I've got to fly with Beth back to New York the day after tomorrow." I try not to let disappointment creep into my voice, but she knows me too well.

"I'm sure it's going to be hard. But remember what I always heard you tell your kids—plan the next trip, or in this case, the next visit, so you have something to look forward to. Maybe a midwinter or spring break can be a time together?"

"Yup, I did always say that to the kids, but I've been trying not to jump ahead. Trying to stay in the moment, enjoy the now." We both start laughing at the message we learned in a yoga class before the holidays. The topic itself has stuck with us, but we've not exactly been shining stars at making changes. Except for relishing in my moments with Beth.

After pointing this out to Isabel, she continues, "Got it. So you've been taking one day at a time for this special break together. How's Everett been when you guys talk to him?"

"He's been really fun to video chat with—enthusiastic about everything Beth and I have done. She proudly shows him every art project and retells him stories that I've told her. She also told him about one evening when we were listening to the song about Emma out on the patio and a cardinal landed on the railing right next to her. It didn't fly away until a minute or two after the song stopped. Before she said anything about it being a sign from Emma, Everett said it himself. I guess my worries that he'd not approve of me talking about those things was unfounded."

Nodding all the while I'm talking, Isabel adds, "It sounds like it's been a good visit. I'm happy for all of you."

"Yeah, I think so. Just last night when we did a video chat, Everett got choked up telling Beth how much he misses her. It was touching, because Beth responded by telling him something she and I talked about earlier in the week. He started to apologize and wipe away his tears, but she told him, 'Daddy, it's okay to cry. Tears aren't all bad. Sometimes crying helps you get the sad out and makes you think more about being happy, too.' I didn't say a word, but I could tell he was surprised—in a good way."

Our chat is interrupted by little feet racing down the staircase.

"Lissa, Isabel, are we gonna go to the art place now? You promised we could get stuff to do one more project before I have to go home. I want to make something special and take it home for Daddy."

"What are you thinking of, Beth? You made him some really pretty kindness rocks. I also uploaded the picture of you and him on Christmas to a website that's going to print it on a pillow and send it to your house. What else do you want to make?"

"I want to go to the store and see what they have, Lissa. But remember when you told me about making tie-dye shirts with Auntie Emma and Uncle Eric? I might like to try that. Is it hard?"

My voice quivers as I reply, "Not hard at all, honey. Let's go see what they have at the store and then decide." The last time we made tie-dye shirts was on the first birthday after Emma passed away. It's a bittersweet memory, but all the times we made them before that were pure joy. The kids always loved turning plain old white t-shirts into splashes of swirling color, then proudly wearing their creations.

"If that's what you like best, we'll get the supplies and dive right in."

Turns out that's what she wants, so that's what we do. We stop by Isabel's house and pick up her kids, Bobby and Lisa, figuring if we're going to set up all that mess, might as well include them too. The more the merrier.

As we sit down to a dinner of pizza and chicken fingers—Beth's usual request, seconded by the other two kids—I look around the table and am transported to a time when this was my kids, well, Emma and Eric at least. The years have brought so many delights and pitfalls, so much joy and so much pain, yet it feels like hardly any time has lapsed. The feeling of well-being predominates. I don't feel sad at all about remembering those times, I'm eternally grateful they happened, and cherish this time right now.

Packing the next day is not quite so joy-filled, but I'm determined not to be openly sad with Beth. She deserves to have fun anticipating being back with her father and her school friends.

"Lissa, my suitcase is too full, can you help me fit everything?"

"You know what, Beth? I only have to bring a couple of things—I'm staying just one night with you and your dad, then heading back here. That leaves plenty of room in my bag for the things you've accumulated since Christmas. No problem fitting it all."

"I think Daddy's tie-dye shirt is the best one of all. I didn't want to hurt Lisa and Bobby's feelings, but theirs were way messier. And the colors I used are his favorite. Mine's second best. Some of the same colors, but not exactly. We don't need to be twins, right? That would be silly." She giggles as she stops admiring them to continue packing.

"No, being twins wouldn't work—he's way too big to be your twin." I giggle, too, but also because I'm not so sure that Everett is a tie-dye kind of guy, but who knows? I'm guessing he'll wear it for her either way, though.

As I'm preparing dinner for our last evening, Beth calls from the other room, "Lissa, your phone's ringing in here. It says it's Daddy. Can I answer it?"

"Absolutely—I told you the pass code the other day, right?"

"I know—1-2-1-2-1-2 . . ."

As she walks in the kitchen, I hear her say, "Yes, it's lots of fun here. Is that why you're coming tonight? You want to have fun, too?"

Looking very focused, she nods her head and hands me the phone.

"Um, hello. Everett? Did I hear Beth say you're coming here? I'm confused."

"It's a long story and I'd rather talk to you both in person. I'm arriving in a couple of hours. I already talked to Eric—he's picking me up. Please keep Beth up—I need to see her, okay?"

I have a million questions, but keep them to myself and tell him, "Of course. We'll be here. She should be fine staying up a little late—wouldn't calm down anyway knowing you're on your way."

I can't read his face when he comes in the door. That is, until he sees Beth. His open arms invite her to run screaming, "Hi, Daddy! Thanks for the surprise! I've lots of stuff to show you."

"Beth, how about if you go do that while I warm up some dinner for your daddy. He's probably hungry."

"Daddy—I have a new book about animals. Can we go read it in my room? I want to tell you about it. Did you know that Auntie Emma once rode an elephant?"

Everett follows a smiling Beth toward the bedroom she's adopted while here. I take my time getting things ready so that they can catch up and she can share her projects and stories with him.

I decide to go poke my head in and see if he's ready to eat yet. They're both in her bed, her eyes are closed with a book flopped on her tummy. Everett is stroking her curls and staring at her. I wave to catch his eye, and he nods his head to let me know he's coming.

Not too long later, Everett comes downstairs, wearing his tie-dye shirt, and sits in the chair next to me.

"Wow—love the shirt! Is she asleep yet? Or is she still too wound up from telling you stories?"

He laughs and shakes his head. "She's definitely full of stories, wants to tell me every single one right away. Each time I thought she was finished, she'd come up with something else. And of course, she insisted I put on this awesome, and kinda flashy, shirt she made."

"She's proud of that shirt! We packed a lot of stories, a lot of projects, a lot of walks into our time. She's a ball of energy and an absolute sponge for information. Definitely kept me on my toes. I loved every second. Thank you for sharing this effervescent child of yours with me. I'm sure you've missed her tremendously while I'm relishing the moments."

"Oh yeah, I've missed her. I want to thank *you*, Lissa. Listening to her just now, this week made her so happy. And it made my work life easy. But the thanks are for more than just the time this week. Of course, it was great to have her be somewhere fun on her vacation. Great to have her exposed to all the things I can't do, or don't have time for, or whatever. But, even more, thank you for sharing your life with her, your life now, and the life you lived before we came into your life. Hearing about your life through Beth, hearing the little lessons you weave into everything you do with her, hearing about Emma and Eric as kids—that makes me know you better. I think I needed that—Beth likes it, but I need it. Does that make sense?"

I think so, and I'm touched, but I want to know more. "Tell me more about what you need, Everett. We're in one another's lives now and I'd like to understand."

"It's, well, when we met—when I found out you were my biological mother—my mom, the mom who raised me, was dying. Even though she wanted me to know you—hell, she orchestrated the whole thing—I felt weird thinking of you as my mother. And you longed for us to be one big family. It sounded cool, but how could that happen? How could I think of you as my mother? Eric as my brother? I hardly knew anything about you, except that you didn't keep me when I was born."

I hope I keep my wince internal at that one. It hurts.

He walks into the kitchen for a drink, returns to the chair next to mine and continues, "Not trying to make you feel bad—I know that's not how you wanted it. But, I wasn't prepared to accept you. The mother I've known all my life dies, and now I'm supposed to be in this family I don't even know, with another mother? I wanted to—for you, for Beth, for Eric, but didn't really know how. And all of you calling me Everett, when I'd grown up as Emery. Your intensity intimidated me. I knew you meant well. I don't know if I'm saying this right."

I hear the sincerity in his voice and absolutely do not want him trying to make me feel better. I want to stay with what he needs.

"You're not making me feel bad. I'm honored you're sharing this with me. There's no doubt that it was, and is, challenging. And the timing was far from ideal. I sure didn't want you to feel pressured to let me in as some kind of replacement mom. No one could—Harriett was a special lady, and I'm more grateful than I can even say that she was in your life when I couldn't be. I also know, because she told me in no uncertain terms, that she wasn't going to leave this earth until she got you and me together."

I pause to gather the ideas swirling in my head and turn them into words. As I'm formulating my thoughts, I start to address him as Everett, but stop myself and don't use either name.

"You know, when we elevate someone into a role in our lives, it doesn't mean we diminish anyone else. Like when you make a new friend, your old ones don't become less precious. If it's your wish to have two people in your life with a mother role, you can do that. Letting me in doesn't mean Harriett is any less the beloved mother she has always been."

He's nodding his head, then offers, "Right, and I get that on a cognitive level. But when I was trying to figure out how to think of you as my mother, I knew nothing about you. Nothing about you, your parents, your other kids. I jumped into your life midstream. Not like if we'd grown together from the time I was born. That's what I feel with Beth. Every day that she grows, so do I. Heck, I didn't know how to be a dad—to say nothing of a dad to a girl. We're learning together as we go. With you—I couldn't figure out how to make up for all that living you did before finding me."

He reaches for my hand, "That's what I'm trying to say feels different now—the sharing. Like at Christmas when you heard the song about Emma performed live in your home—I *shared* that emotional moment with you and Eric and the others. It was our moment all together. And now I'm hearing directly from you about Emma and Eric growing up. Beth showed me photos of you as a young mom with them looking over Niagara Falls. It feels like I'm beginning to be a part of your story and of making *our* story. I can share your past as well as the future. I like getting to know you, and I'm liking it for Beth. Actually, I love it."

After all my doubts and anxiety, I'm basking in his revelations. I couldn't ask for more.

"Everett, this makes me very happy. I haven't been able to figure out how much sharing is too much or too little. Or, how much you want me to help you and Beth. And I can't stop myself from saying Everett, even though I know you've been Emery for decades—it just comes out. I'm flying by the seat of my pants here—fighting my desire to see you both every possible minute, because I know I need to respect that you have your own lives—maybe I'm part of it, maybe not. I guess all we can do is keep reaching out and being honest about our comfort levels. I'm grateful that we're figuring it out."

"Yeah, but Larissa, you have a lot of experience being a parent, and taking care of everyone around you. Talk about flying by the seat of your pants, when Addie, Beth's mom died, I didn't know what I was doing. Sad, missing my wife, and now I gotta do this by myself? I gotta figure out how to braid her hair today and who knows what later? I'm a total newbie—every step of the way."

He must have felt so overwhelmed. And who could help him? Addie's mom kept her distance, and still does. His own mother was over a thousand miles away, and already sick, and me, well, we didn't even know each other.

"I think you're doing pretty damn well, my dear. She's a smart, beautiful child. And by the way, you did braid her hair for Eric's wedding, and there's an adorable photo to prove it."

"Well, I saw you sneak in and smooth out that hair before the ceremony. But, thanks. I try, Lissa. I do try."

"I think you're doing great."

Everett takes a few deep breaths. His eyes capture mine and grab my attention.

Clearly, there is more. "What, what is it? What did you need to come talk to us about, Everett?"

"I need to ask you a favor, a pretty huge favor. And, you might change your mind about me doing great as a parent."

This sounds more serious than I'd expected.

"Go ahead . . . ask me."

"I should have made the decision sooner, I know that. It was too hard. Oh, God, I just have to spit it out. Can Beth stay with you for a longer time? Like, well, I don't know exactly how long. But, at least a couple of months?"

A couple of months? At least?

8

*H*is request, and the story related to it, spills out in bits and pieces. His marketing strategies have brought him plenty of accolades here and they want him to share his approaches abroad. While he's flattered, it's been tough for him to come to this moment. A huge career opportunity at odds with his monumental efforts to be the best single parent he possibly can be. And that's not even mentioning his repeated apologies about putting this on me. I've got a few questions, but I'm thrilled at the chance to help him and to spend precious time with Beth. A few of my own work commitments are swirling around in my head, but nothing that can't be accommodated if he's sure this is what he wants or needs to do.

"Everett, I think I've got it all now. This new marketing, or launch involves several weeks of European travel starting when, again?"

"I'd need to leave in a few weeks. I answered my boss that I was seriously interested in going, but need some time to make arrangements with family before I would commit. I didn't just assume this could work out. It's a big ask."

Treading lightly, I ask for more information. "And did you think about taking Beth with you? Living abroad is a once in a lifetime opportunity and, I mean, there are well-thought-of schools in those countries for children of Americans working there."

"Yeah, kinda, but not really. I don't think there's enough time to investigate options like that. Wouldn't it take research and jumping a bunch of hurdles for admission? Sounds overwhelming. Where would I even start? I can't predict my schedule, and I'll probably be moving around between locations."

"You're right—could be a lot under these circumstances. So, what about Beth and school if she's staying here? Thoughts?"

"That's one of the reasons I waited a few more days before asking you. I met with her teacher and principal yesterday. There's a couple of options. You and Beth need to be part of the decision. Because there are some kids from her school at home that are sick or have disabilities that make coming to school tough, she could participate in school the way they do, by video, but it's designed for short-term situations. We could try it and see. Or, she can do a temporary transfer to school here—like whatever school Eric and Emma went to? If that's not a hassle for you."

He wrings his hands, then rubs them together, just like Eric does. Could that be genetic?

"And I know beggars can't be choosers, but I kinda prefer public schools. I know a lot of, well, people in the South who are able, send their kids to private school, but I don't think that's the best idea. The best thing about public school in New York

City is, well, there are a lot of kids, as well as teachers, who look to be from families of mixed races, or first generation in the U.S. She's far from the only kid in her school who looks like she does. I think that's good for her—and it sure wouldn't have been that way if we lived where I grew up. I'm thinking public school here would be the same."

I nod attentively. I want him to keep going—we've never spoken directly about Beth's racial background, and it might be important as we figure this thing out.

"Anyway, if it's just up to me, I think it's best she enrolls in school here, but she might be afraid or worried. What do you think?"

I think through my opinion for a minute and offer it carefully.

"We definitely need to ask her, but not imply she has free rein. We need to present our preference convincingly. I agree with you about public school. As a single mother, I couldn't afford to send the kids to a private school, but don't think I would have anyway. Beth has already made friends with kids who go to the school we'd place her in: Isabel's kids, Lisa and Bobby. Isabel is Puerto Rican, and their father is also Latino. Beth won't be the only one here, either."

He nods his head and his facial features soften.

Thinking about it further, I add, "All that aside, back to the virtual option, I think she should be around kids her age. There's so much more to school than the formal curriculum. Good news is, vast majority of the time, my work schedule is very flexible. One exception—I was supposed to go on a trip to do training next week. It would be good if I keep that commitment."

"Oh, yes, definitely—do the trip. Like I said, I have a little time. Beth and I will go back to home till the schedule gets finalized. We can figure that out."

"Yeah, how about we call it a night and regroup in the morning? I'm happy to do it, Everett, if you're sure you want to move into the managing side of marketing. We can work out details as they come up. I have a lot of support here. If something comes up, Eric and Hilary, Isabel, and Renee are around all the time. Then, there's all the other folks who pop in and out. As the saying goes, *it takes a village.* I'm blessed here with a great group of villagers."

"Thank you for listening, not judging. I called Kristy about this and she yelled at me for ten minutes about being selfish before she calmed down and listened to me, listened to how Beth spent her time with you the last ten days. By the end, she was offering to help too. Hell, she's not all that far away if you want a getaway back to Florida."

I pull him toward me for a goodnight hug, but it's so much more. Here is life, once again, throwing a monkey-wrench into our paths. The hug is affirmation that we will figure out a way. A way to navigate challenges and stand strong together.

A list of more questions and a tentative to-do list keep popping into my head when I close my eyes. It's as if a huge movie screen is projecting all of these distractions onto the back of my eyelids to derail my attempts at sleep. Instead of my usual deep breathing, I repeat a couple of silent mantras over and over: *wipe the screen clean; blank screen equals blank mind.*

Either the mantras worked or sheer exhaustion won the battle with my racing mind. I awaken to the muffled sound of voices downstairs and the whole list of questions leapfrogs right back to the forefront of my thoughts. The two downstairs and I have a busy day of talking and decision-making ahead of us.

As I walk slowly toward the coffee pot, Beth grabs my legs and says, "Daddy got a travel bug too, Lissa. He told me he's going on a big trip. I can't go cuz it's work. He said I can stay here."

I'm caught off guard. I thought we'd have the conversation together. But, maybe he wanted to start alone with her. It's his call, not mine. Time to follow his lead. My comments will be simple and neutral.

"Yes, he told me about his work trip last night. What do you think?"

"I think it's okay, I guess. He said we'd talk more when you got up. Can we have waffles?"

After consuming the pile of sticky breakfast deliciousness, we stack the dishes in the sink. Everett suggests we go in the living room and talk. He calls it a strategy meeting.

Once he's answered Beth's demand to define *strategy*, he starts, most likely where he and Beth left off before I came downstairs.

"So, like I told you and Lissa, I have a chance to share what I've learned here with people in new places. It will also let other important workers at the company learn more about what I might be able to do in the future. Remember when I told you that my work is called marketing? That's a fancy word for selling. They are asking me to go teach sellers in other countries about how I've done it here. If I spend this time away now, then afterwards, I might be able to do things in the company that I've hoped to do for a long time. And we might be able to live someplace else if we want to. So, while it's going to be hard to be away from you, there might be some good things that come out of it down the road."

I'm hanging on every word out of Everett's mouth. He's doing a great job explaining something pretty complicated to her. I need to remember what he's saying in case I need to repeat it, or follow up later.

"Daddy, Lissa and I had a tea bag that kinda said that. It said if you like how a rose smells, then you have to like the thorns, too. Right, Lissa?"

The coffee nearly blasts from my nose as I burst out laughing. That tea bag lesson—it fits the situation perfectly.

Everett looks over at me. "Tea bag?"

"We started having mint tea in the afternoon when we needed breaks between our projects. She liked the ones that come with little sayings or proverbs on them. And she's right. There was one that helped us understand that with good things, there are sometimes bad things. It does fit. Thanks for reminding us, Beth."

After covering a few more details, Everett brings up school.

Beth listens attentively, likes the idea of going to school with Lisa and Bobby. She then brings up her own concern, one we hadn't gotten to yet. "It's all okay, Daddy. Don't look so sad. But there's stuff at home that I want to have here. Like the stuffed animals you said had to stay home when we came down here, my books, my other clothes, my corner desk, my--"

"Whoa—you can't bring everything. You won't be gone forever, you know."

At the word *can't*, tears slip down Beth's cheeks. And before she can catch them, she really starts a heaving cry. "You said my stuffed giraffe and sloth would be fine alone for ten days while I visited Lissa. But this is too long, Daddy. They'll miss me too much. It's not fair."

I've been letting him take the lead and don't want to make things worse, but I have to suggest something. I can't watch this whole plan disintegrate, or at least her investment in it be lost, over her prized possessions. Who doesn't want their special things with them?

"Everett, there's got to be a way to get Beth's things here. We have some time to think about it before you need to leave. You two are going home while I'm getting my work travel checked off my list. You can sort through things, Beth can go to school, have the chance to say goodbye to her teacher and friends. Then, either you bring her back here, or maybe I come up there? Heck, I could fly there and we can drive back. I'll rent a car? Beth and I can make a stop or two along the way. It could work. We've got three good brains here. Let's put them together and make a plan—isn't that what strategy meetings are all about?"

The tear-streaked face looks up at him and says, "Can we, Daddy? Can we do Lissa's plan?"

Although we adjourn the official strategy meeting, we keep working out the details as Beth and I take Everett to the park for a walk, then stop for dinner with Eric and Hilary. While Eric is showing Everett and Beth around their house, I fill Hilary in on the new twist my life is about to take—at least for the next few months.

After expressing her happiness for me and the time I'll have with Beth, she makes an interesting comment. "How do you think Everett is going to do with this? He's never traveled the way you have. He grew up in that small fishing town in Florida, went to college nearby, and has been in New York ever since. Not only is he going to be away from his little girl for the longest time ever, he's going to be figuring out what it's like to be in foreign countries. You couldn't see his face at Christmas when you were talking about all the places you've been. He looked kinda terrified, if you ask me."

"Jeepers. I hadn't even thought about that. I've been so focused on Beth, and figuring out how that is going to unfold. He may have some struggles he hasn't even thought about yet. Guess we'll be supporting him in more than one way."

"Didn't mean to put something else in your head to worry about. You're a good grandma to do this. He's lucky to have you."

9

The meaning of life is to find your gift.
The purpose of life is to give it away.
PABLO PICASSO

It takes a bit of time to adjust to the quieter house. But I'm far from lonely. The ties created while Beth was here, and the prospect of not only having more time with her but also helping Everett reach his career aspirations, have filled me with hope for the future. So many times I've been afraid to hope, afraid of disappointment if things don't go as envisioned. This time, there's no room for fear. I need to forge ahead with resolve and get things in place for our new arrangement.

At my appointment with Marie the day before I need to travel for work, she asks me about our holidays and my time with Beth.

After recounting how Beth showed enthusiastic interest in almost everything, I ponder my newfound confidence as a grandma. "Before Christmas, I had the feeling that Everett was concerned about Beth's visit, maybe even reluctant to let me into their lives. And I was hesitant to share much about our lives as a family when Emma and Eric were young. I worried it might make Everett feel left out. I could only hope that I'd get closer to Beth and learn how to connect with her, but the unexpected joy is that Everett shared how much closer *he* feels. Now it looks like that closeness has evolved into something even bigger. I'm pretty happy right now, Marie. I can't tell you the last time I could say that." Just as I'm about to fill her in on what I mean by 'bigger', she interjects.

"It's wonderful to hear the time together has made such an impact on you, Larissa. It sounds like it has on them as well. What a blessing it worked out that way! Do you think there's anything else making you happy, besides the art projects and outings, and Everett's reflections? Not that those are at all trivial, I just think there's more to it than you've considered."

"Well, those art projects and nature walks and museum visits let me build a story with Beth and Everett. That makes me happy. But . . ."

"Of course. Shared stories, shared history are big parts of family relationships and will likely continue to deepen your ties. I think there's something else I'm hearing, though, that I haven't heard from you in awhile—maybe since Eric came home and needed to reconnect with you. I'm hearing you say that you have an expanded purpose. It sounds to me as if Beth and Everett both want and need you in their lives. And being needed is something that's important to you—without Emma, and with Eric missing, I think you questioned why you even existed."

Questioned why? That's an understatement. I didn't even want to exist without them.

"When you started working again and Eric returned, you began to have more of a reason to move forward. And when searching for Everett, there was purpose—my heavens, you were driven to find that son of yours. Once you found him, though, I think you floundered again. Eric moved out of your house and in with his wife. And you were uncertain of your role with Everett and Beth. But, given the chance, you dove into being part of Beth's life. You shared your past, your love of travel, and Everett appreciated it all. You're finding purpose again. I think purpose may be one of the few parts of happiness over which we have some control. Pat yourself on the back. You haven't given up, in spite of many times that it might have felt as if giving up was the answer. Rejoice in your purpose!"

I feel my head nodding as I try to respond to her. "Thank you. Maybe that idea is obvious to you, but I hadn't thought of a sense of purpose in quite that way before. Maybe because I took it for granted for so many years—there was no real questioning or searching for purpose—it was right in my face, day in and day out. Raising the kids and working, I was like a hamster on a wheel. If anything, maybe I wished for a break from my purpose. Huh—another thing I didn't appreciate till it was gone."

"You're certainly not alone in that, Larissa. So often, when people are telling me they need to 'find themselves,' I think it has to do with figuring out a reason for getting up every day and contributing in some meaningful way to the world. When our roles change because of loss or major life changes, the whole idea of purpose gets overlooked in the wreckage. It sounds like you've been given the gift of purpose as your Christmas present."

"The other gift is that Beth will be spending more time with me. She's going to live here temporarily while Everett takes an extended work assignment. So, I'm going to have purpose, all right!"

That evening, I share my conversation about finding purpose with Eric and Hilary. I see a sly smile on Eric's lips and Hilary returning a look to him that I can't quite interpret.

Eric comments, "And you're still working. And Beth is coming to stay. You've got a lot going on and quite a bit of purpose, if you ask me. Think you can handle it all?"

"Yes, Eric, I can handle this and more. Always have—well, until you flew the coop and Emma passed away. Like Marie said, I was floundering there for awhile. Talk about the rug being yanked out from under me, going from a mom of two lovely, but headstrong, young adults, to having no one anywhere in my reach, you could say my purpose was unabashedly squashed! Pretty damn brutal. Now—being in the midst of you two, Everett, Beth—I'm loving all of this purpose. At this stage of my life, work isn't my purpose anymore—it's a means to an end. A way to support myself, take care of my home, but not my purpose."

"Glad to hear it, Mom. We love you and like seeing you so enthusiastic again. Wondering though, well, if you can handle more."

"What do you mean, more? I don't need a pet, if that's what you're talking about. I'm perfectly happy that you guys took Valentino off my hands. He's a sweet dog, but he always preferred you and Emma to anyone else."

"No, Mom, I'm not talking about Valentino. Hilary and I, well, looks like we're going to make you a grandmother—I mean, I know you're already Beth's, but I'm thinking this one will call you something other than Lissa, and this little nugget will be around longer than a couple of months."

Surprise, joy, love, all well up inside me and I erupt with, "What? Are you kidding? You're going to? I'm going to? Oh, my good heavens, I've got no words. And, hell yes, I'd like more of this kind of purpose. Tell me the details—and by the way, I kinda like being called 'Lissa,' but I'm not going to quibble with whatever this baby ends up calling me—as long as I get called!"

I make a pot of decaf and wait for more info. Hilary fills me in on how she's feeling, the expected due date, and what she thinks of her doctor. She adds, "We came to tell you first. With my mom gone, well, I adore my dad, but for some reason, I wanted to tell you first. I really love how you welcomed me into your family. It's special. We're going to go over and tell Dad now. We're not just dropping the news, then rushing out on you, but I know he'll be ecstatic too."

I'm glowing with Hilary's admission that she wanted to tell me first. Tragic she lost her mother far too young, but I'm grateful for this—yet another purpose.

Always thinking I should remind him, I also suggest, "And Eric, what about telling Steven? You can't forget--"

He cuts me off. "I'm not forgetting, Mom. Geez—give me some credit. I texted Dad this afternoon to ask when he could talk—he's working late, so after we go see Paul, I'll be calling him. Then, we're heading to bed. This mamma over here has been exhausted every night. Got to get her to bed."

After they leave, I grab my phone to call Renee or Isabel. But stop myself and grab a sweatshirt instead. I want to reflect a bit out on the patio—my sanctuary, where I've contemplated so many of life's pivotal moments—good and bad and everything in between. This particular moment is definitely right up there at the top. It strikes me yet again how tough it is to fathom being this happy, this overjoyed, yet knowing that in the next minute, something could remind me of Emma and I'll feel miserable about being so happy. The constant pull between emotions is agonizing, even after all this time. Time has nothing to do with the depth of the feelings of grief. It may not be the acute pain it once was, but the hurt lingers nonetheless. Thinking of Emma reminds me of my resolve to go see a psychic about the song.

Life has been so full since the holidays that it totally slipped my mind. I'd like to do that before Beth comes to stay. Next time I see Renee, I'm going to bring it up and see what we can work out.

My ringing phone jolts me back from my thoughts, and I see that it's Renee calling. Of course it is—I swear she has some innate sense about when there's news to share.

Trying to wrap up after sharing details about Beth and the fabulous news from Eric and Hilary, I continue, "Yeah, so, for the first time in a very long time, I can say I'm in a pretty darn good place, my friend. I feel a little guilty, like it somehow violates Emma, but something tells me she's watching over this whole thing. I feel her when I'm with Beth, and before you called, I felt her with me out here on the patio. Finding a meaningful purpose also honors her, I think. Don't you?"

"I sure do. It stinks, but we can't change how Emma's life went, we can't make Isabel's ex be a decent guy, and we can't bring back Everett's wife. But we can make the most of what we're doing here and now. Every time you make a decision to do something good, something positive, you're honoring this gift of life—for you, your kids, your grandkids. We do have purpose, and we can be happy about it without needing to feel guilty or regretful. At least that's how I look at it."

"While we're talking about Emma, remember when you offered at Thanksgiving to go with me to a psychic? To ask about the song? Will you still do that if I can get an appointment soon?"

She agrees enthusiastically and I tell her I'll try to get a time scheduled and get back to her.

As soon as I hang up, I look for a scrap pad to make a note to myself to call in the morning. So much is happening so quickly, to-do lists are the only way I accomplish anything. As I finish picking up the house, I spot the photo albums that Beth and I pored over. A soft, mauve-colored book, embossed with gold swirls, is right on top. Emma gave it to me shortly after she came back from an inpatient stay. In letters resembling calligraphy, she'd titled it "Things I'm grateful for." As I flip through the photos of what she'd assembled, I'm touched by all that she'd included. Photos of her, and Eric, and me, but also of a butterfly perched on a flower and a cardinal in the birdbath in our yard, and a close-up of my hand holding hers. A sort of tribute to the insight her rehab experience had given her into gratitude for everyday moments.

Huh—I didn't look at this album with Beth; in fact, I'd forgotten about it until just now. How did it get on top of this pile? Did Beth look at it on her own? Did Eric pull it out? Or is this a sign from Emma that she approves of what's going on right now? A message she wants to connect with me as well? I choose that explanation. As I lie down in bed and try to calm down from the excitement, I embrace the message from Emma with all my heart, and gratitude lulls me to sleep.

10

Music is well said to be the speech of angels.
THOMAS CARLYLE

The note to make an appointment is waiting on the counter when I pour my first cup of coffee. The contact info for the local person recommended by the psychic I visited while in the Finger Lakes is still in my phone. After five rings, a recording comes on to tell me to leave a message and Miss Lillian will get back to me.

A woman's breathless voice interrupts the recording with, "Oh, hello. It's me, Miss Lillian. What may I help you with?"

Even though she is slightly breathless, the tone of her voice is calming and I immediately feel at ease. This is a good decision.

"I'm looking for an appointment with you. Another psychic I visited while out of town recommended you. Do you have any openings? Preferably this week?"

"I've been very busy, but just a few minutes ago, had a cancellation for my last appointment today. I don't know if you have a flexible schedule or not, but can you make it today? Otherwise, I'm booked solid for the next two weeks. Something about holiday time and a new year starting, I guess."

I silently scan through my calendar. There is plenty I should get done today, but no specific commitments. *Heck, might as well go today and see what happens!*

"I can be there. I'm looking forward to this."

"Great—your voice tells me that you have someone special in the spirit world, so I'm happy we can make it happen today. Many blessings to you and be well until we meet."

I hang up the phone and feel warmth settle over me. This is the right thing for me right now.

As I pull into Miss Lillian's driveway, I'm relieved to be going alone—Renee couldn't make it with so little notice. The first time, I needed her beside me. I had so much trepidation, no clue what to expect. But this time, I want to immerse myself totally and not be thinking about someone else.

The walkway to the purple front door is bordered by colorful stepping stones. Each one has a different image of something from nature—flowers, butterflies, birds, shells, and turtles. I immediately feel at home.

The door flings open and a woman who must be Lillian emerges with tie-dyed, flowing pants, an embroidered smock top and bare feet. Her toenails match her purple door and her fingernails are silver glitter. I can't help but smile at her mere presence.

"Hello, hello, welcome. Come in and settle yourself. I'm making some herbal tea. Would you like some?"

We walk into a small room off of the entry hall and settle into corduroy loveseats—mine pale green, hers purple. She hands me my tea, and her gray-blue eyes hold mine for several seconds.

"You said you'd been to a psychic before. We are all devoted to communicating with those in spirit, to connecting worlds, to bringing angel messages, yet we also differ. I'll quickly explain what you can expect here, then let's get going, see who wants to enter our space today."

I sip the hot, floral tea and listen carefully. Much of what she says is similar to the others I've visited.

"You're nodding your head, so I'm guessing you're comfortable? I will open with a greeting to the angels, sort of a prayer, and see who wants to be with us. Sometimes there are spirits with whom you do not want to connect, or who do not seem familiar to you. That's fine, this is your time. I'll ask you if what I am seeing and hearing makes sense to you, and you can confirm or turn down any particular soul. Ready?"

I nod my head again, find my pen and paper, then turn on the recording feature on my phone. I do not want to miss any detail.

"I see an older couple. They're holding hands and reaching toward you. Maybe parents or grandparents?"

"Probably my parents. We had some differences in my teens, but were very close otherwise."

"The woman is putting her arms out as if she wants to embrace you. She's touching a necklace, looks like a heart charm on it?"

Smiling at the memory, I confirm that the locket makes sense, "Yes, my kids and I gave her a heart locket on the last Mother's Day she was still with us."

Lillian is quiet for a moment, then continues, "She's gesturing to someone else. A young woman with long, wavy hair. Almost like she's encouraging her to come forward. The young woman is approaching slowly. The older woman continues to pull her closer."

Tears are welling in the back of my eyes and throat. "Probably my daughter."

Lillian nods her head and gives me more information, "I feel like a name that begins with 'E'? Emily or Emma?"

"Yes, yes, it's her. My daughter is Emma." My voice is quavering. The same feeling that overtook me the last time, almost like low-level electricity coursing through my body, puts me on the edge of the soft furniture. I want to hear her so much; I crave this connection. Lillian is my bridge to Emma.

"Emma wants you to know that she watches you all the time. She says that when you're happy, she's happy. She says that she sends you signs every day. Sometimes, several a day."

"Yes, I believe she does. What kind of signs, does she say? I want to be sure I recognize them."

"Emma says that living things are the easiest for her. She particularly likes butterflies and birds; wants you to see them as her, but sometimes it's other things. Do you see cardinals and think of her? And are you ever near the water? She is making me think turtles or dolphins? Does this make any sense to you? There's not much water or even beaches close by."

"Yes, it does makes sense. When I do go to the beach, I feel like she's there as well, just in a bit different form. One of my favorite places has dolphins on one side of the island and turtles on the other."

I'm compelled to look upward. "Oh, thank you, honey. I love feeling you there."

"She's also holding up three fingers. I think she's saying that three is an important number and that you should look for things in threes. Like three butterflies together, or even three pennies."

Hmm. I instantly get the image of Beth and I finding pennies on our picnic, there were three. I knew they were pennies from heaven.

"Do you want to ask her anything? She's continuing, but if you want to know anything in particular, now might be a good time."

I'm so caught up in what has been shared already, that I almost forget my main reason for coming.

"Oh, yes, thank you for reminding me. Someone has written a special song. I'd like to know if Emma knows about it."

Lillian is still again, her eyes are closed, with her head leaning back. She is clearly listening intently. A smile breaks out over her face.

"Emma is humming a tune. Its rhythm is both energizing and calming. Wait, I'm catching some words. Something about smiles are stories from the heart, something about stories and songs being connectors, she's making a bridge-like gesture with her fingers together and elbows splayed. Wait, then she's repeating her name and smiling. Do you think that's about the song you mentioned?"

My head nods, but I can't speak. I can't find any words. I can smile, but I can't talk. I sense Lillian waiting, but not pushing for a response. No idea how much time lapses while I try to articulate how grateful I am for this message from Emma. The strength of the reassurance is beyond anything I might have expected.

"That is most definitely the song. I was worried that maybe it would make Emma ashamed or embarrassed in some way. A former counselor, no, a friend of hers, has written and recorded it. While I agreed right away that it was beautiful, my fears about it being too personal were stopping me from encouraging Monica any further."

"Emma says this—I'm going to try to repeat her words exactly: 'Let it be, Mamma, let Monica sing it; I'm happy she wants to connect with me. Just like I'm happy when you connect with me. Let everyone enjoy it. Songs are bridges between our hearts.'"

I don't want this to end. Lillian begins to tire and closes the reading with another short prayer. I feel like I'm being cut off from Emma, but I'm also exhausted. I need to get home and rest.

This is when I really need Renee, to be my driver after another extraordinary experience.

Home is where I need to be more than ever. I feel Emma as I walk in the front door. Her portrait over the fireplace brings me back into Lillian's sitting room. Her presence is unmistakable here, and was unmistakable there. I start to call Renee, then stop. I search for Eric's number in my "recents," but pull my finger back. I want to share this, but I simply can't yet.

Playing the recording is my decision. Listening to Emma's words via Lillian's voice is the balm for my anguish. Her presence and her words deliver assurance of her support for the song being shared. I'm bolstered enough to face whatever comes along with Monica's release.

Don't move the way that fear moves you.
RUMI

The following week, while packing my work suits, I catch the end of a report on TV that makes me pause. Ever since Emma died, I've shielded myself from too much news. The constant tragedies take my breath away. Mass shootings, school bullying, I just don't have the ability to get through those stories. And the nasty politics have gotten almost unreal to me. The day when I caught myself screaming at the TV, "Do you really think more hate is going to change anything?" was the day I decided to take a break. So, mostly, I just skim headlines on a device and move on. Yet ever since I declared my wish to travel again, I've paid more attention. Gotta know what's going on in the world if you're going to satisfy that travel bug. Globe-trotting might have to wait now until Everett returns, but it doesn't hurt to dream a little. And after all, I might get a chance to do some travel with Beth. I've got to remember to look up the best route to drive from New York back here and see what interesting places there may be to stop.

The report that causes me to take pause is talking about some mysterious virus in China. It's halfway around the world—but they're speculating it might be a global health emergency. *What the heck? This feels surreal, like they're sensationalizing.*

The next day, strangely enough, in the midst of a training session about our company's latest wheelchair innovations, an equipment sales person who recently traveled abroad brought up the virus news. If I hadn't seen it yesterday, I'd have had no clue what she was even talking about.

"Yeah, I just got back from a trip to Germany and the UK, and people there are talking about their governments possibly not allowing any flights to come in from China. It's pretty weird. Do we distribute mobility devices in China, Larissa?"

"China? No, not really. Staff are constantly searching for new market opportunities, but as far as I've heard, that's not planned anytime soon. I've heard nothing in-house about whatever havoc this virus is causing. And honestly, I'm surprised at the language in the press about a health emergency. Sounds like the news just wants to scare us. I don't know about all of you, but putting aside work travel, I was hoping to go on vacation soon."

A light-hearted chuckle goes around the room before we return to the day's agenda. Back in my hotel room that evening, I call Isabel to tell her we're going to have to postpone yoga for a couple of weeks with all that's going on in my life.

"Well, your life is certainly going in a new direction. A road trip with a granddaughter, then caretaking for weeks, maybe months. What are you thinking of all that?"

"To be honest, I'm excited of course, but also still just trying to believe it all. Wasn't that long ago that I felt like I'd never see Everett and Beth enough—now this. It's definitely a big change, but, well, I can't wait!"

We laugh and agree that we will be seeing lots more of each other with her kids and Beth in school together.

"Let me know if there's anything I can do to help you get her enrolled, or to connect with some of the after-school activities. We can share carpooling too!"

After we hang up, the thought of getting back into all the activities that kids want to be part of makes me tired. I settle down into my comfortable hotel bed with a glass of wine to get a much-needed night of sleep before another long training day tomorrow and a late flight home.

Looking at my phone as soon as I wake up, there are texts from Everett and Eric, and before I finish reading them, my alarm—the least obnoxious tone I could find, but it's still abrasive—sounds as well.

Eric's text wants to know my return time, and Everett's is pretty benign as well, just asking me to call him when I get a chance. I answer "will do" with a reminder that I'm traveling and getting back home tonight.

Once the meeting is done, and scrolling through more news while taking a ride-share to the airport, my attention is grabbed, then captivated by the song coming out of the car radio.

"Hey, sir, can you turn that song up?"

Confused, the driver meets my eyes in his rear view and seeing me nod with a ridiculously wide grin on my face, he responds, "Yeah, sure, usually my riders want me to keep it down."

I put my finger to my lips to quiet him, then to my ear so he knows I want to listen. I set my phone on the seat next to me and allow Monica's melody for Emma to come through the speakers and surround me. It is magical to hear this song, this tribute, at this moment. *At any moment, Larissa.* If I'm hearing it on my way to the airport, I may hear it in elevators, stores, or anywhere else that pipes in music. It's surreal, yet very real.

When the song finishes, the driver says, "Hey, that's a pretty tune. How do you know it? I mean, if it's not being too nosy," his voice trails off as if he's second-guessing asking me the question.

"Well, it's kind of a long story, but I'll keep it short. Someone wrote that song about my daughter."

"Wow! That's way cool. I'm up for a story—we still got a half hour to the airport. About your daughter?"

Hesitating while I figure out how much I want to say, I then come out with, "Yes, the song is cool, the story is bittersweet. My daughter passed away a couple of years ago. A woman wrote and recorded that song about her, about Emma. The title is about Emma's smile—the writer called it 'Smiles from Her Heart.'" I'm smiling while I say it. I might cry later thinking about it all, but right now, the joy of hearing this song when I least expected it is, well, unexpected but so welcome.

"Oh, wow, well, I'm sorry about your daughter. That's totally sad. But, that song, it's amazing. I'll keep hearing it in my head the rest of the day. It's catchy, you know? And I know someone with a smile like that—a smile that makes you feel instantly connected. My sister has that kind of smile. She's sick and in the hospital, but when she smiles, it's like that. I'm gonna download that song and play it for her tonight after work."

"You're a good brother. I hope you both smile when you listen to it. And I hope she gets well soon."

For the rest of the ride, I contemplate the whole idea of this song. It's happening, it's getting out into the world. And if this driver is any indication, it has the power to touch people. He's taking it to play to his sick sister, for Pete's sake. The magic of music and how it makes people feel. Seems like this one wrapped around his heart—and he's a total stranger. Sure, our whole family was enraptured, but we were hardly an objective audience. This is genuine, spontaneous feedback. I need to get in touch with Monica and let her know.

The driver gets me to the airport in great time, and I leave him an extra tip. He was also a kind man, a good soul. I could feel it when he spoke about his sister so tenderly. As I get out of the car, I offer one more time, "Hey, take care of yourself and your sister."

The driver a few hours later—from the airport to home—is not quite so nice. He barely speaks except to mutter under his breath, "I hate going this far outta downtown late at night."

I'm tempted to mutter something back, but keep my mouth shut and stare out the window, breathing a sigh of relief as the sign for my street comes into view.

Not long later, I settle on the couch, rifling through the little bit of mail that had accumulated while I was gone, and my phone lights up with an incoming call from Everett.

I pick up with, "Hey, sorry I didn't call—I got in just a few minutes ago and thought it was too late to talk. Everything good with you?"

"It is kinda late, but I'm just wondering, have you heard about this COVID stuff? That virus? I mean you're kind of in health care, and I thought maybe--"

"Oh, honey, I'm far from a health care professional. I just sell some equipment—walkers and wheelchairs. Why? The little bit I've seen doesn't seem too alarming, at least not here. I wouldn't want to be going to China, but what are you hearing?"

"I don't really get the whole thing, but people here are talking about it—in the line at the grocery store, on the subway. There are rumors that airports in big cities might start screening anyone who's been out of the country. I don't know what to make of it."

Although his questions make me wonder, and raise more in my mind, I quickly take on a calming mother role.

"Well, it is unusual to hear all of this, but I think the news has gotten exaggerated lately. Every story gets blown up for the drama. Maybe we need to just listen and learn from reporters who are most objective. We're in a country with amazing medical resources, I doubt it'll be an issue here. Wasn't there some big flu scare in Asian countries a few years back? Never became the big thing that was predicted. There's no sense in getting upset about all of this."

"Yeah, I guess. It scares me a little, just when I'm getting ready to go on a trip. What the heck?"

I jump right in, "Let's not think the worst. And there's no way your company is going to send you to China, right? It's Europe? UK? Netherlands?"

"Yeah, it's Europe for sure. It's just, well, I've never gone anywhere this far. Moved here for this job straight from Florida. Oh, once I went to Las Vegas with a friend in college. What if I get sick in another country?"

Yup, Hilary was right. He is nervous about going abroad. And now, this whole weird virus thing to give him more anxiety. Time to switch topics to something less stressful.

"Hey, have you talked to your brother, to Eric? Did he share his news?"

"Yeah—whoa! He called me. There's gonna be a baby in the family, huh? Like July, I think? All good, but man, his life will be different. He'll be the one asking you for parenting advice."

Laughing at the idea of Eric figuring out fatherhood, I agree, "Yes, it'll be a whole new world for him. He can do it, we all find a way. It should be fun to watch him though. Seriously, I'm excited! And, Beth will have a cousin." There I go pushing family stuff on him again.

I'm relieved when he responds, "I told her and she's excited, too. She asked twenty questions about when will the baby come, will it be a boy or girl, you know how she wants to understand everything right away."

We chat a few more minutes and agree to talk in a couple of days about which day I'll fly up to get Beth back to Atlanta. Glad that we changed to the lighter topic of Eric's impending fatherhood, the conversation ends on a pleasant note. I text Eric that I made it home fine and add, "Hey, I heard 'Smiles from Her Heart' on the taxi's radio today—amazing." The reply is a heart emoji with a note to talk in the morning. Yup, he's definitely changing his routine already. The former night owl is turning in earlier and earlier.

12

*The only way to make sense out of change is
to plunge into it, move with it, and join the dance.*
ALAN WATTS

The next day, Eric stops by for coffee on his way to work. He
offers to go with me to New York for the moving adventure.
I assure him I'll be fine and remind him of all the fun he, Emma,
and I had on road trips when they were Beth's age.

"Ha, yeah, sometimes it was fun. Other times it was torture
being closed in a car with that little monster. What age was Emma
when she had that high-pitched squeal—sounded like fingernails
on a chalkboard?"

His tone of voice makes me laugh. Then, I notice his silence.

"Damn, I miss her, Mom. I just don't get it."

My hand reaches for his as I whisper, "I don't either, honey.
There is no getting it."

Jerkily shaking his head side to side, he abruptly yanks us
back from that sad place with a glance upward, toward the sky.

"Emma, you little goon, it was a great ride while it lasted."

His reference to a ride and to Emma give me the perfect chance to tell him about my own ride.

"Yesterday, on the way to the airport, Emma's song started playing. The ride-share driver listened along with me when it came on the radio. Naturally, he asked the story behind why the song is special to me. I told him a short version. He was pretty impressed. Said he was going to share it with his sister."

I fiddle with my coffee cup and spoon.

"Eric, I went to a psychic medium the other day. I was worrying myself into a frenzy about the thought of the song becoming a hit—even a huge hit. Maybe that was a pretty far-fetched worry, maybe looking for a problem where there isn't one. But the more I hear it, the more I realize it could happen. I wasn't sure if I'd know how to handle a public demonstration of such a private, intimate work of artistry. Does anybody else have that reaction, or is it just me?"

Eric offers a thought, "Well, aren't most works of art an expression of the artist's experience or interpretation of a person or an event? I mean, isn't there always probably a private story behind creations?"

"Yeah, maybe, but this is my daughter, your sister. I never thought about the story behind songs before. Her story ended in a tragic way, but that's not her whole story. And people are so judgy—like they think she brought the end on herself or something and that makes her bad. I'm scared—wanting to edit the story so people aren't biased about her. I want them to care."

"Right—so maybe other people won't think about the backstory either. For most, like that driver, it'll just be a pretty song about a pretty smile. And after all, regardless of what part of the story is told or not told, her smile did speak a thousand words, made words less important. So, you're saying that you *were* worrying? Did going to the psychic change that?"

"Yeah, sort of. I mean Emma spoke to me through the psychic and said I should let people enjoy it. I should just let it be what it will be. This niggling uneasiness is difficult for me to shake, but hearing those words did help. I have no control over any of this anyway. The song is making it to the airwaves regardless of my fears. And I have to agree, it's appealing in so many ways."

An email the following day from Monica causes me to start thinking about it all over again. I pick up my phone and call Eric.

"What's up, Mom? It's kinda early." His sleepy voice tells me I've definitely woken him up. Too bad, big guy. Better get used to being awakened at any hour.

"Eric, I got an email from Monica. It's like we were talking about last night. 'Smiles from Her Heart' is being downloaded at some crazy rate, it's being played on radio stations, and she got a call from her publicist that someone wants to interview her about the song—like how she wrote it, her inspiration. She's asking me for permission to talk about Emma—does she even need that?"

I can almost envision him running his hands through his hair and rubbing his eyes, trying to figure out what I've said and then how to respond.

"I don't know. She wrote the song, I'm guessing she has a copyright or something. She's asking out of respect. Why don't you see if you guys can meet in person to talk about this? You need to share your thoughts with her. It means too much to you to go back and forth by email. Suggest a visit."

"You think she'd really come see me? Isn't that asking a lot?"

"She can come to you or you go to her. Heck, I think she's in New York pretty often. You could go to her, when you go up to get Beth. Or maybe she wants to come to Atlanta—it's not like you're in the middle of nowhere, right?"

More and more often, it's clear to me that his logical, practical approach to problem-solving is a really good balance with my emotional reaction to pretty much everything. Who woulda thought a few years ago that I'd be counting on him this way? Not me, that's for sure.

"Yeah, that makes sense. Thank you, honey. I'm going to suggest we talk about it in person. Go finish your beauty sleep!"

"Ha—Hilary is up and getting ready for work. She brought me some coffee, so I'll be good soon."

After sending an email that both congratulates Monica on her success and suggests a personal meeting, I delve into work emails. Before I accomplish much at all, there's another email from Monica in my inbox. It's pretty brief—telling me to call her and we'll figure out something.

When I dial her number, the call rings a handful of times before going to voicemail. Midway through leaving my message, she is calling me back.

Slightly out of breath, she starts right in, "Hello, Larissa, oh my gosh, things are pretty crazy! You read my email, so you know that the song is doing very well—better than I ever expected. 'Smiles from Her Heart' seems to be *speaking* to people's hearts. You wanted to talk about it?"

"Yeah, like I said in the email, I'm super happy for you. It's gotta feel great to have people loving your song. I can't even imagine! I just want to talk about what you asked—like, maybe in person? It's hard to explain how I feel over the phone, without seeing your face. It'd be helpful for me to know what you want to say about the song and the inspiration. It might be asking too much--"

"No, I get it. I mean, I think I get it. Let's face it—the song is about your baby. Sort of. It's also about the feelings a magical, enigmatic smile brought to me, and that song is my baby—sort of. I'm at a meeting on the West Coast this week, but if you could either come to New York after that, or maybe I can return from that trip through Atlanta? Would either of those work?"

Relieved that she's willing to talk with me, I offer, "Let me check with Everett—I'm going to New York soon. If the timing doesn't work out, then we could do it the other way you suggested. Is that okay? Like I could get back to you tomorrow?"

"That works—I need to book my flights by tomorrow at the latest, so please let me know as soon as you know. This is gonna be fine, Larissa. All I want to do is honor Emma, her smile, and the song."

"Talking about honoring her—one more thing. Not sure if you know, but it's getting pretty close to her birthday. It's, well, always bittersweet for me. I want to celebrate her life, because she's worth celebrating. Yet, it's a day that makes the hurt come back to the forefront, the emptiness deeper, if that's even possible. It might not seem important to you, but it makes a difference to me what happens on or around that date."

"I didn't know, Larissa. I knew the angel-versary is in a couple of months, but I didn't know her birthday. It is absolutely important to me and I appreciate the heads-up. I agree. If anything regarding the song gets planned on or around her birthday, I sure as heck want to do it right, do her proud. Our girl deserves our best."

Feeling reassured after talking to Monica, I text Everett and ask if we can talk tonight after they're home and settled. Not long after, I receive a thumbs up. Great—I should be able to give Monica an answer and not impact her timeline.

A tone on my phone indicating an incoming request to video chat breaks into my musings. When I see that it's Everett's number, I'm happy he's getting back to me so soon.

"Hello, you two! How's it going? Is it freezing up there?"

"Yes, guess what? I went back to school, Lissa. We built snow people on the school playground today. Some kids don't like going outside much in the winter, but the teacher said fresh air is important. It was fun!" Beth's unbridled enthusiasm is delightful. Makes me excited about our time together.

Everett's voice is in the background, "Okay, little one, tell your grandmother about your journal and then go get your pjs on while we talk for a minute."

Beth describes the journals they've been doing in school. "Each day the teacher tells us what she wants us to write about. She says we should write the first thing that pops into our head 'cuz that's probably the most important answer. Then, she only gives us fifteen minutes to write or draw. Today, it was to describe the most fun thing we did on Christmas break. Guess what I did? I wrote about going to see you and drew photo albums and tie-dye shirts in a pile. I couldn't decide which was my favorite, so drawing them together was the quickest." She punctuates the end of the sentence with a giggle, like she'd pulled one over on the teacher by getting two things in—what a character.

Everett reminds her to scoot while we talk and then gets back on the phone. "So, what's up?"

"I have a question to ask you. Monica's song is making inroads in the music world—getting thousands of listens, downloads, whatever, every day! She's been invited to do an interview about the song. I want to talk with her in person before she, well, goes public with anything about Emma. Does that seem weird of me? Part of me is so happy, but part of me is scared of the story being out there."

"I can see why you'd be hesitant. There's a lot wrapped up in those three-plus minutes of music."

His empathy surprises and pleases me. I'm still learning about how he reacts to things.

"Anyway, Monica's going to be in New York in a couple of days. I'm thinking I'll come a little earlier than you need me to meet up with her. I'd get a hotel nearby."

"Yeah, sure, come whenever it works for you. I wish I could say no way to the hotel, but you wouldn't believe how small this place is."

"A hotel is better—I want you guys to have your last few days together without me underfoot. Does it matter what day I come? I'm pretty flexible. Since the training is finished, I'm working from home for awhile."

"Nope—come whenever. Just let me know when you pin down your plan. It will be fun to go tell little missy. She's getting pretty excited about the whole thing. And, probably good you decided to rent a car. Never would have gotten all her stuff in a couple of suitcases to fly back."

"Aww . . . well, she wants her stuff and we want her to be comfortable, right? By the way, did you know she told me her mama used to call her 'sunshine girl'? We were cuddling in bed one morning telling stories and she shared that. It's the perfect name for her and how she makes me feel, you know."

"She did tell me. Told me that she liked cuddling in bed with you. That's how I know she's going to be fine while I'm gone. It'll be good for her."

"One more thing. I've been thinking more about our drive back to Atlanta. I'd like to take a couple of days for the trip and stop along the way, find interesting places to explore with Beth. Do you have any problem with that?"

He's quiet for a minute, then replies, "Yeah, sure. See what I mean? You're already planning things for the two of you to do!

I'm fine with her getting out of New York for awhile—just don't go getting her all worked up and ready to travel the world with you. Let's take this one step at a time." He laughs as he finishes the response.

Laughed, but is there some hesitancy coming through? It's going to be tricky to navigate all of this. He's her parent, I'm the grandparent. I'm under the same roof, he's across the ocean. It's good I'm going a few days early. Maybe I can get more hints from him about his expectations. If not, I'll just need to be direct and ask. The transition is going to be interesting for all of us.

13

Instead of asking why they left, now I ask,
"What beauty will I create in the space
they no longer occupy?"
RUDY FRANCISCO

A delayed flight gets me into the hotel two blocks from
Everett and Beth much later than expected, so I won't see
them until tomorrow. Years of work travel taught me to be glad
I've arrived and not waste my time worrying about late. It's just
the way it is.

I call Everett to coordinate our schedule for tomorrow. "Hey,
I got in too late to come over tonight. Can I pick up Beth from
school? The two of us can shop and get dinner started for you,
if that sounds good."

"Sure; I just need to let the school office and her teacher
know that you will be coming to get her as soon as class is over,
instead of when I usually get her from the afterschool program.
And, yeah, I love the idea of dinner waiting for me!"

We cover a few more details and I settle in for the night. I'm
exhausted and want to simply collapse on a comfortable surface.

My meeting for coffee with Monica at ten in the morning will be here soon.

After a round of hugs and catching up on her last few weeks, we start talking about the song. The language around song release, streaming, and sales is a foreign one for me, but her summary certainly seems promising.

"Yeah, so, I had to get an agent. An *agent*. I'm sure not used to saying that yet, but that's the advice I got from people who know more than I do. Within a few days of signing on with her, she called to tell me that a local radio host wants to have me on the morning show—one of the biggest listening audiences in the metro area. Says that it's often a stepping stone to more national exposure—like even some of the big afternoon talk shows. Not gonna lie—I'm scared, but excited—it's more than I could have hoped. I dropped you the email because I didn't want you to hear it somehow and feel blindsided."

So, as I'd guessed, she really isn't asking my permission in any sense of the word. I'm grateful nonetheless that she let me know. "Thank you for thinking of me, us. It affects the whole family. I'm having trouble putting into words why it feels so strange. It's just that this churns up a very sad part of our lives. Losing Emma is by far the hardest--"

"I don't mean to cut you off, Larissa, but I think I can clarify my intentions and answer some of your concerns. This song is not about the sadness—not at all. It's not about her private struggles. It's about a young woman who made an impact on me. She was at a tough point in her life, yet she blessed me with an endearing smile that reflected her huge heart and welcoming spirit. It was my *job* to listen and help her at her time in need, yet it was anything but work—she did far more for me than I recog- nized at the time. The song is a tribute, a thank you to her. Some might say too late because she's not physically on this earth, but I know she's hearing every word and cheering me on. My hope in recording this was that my voice and the words might be a bridge between where we are here and where she is. I don't pretend to understand where that is exactly, but I don't need to know. I need to build the bridge and connect with her through my music."

Monica closes her eyes and tips her head back.

"When I close my eyes while singing, I see her. Every single time. Back then, she recognized that my music was healing for me, for her, and for others; and her encouragement inspired me. People lifting other people up. That's the story I'll bring to the interviewer. Not private details about Emma's inner turmoil, not the pain that some of her decisions brought to you and your family."

"Wow! I hear the conviction in your voice. It lifts me up. I was worried about the world hearing dark stuff, like that Emma was in rehab, her passing, and then she'd be judged. She's so much more than what ended her life. You realized that without me pointing it out, and your song says it, well, beautifully. I finally went to a psychic because I thought maybe I could find out Emma's reaction to the song."

"So, did you find out? Did you connect?"

"I did, Monica. It was helpful. She said the usual things I've heard before about sending signs. Then I asked about the song. Lillian, the psychic, said that Emma began to hum! And she told me to let it be, to let people enjoy the song. She told me, almost exactly what you just did—that it's a way to connect with people."

"Those are exactly the same messages that I receive from her. She's cheering us on from afar, but letting us know she's close."

"You know, there's one other thing she said that I hadn't heard from her before. She said she tries to send messages in threes, like three pennies or whatever. What do you think of that?"

Monica isn't at all surprised and chuckles knowingly. "Well, three is a sacred number. It can symbolize body, mind, and spirit. It can mean birth, life, and death. I've even seen some sources say it is creativity, self-reliance, and positivity. Any one of those interpretations is good enough for me."

"Thank you for explaining. I'd never heard that before. Only a few weeks ago, Beth and I found three pennies under a blanket in the park. And, more than once, when I see butterflies, it's groups of three."

"And did you ever look at the length of the song, Larissa?"

"Well, I know it is three minutes and something. What are you saying?"

"It's three minutes and thirty-three seconds. I never tried for that, didn't even see it until the sound engineers sent me the final version. If three alone carries such deep meaning, what can three, threes imply? It feels like something divine to me, feels like the highest level of support we can get." She reaches for my hands yet again.

"Emma was blessed to know you, Monica. I'm still overwhelmed by all of this, but now in such a positive way. We're fortunate that you decided to find us, and help us understand the way that you and she lifted one another up." I bow my head to collect my thoughts further.

In a barely audible tone, Monica responds, "I'm blessed to know Emma, I still hear her, and know her heart, as you do. You raised a wonderfully sensitive human being. Sometimes I think that it's the sensitive, compassionate people, the ones who feel things so deeply, that find our world most challenging. Everyday life is stressful for all of us, but for those deep feelers, it's too much. Just too much." Her voice trails off and her head drops as mine did.

The silence that surrounds us is sacred. Neither of us interrupts the stillness for several long, deliberate breaths. Even the coffee shop is hushed for those moments.

Not quite ready for this conversation to end, I slowly, carefully add, "Thank you. I'm honored that you've chosen to share your thoughts with me, and the song with the world. I think it might serve as a bridge in many more ways than we know. You're a thoughtful, talented woman, and we're all better for how you've chosen to share those gifts. I wish you much success."

We stand to give a hug goodbye, much as when we greeted one another, but this time, we each hold on as if we never want to release the other. Meeting in person was absolutely the right thing to do. Thank you, Eric, for guiding me here.

I've got a few hours before I go meet Beth after school, so decide to take the subway and get off near Central Park and wander. It's sunny and relatively warm for late January, a good day for a walk. A little bistro along the way tempts me, and I emerge with coffee and a pastry to go. I hardly ever treat myself to such decadent treats, but there's nothing like fresh baked goods in the city.

My feet lead me to one of the most beautiful spots in Central Park—the Bow Bridge over the lake. A bench nearby beckons me. The lake offers intermittent reflections of the sky and the bench is an ideal viewing spot to people watch. While nibbling, there's a chance to finally search the best roads for our drive back. Scanning the various apps, I realize one route that could be promising goes right near Washington, DC. Not that I relish that traffic, but, wow, there are so many amazing attractions. Should we give that a try? Museums, monuments, walking tours. Talk about an educational side trip! I can't wait to run this idea by Beth and Everett.

As I get up to toss the bag in the litter bin, I look back up at the sky. It had been filled with puffy, white clouds when I sat down. Most have now turned wispy. But straight above me, there are still a few thick ones. Before my eyes, they open ever so slightly, and then gradually more, to reveal an almost perfect heart shape right in the center. A rosy-colored beam emerges from that heart. My eyes dart to the lake and catch the heart reflecting back.

I reach for my camera to capture this beautiful spectacle. As I check the camera roll to be sure that I got it, I see the clouds come back together and the heart disappears.

The timing is simply amazing. If I'd gazed at the bakery case any longer, walked any more slowly, or glanced up just a few seconds later, I'd never have seen that heart. A heart stretching its reach from the sky to connect with earth, Emma's heart connecting with mine. This stuff simply cannot be coincidence. It's most assuredly a sign. Emma approving of Monica's song. Or one of my parents approving of the plan to help Everett with Beth. Not sure who from, but the message is simple—they're watching over us.

The inner glow transmitted by the beam of that heart lingers with me all the way to Beth's school. My life may not be perfect, but when signs come from angels, I'm content. Content is good enough. A choice to be content with what is. If I wallowed in all that is not right, I'd have no space for the gifts of today.

I spy Beth before she sees me. Moments of watching her before she senses my presence are one of those gifts. Little circles of pink adorning her bronzy cheeks and the long braids barely constraining her curls tug at my heart. I call out to her just as she spots me and starts running—purple winter coat blowing open and a mitten hitting the ground. The love for this child envelops me. The influence of that heart from the sky compels me to pick up my pace because I can't get to her fast enough. I scoop her, the mitten, and her backpack up in my arms and exclaim, "Hello, little sunshine girl! Just a few days, but I missed you!"

"I missed you, too! Put me down, Lissa, I'm not a baby, you know."

She's right on that one. "I know you're not. And, you're too heavy for me. I won't do that again, I promise."

"But, you can hug me. Um, please."

"Of course, I will. You'll never be too big for a hug. Let's go sit for a minute and get your clothes straightened out. You won't stay warm this way. How was your day?"

Beth launches into a narrative with enough detail to take me right into the classroom that she clearly enjoys. I stifle my laughs more than once as she imitates her teacher and some of her classmates.

Once back at the apartment, I suggest something warm to drink with a snack.

"I think hot chocolate, Lissa. Our tea bags don't have special messages on them like yours. And I want to show you my papers from today."

She pulls out her worksheets, an art project, and a journal.

"Would you read your journal entry to me while I cut up vegetables for dinner? Then you can help me stir the sauce."

Making dinner and getting the table ready with Beth as an assistant is another gift of the day. The evening flies by, full of Everett talking about work, Beth about school, and then preparation for the next day. I'd forgotten how full an evening can be. After Emma died and Eric was still missing, I hated the hours from five to seven p.m. They were so lonely, so empty, compared to the hubbub of those hours when they were growing up. There was never enough time to check all the 'to-do boxes,' have a decent meal, and get ready for the next day. This is a déjà vu moment—one that makes me appreciate the past and the present.

After dinner, Everett and Beth put her suitcases and boxes by the front door. I'll go back to the hotel tonight, check out in the morning, pick up the rental car, then come here to load up. Everett's staying home in the morning to see us off.

"That's quite the pile of stuff, little sunshine girl. I hope there's room for you and me in that car."

She laughs, and suggests, "Well, I can always hold my doll and animals on my lap. Maybe they'd like that better anyway."

"They would, or you would?" Everett picks her up for a snuggle and walks toward her bedroom.

"Lissa, can you hang out for a minute, while I put her to bed? Just a couple more details I need to go over. A folder full of papers, like her birth certificate, report cards, a bunch of random stuff I thought you might need."

When Everett comes out from the goodnight routine, he plops himself down into a chair heavily—as if he's carrying the weight of the world. He grabs the folder, and starts reviewing each one in almost excruciating detail, as if it is perhaps the first time I'd seen a school record or a child's immunization chart.

"What's up, Everett? Seems to me as if there's a message between the lines that you're not sharing. Tell me what's going on—please? I'm here to help."

He looks up from the folder and says, "I need a beer, you want anything?"

"I'll take a half glass of wine. I've got a busy, early morning coming up."

"This isn't easy. Am I making the right decision? It's not about you, Lissa. I have full confidence that you'll do right by Beth—not one doubt. In fact, maybe I'm scared it'll all go too well. Like, will she be so happy in the sunny south that she won't want to come back here? Will she love being with you, surrounded by family and friends that are so much a part of your life? She doesn't have anything like that here. She's got a grandma here who on any given day can't decide if she wants to see us or not. She's got a single dad who works until five, gets her dinner, puts her to bed, and then does it all over again. Damn—maybe she won't even miss me."

How to answer him? How to help him over this hump?

"Every decision we make about working, once there are kids in the mix, is tough. We try to do what's right for our careers, because that means things like better income, or schedules, even more vacation time with them. I've never known a dedicated parent who doesn't doubt her or himself, who doesn't feel like decisions are fraught with worries about whose needs to put first."

He's listening, but still shaking his head.

"I won't tell you not to worry. But I'm going to suggest not getting ahead of yourself on the what-ifs. Someone once told me that worried thoughts are rarely true or accurate. They're the product of conjuring up worst-case scenarios and then believing they're true. What we do know is that she's excited about this and is thinking of it as an adventure. Let's treat it that way, then take it day by day, week by week."

He nods his head silently and reaches across to take my hand.

"Let's both vow not to get ahead of ourselves. We'll video chat as often as you can; I'll have her send you stories of her days—best way there is to practice writing. I'll enjoy my moments with her and you enjoy the learning you're being exposed to—and traveling to other parts of the world for the first time. Make a list of places you want to share with Beth someday and tell her about them when we talk. Send her postcards from each place. We'll look them up and make a scrapbook. This will work out."

"Good ideas—her writing stories. Thank you for listening to me. I'm still not sure of a lot of things about all of this, but I'm incredibly glad that you're in this world for Beth."

"I was missing from your life for way too long, Everett. I wish it wasn't so, but can't change a thing about that. I've been given another chance. A chance to be your mother and her grandmother. I promise I'll do my very best to make the most of every moment we have together now."

14

Today is our bridge to tomorrow,
a span we walk for a lifetime.
Pepper Blair

The hotel is a quick walk. I settle in to plan our travel route. It's about four hours to DC from here. Checking the list of fun places to take kids, there are sights I know about, as well as several I don't. Like the International Spy Museum? What kid wouldn't want to see that? Jeepers—we could stay a few days. It makes no sense for her to start school midweek anyway.

Damn—I'd totally forgotten to tell him I'd decided on Washington for the stop on our way south. I send a text to Everett to double check. I don't want to bring it up to Beth if he has any worries about that plan. Within a few moments, I receive a thumbs up in reply, then a smiley face.

After making a hotel reservation near the Smithsonian, it's lights out. Sleep does not come quickly. I toss and turn, and turn some more. The room is quiet and comfortable—it's my brain on overdrive. I turn on the light and recheck the best route. I look up the attractions again and remember the great zoo in DC. I close my eyes and get an image of Eric and Emma walking hand in hand near a lion cage. The memory is so clear. I hear Eric helping her practice how to make a roar so that she isn't scared when the lions do it. All these years later and it's as vivid as if it happened today. We didn't know then that it was memory-making. It was simply having fun and enjoying time together. Okay, Larissa, deep breath. Be glad it happened, that you've likely got photos of it somewhere in those albums. Now you have the chance to do the National Zoo with Beth, and collect more photos.

A sliver of light is sneaking in past the hotel's blackout shades and the phone is ringing. It's Everett's number. Beth's voice squeals with excitement, "Lissa, Daddy says we're going to big museums and maybe a zoo on our way to your house. I like that. When are you getting here?"

Feels like only a matter of moments since shutting out one memory so that sleep would come, now awakening to the possibility of making a new memory. While thinking, 'such is the way of life,' I find words to match her enthusiasm.

"Yes, if you want to do those things with me, it's a deal. When I get to your house, we're going to walk to the diner on the corner and get breakfast before we start. While we're eating, we'll decide what we want to do on this trip. It can last a couple of extra days, then we need to be back for you to start school. Along the way, you'll be our list maker to practice writing and spelling. We'll be a traveling school room. Let me get ready, pick up the car, and I'll see you soon."

It's been a long while since I'd driven in New York City. After renting the car, I easily navigate the streets and find parking. I'm pleasantly surprised at my success and happily find Everett and Beth waiting.

It's obvious that they've talked about the departure. Everett hugs her and uses sweet parting words, "I love you and I'll see you soon. Remember what we practiced—no sad goodbyes."

"Right, Daddy. Till we meet again! I like the sound of that one best. I love you, too, and can't wait to send you lots of pictures."

Once seated with waffles and bacon, I decide to engage her in making decisions about our trip, to distract her from the reality of leaving her father and her home. I point to the map and explain, "You know we have to go past the river to get from New York to New Jersey, then on to the rest of the states. So, how do you think we connect to New Jersey? I'll give you a hint—there's two options."

"Is one of them a bridge? A high one? I don't really like those."

I didn't know that was coming. Challenged already because I don't really like tunnels. The first conflict of the trip to resolve. "Yes, one is a bridge—the George Washington Bridge. The other is a tunnel. Why don't you like bridges?"

"Cuz, it scares me to be up so high. But, I did like the one in Florida going out to Hutchinson Island. When we first came to see you, Daddy told me that a bridge was the only way to get to your beach house. And when we were done visiting, the bridge took us back to Aunt Kristy. It felt less scary when I was going to a special place, to see people I wanted to see."

"This one is doing that too—only it's going to my real house and to the house you'll be living in for awhile. That's the nice thing about bridges—they connect places, and by doing that, they connect people with one another. Sometimes we have to build bridges to get to the people we love."

"Lissa, that sounds like a message on a tea bag tag again. Okay, I'll try. It's also cool because its name is Washington and it's taking us to Washington."

"Thanks for agreeing to give it a try, Beth. You know, every time I cross a bridge, I find something new that I like. Even though it might be scary to be high, it's nice to look across and see the place you're going. To be honest, I don't like tunnels very much; maybe because I can't see where I'm going. So, one of us gets to have our wish and one doesn't. I'll owe you a wish!"

We're on the road shortly, bellies full and list in hand. I have to focus carefully on the turns till we get to I-95. Looking in the rearview mirror, I see Beth has fallen asleep already. I envy the effortless sleep of little ones. When does that lack of effort transform into the constant struggle to access a full and restful slumber?

I turn the radio down so as to hear the peaceful rhythm of her slumber breaths. They aren't notes strung into songs, but music nonetheless. My mind wanders back to the days with two little heads bent into a sleepy posture in the back seat during road trips. Emma and Eric started most trips loud, chatty, sometimes quibbling, but the monotone hum of the car inevitably lulled them to sleep. *What would it have been like if Everett was in the back seat with them, three beloved siblings? More arguing? Or maybe older enough that he would have insisted on being in the front like a grown up?*

Memories are disorienting at times. One child has died, another came back into my life as an adult. Nonetheless, my three children. At the psychic reading, Emma said three is important. Is there anything more important to me than my three children? My heart wants to remember them all in the same place, but can't have its way.

Stopping in DC makes the first leg of the trip fairly short. Beth wakes up when she senses the change from highway driving and asks the predictable, "Are we there yet?"

I can't help but laugh, and then tell her, "Almost! You missed three states—New Jersey, Pennsylvania, and Delaware; now we're in Maryland. I think it's still fair to check them off on your state list because you were in them while we drove. What do you think?"

"Yes! I want to make checkmarks on the list and get as many states as I can. How many have you been to?"

"Uh, last time I looked at my list, it was forty-seven. So, can you do the subtraction? How many do I have left?"

She got out her pencil and paper and within a few seconds asked, "Three, right? I have so many left to go. I've been in Florida and New York, now four more this morning. So I have forty-four to go." Her voice and head dropped as if that number totally defeated her.

"Well, guess what, after our adventure in Washington, you'll be going through more states. Just keep the checklist handy, my little friend. I have to turn the GPS back on and listen closely now to get us to the hotel."

I'd requested an early check-in, and they're able to accommodate. We carry our overnight bags up to the room and make our way to a restaurant nearby for lunch.

After I finish my sandwich and tea, I suggest, "Since we've been in the car all morning, how about we walk around the zoo on this sunny afternoon?"

"That would be fun. I want to see the elephants. But you won't forget all the other places we talked about, right? Like the big dinosaurs and the spy stuff? When can we go there?"

Maybe I'd made a strategic error telling her about every place we might get to see. To moderate her expectations a bit, I respond, "How about after the zoo, we take a rest at the hotel and pick our favorite places to go tomorrow? We should start driving again the next day. Uncle Eric is waiting to see you, then Lisa and Bobby want to tell you all about your new school."

The rapid head nod tells me we're on the same page, and her smile, while trying not to lose her potato chips, emphasizes her agreement.

A couple of hours later—after seeing most of the animals—we're on a bench looking at the map to figure out our next path while making our way toward the exit.

Pointing at the animal picture, she reminds me, "Can we go to the elephants now?"

It's easy to show her our route by following her little finger with my own. "Absolutely! I think if we walk over here to see the lions, go this way to the elephants, then we will have seen everything."

"Will you tell me when we are getting close to the lions? I need to be ready."

"Ready? Ready for what?"

She doesn't answer me right away. Then, she turns to look at me, lifts her fingers up like they're claws and makes a little-girl attempt at a roar, "GRRRRR!"

Startled, I ask, "What's all that about?"

"I told Daddy I was excited to see all the animals, except for the lions. I saw on TV that they eat other animals; they're scary. He told me I shouldn't be scared, they're in a cage. But that maybe I'll feel braver if I roar like them. Maybe they'll think I'm talking to them. I need to be ready."

My mind races back to last night's recollection of Eric teaching Emma to roar for the same reason. Did that actually happen? Is my mind playing tricks on me? Is this for real? The similarities between the memory of Eric teaching Emma and Everett teaching Beth are beyond explanation, but after contemplating for a few seconds, I just don't care. A memory of the past, somehow coming true in real time today, feels awesome. It feels like somewhere, somehow, Emma is sending me another message. She's with us, connected to Everett and Beth. I'll shove away the doubt and embrace the message, the here and now.

"Got it—I'll let you know. It looks like as soon as we pass the next food stand, the lion enclosure will be on our left."

I snap a photo of Beth mid-roar so I can send it along to Everett at the end of the day. Whether the roaring strategy worked, or the appearance of a mother with her cute cubs makes a difference, Beth happily skips by the lions and on to the elephants. In the gift shop just before the exit, she lingers over many souvenir options, then picks out a stuffed sloth on a log that raises money to rescue and rehabilitate injured sloths. Beth explains her choice. "I liked all the animals, but my old sloth needs a new friend. Do you want to get an animal?"

"You know what? Maybe I will. On that same shelf, there's a turtle. The money from that one helps rescue turtles. Remember the sea turtles when we were on Hutchinson Island? They're endangered, and people work hard to help them survive. They don't look cuddly like the sloth, but there's something about them that makes me smile when I see them."

"Oh, yeah, I remember seeing turtle tracks in the sand. Can we go there again someday?"

"Oh, I think probably. That's where your daddy grew up. Plus, he and Uncle Eric like to fish there." The attachments we now have to that beautiful part of the country make me smile. Not only did my parents once vacation there, it's where Everett grew up, and it's where we all came together—where we met for the first time, and then where Eric and Hilary got married. All fond memories.

Back at the hotel after dinner, we plan the next day, and call so she can tell her daddy all about her day. From the bathroom, I hear her excited voice, then quiet moments, then more squealing. One lovely day, for sure.

"Lissa, come here! Daddy wants to talk to you, too."

I obediently return to the main room, and she swings the phone camera in my direction, "Here, you talk!"

Everett laughs at her command for me to be part of the call. "Well, she sure sounds like a happy girl. I hear she got over her fear of lions and that the sloth is still her favorite animal. Good day for you too?"

"It was so much fun. Especially seeing things through her eyes. I took a bunch of pictures—I'll send them as soon as we're off the phone. I'm thinking we'll do some more sightseeing tomorrow and then get on the road the next day. What do you think of that plan?" I'm still running things by him. Not sure I know the boundaries of my decision-making. If I'm going to make a mistake, it's going to be on the side of including him too much. Might not be possible once he's working overseas, but at least that's my target for now.

"It sounds good to me, it's fine. I do want to know where Beth is and what she's doing, but I trust you, you know. Guess it's new for both of us."

"Oh yeah, it really is. We'll figure it out as we go, right?" What a relief—he's making it easy on me.

I send the photos after we finish, just as promised, then urge Beth to get ready for bed.

"We have another big day planned for tomorrow, little miss sunshine girl. Tell me the favorite part of your day, then lights out."

"My favorite is too hard. Can I maybe have five favorites? I liked the sloth baby holding on to his mama, I like the peacock feathers, the baby elephant's trunk finding the banana, the panda bear, and I was proud that I wasn't scared of the lions. I liked them, too. What was your favorite?"

"My favorite was watching you find your favorites. That was fun for me, cuz you're my favorite!"

15

We must be willing to get rid of the life we've planned
so as to have the life that is waiting for us.
JOSEPH CAMPBELL

Three days later, Beth is telling a table-full of family and friends about her trip. We'd returned the night before, weary and happy to be in a house instead of a hotel. Eric's suggestion when I let him know we were back, safe and sound, was to bring take-out dinner over the following night. I invited Renee, Isabel, and her kids over as well to catch up.

"We stayed up really late one night, rode a bus, and saw all the statues lit up. It was really cool, and Lissa said I did better than you and Auntie Emma did, Uncle Eric."

With a look of exaggerated indignance, he responded, "What's that supposed to mean, Mom?"

"Well, if I remember correctly, we did that tour many years ago. Emma fell asleep and you made loud, wise-guy comments most of the way. The only thing you liked was the statue of Abraham Lincoln because you were just learning about him in school, but the rest of the experience was pretty much me wishing the whole thing was over so I could yank you off that bus. Beth, however, was pretty into it, and wide awake. Well, mostly—I think she nodded off the last fifteen minutes or so."

"Huh—well, Mom, sounds like you might have found a fellow traveler. Be careful, Beth. If you catch the travel bug, she might start dragging you all around."

"Not anytime soon, mister. She needs to start in school here and settle in. Maybe someday, though. I told her that when she gets to be an age that's double digits, maybe we'll go on a big trip. Anyone else who wants to come along is welcome. If you still hate the idea of bus tours, we're counting you out."

Everyone laughs, this time at Eric's expense, and he chuckles along. He stands and reminds us that it's getting late for Hilary.

Renee excuses them from doing dishes. "Get the little mamma on home, Eric. I'll do the dishes. Isabel, I'm guessing you want to get these guys home, and Larissa needs to get Beth to bed."

After telling more bedtime stories than I'd planned, I join Renee in the kitchen. She's pouring herself a glass of wine and raises her eyebrow toward the bottle to inquire as to whether I'll join her.

"Half a glass, my friend. There's plenty to do tomorrow to get ready for school."

We settle into chairs with hassocks to prop up our legs, enjoying the quiet before either of us speaks. The comfort of good friends allows for easy silence.

"Sounds like your trip back was fun for both of you. Is it tiring to be with a little one again twenty-four/seven?"

"She's a great traveler, Renee. Interested in everything. Maybe it's the novelty of being with a grandparent? I don't know, but it was really fun, and I'm not tired. We pretty much collapsed in bed after each action-packed day. So, I'll just knock on wood that things keep going so well." I do knock on the coffee table to emphasize my hope.

Renee looks down and runs her fingertip around the rim of the wine glass. "I need to tell you something. I jumped into something I may regret. I hope not, but maybe."

"Well, tell me. Won't be the first time you jumped into something. I won't mention any jobs or men's names, though." My attempt to be funny could not have gone worse—totally fell flat.

"This is a big deal, Larissa. Remember all the times I've said I never wanted to be a mom? Well, sometimes that was true, other times it's been a big lie."

I'm speechless. Probably for the best, because she continues quickly.

"I know I've often joked that maybe I should just adopt or get a surrogate or something. That was a cover up, or saving face, or whatever. Many, many times, I've wanted to hold a sweet, soft little one of my own. But, since the right person never came along, I just kinda gave up. Gave up thinking it would ever happen, and felt like my clock was ticking. Forty-four last year? No way, right?"

I've forgotten she's quite a bit younger than me and past the age when it's advisable to become pregnant.

"Then someone at work started talking about her single sister adopting, and it planted a seed. I thought about when you were searching for Everett, and the whole complicated process of adoption and who has access to records, and all that stuff. But then I kept thinking about how empty I feel sometimes. Like my life means nothing, no purpose. So, maybe adoption? And, not necessarily a little baby, but maybe a child a little older. I don't care about race, either. Do you think I'm nuts?"

I don't have a clue how to answer her. Damn, I wish Isabel was still here. She's better at this stuff than I am. Trying to navigate this delicately, I draw on my experience being questioned by counselors for the last few years and try the reflective stuff they do. Help me bide my time or pull more information out of her before I stick my foot in my mouth.

"So, you're thinking about adoption. What have you done as far as moving forward with this? You said you jumped in?"

She stands up and starts pacing.

"I left a message for the social worker that my friend's sister is using. She called me back last week. I'm tempted, then I think about all that could go wrong. She suggested I go to a group later this week for people who want to adopt. I'll meet and hang out with people who've taken this plunge. It's like a presentation and then time for questions. I'll ask again—do you think I'm nuts?"

"No—I think you'd be nuts—or let's say foolhardy, if you *weren't* thinking about both the pros and the cons. You're a loving, fun, energetic woman, Renee. You could make a huge difference for a child, and he or she could make a huge difference in your life. Maybe fill that empty spot. But it *is* really complicated. I think it's awesome that you're considering it, and wise that you're going to this meeting. Find out all you can. Knowledge is power. Ask a ton of questions at the group and when you meet with the social worker again. You can even ask Everett some questions. Your decision will impact at least two lives enormously. It's worth taking your time."

By the time we're done pulling the idea of adoption all apart and looking at it from every possible angle, another hour has passed. I need to push her out the door.

"Thank you for confiding in me, Renee. It's hard to open up and be vulnerable. But, now, I have to chase you out or let you sleep in the spare room. My morning is full with school stuff for Beth and getting her settled in her space here. I have lists upon lists!"

As I start up the stairs, still thinking about Renee, my phone pings. Who now? I need to get some sleep! The text is from Steven. After apologizing for the lateness, he writes: *Hey, I hear we're going to be sharing a grandchild. Can't think of anyone I'd rather be sending this message to,* followed by a clapping hands symbol. Oh my gosh, I'd been so wrapped up in Beth that I'd forgotten to contact Steven after Eric told him. I want to talk to him, but suggest tomorrow, *When I'm not half asleep.*

The alarm goes off bright and early and I'm transported back in time once again. My routine is going to be reminiscent of school mornings long ago. Two sips of coffee alone before needing to awaken a sleeping child to get ready for school. Neither Emma nor Eric was ever easy to get going in the morning. Let's hope Beth doesn't take after them.

No worries. Sounds of rustling in her room confirm that she's ready. I peek in and see her sitting up in bed. Her open backpack is next to her with school supplies in neat little stacks. She looks up at the sound of the door and says, "I'm almost ready. I'm arranging my pens and pencils. I like them sorted into different compartments."

So much for thinking she might be anything like her aunt and uncle. At least not at this age. Eric—well, I would have been happy if he'd even thought about bringing a pen to school! Emma—at this young age, she treasured new school supplies. Later on, she became obsessive about everything, including pens and pencils being sorted by color. It's a new adventure with each kid, I guess.

"Well, arrange them the way you want and get dressed in the outfit we picked last night. I'll go get your breakfast going."

With a big grin on her face, she comes back with, "Okay, I'll be ready in a jiffy!"

16

If your heart is broken, make art with the pieces.
SHANE KOYCZAN

Registering Beth at school goes smoothly. The principal has a little girl from her class come to the office to show her around the building and take her through the hallways. I'm a little shaky anticipating the goodbye, but remembered how she and Everett so bravely said, "Till we meet again" when they parted.

I'm only leaving her for a few hours, I can do this. "Have a great day, little sunshine girl," succeeding at sounding far more cheerful than I feel.

"You too, Lissa." The other girl grabs her hand and off they go.

I remember my promise from last night to call Steven and dial him up to talk while driving back to the house.

I hear his cheery voice, "So, are you awake now?" followed by a chuckle.

"Oh yes, sure am. Quite a bit has happened since we last spoke."

"Right? I can't believe we're going to be grandparents. I mean, I know you've got Beth, but we kinda just figured out how to be parents together for Eric, and now we've got another shared family member on the way. Who woulda thought any of this a few years ago?"

"Certainly not me, I'll tell you that much! There were several months when I thought I literally had no one left in my life—no one related, anyway. Lots of wonderful friends, but well, you know what I mean."

"Sure do. And I thought I had no children of my own and was way too old to even worry about it. Now there's a grandbaby?"

"And don't forget sweet Nina." How crazy it still is to think that at the same time as Eric and I were relying on DNA testing to try to find Everett, Eric's test would also reveal a sister? A child Steven didn't even know he'd fathered.

"No, never—she's actually up here visiting right now. She nearly exploded with joy when Eric told her she's about to be an aunt. That child is gonna be loved!"

I stifle my tears. Emma would have loved being an aunt too. The things she's missed already break my heart. Some days it's hard to be happy for those who are able to experience such joys.

But I redirect my reaction and find it in myself to be grateful for what is, not sad about what isn't.

"That's great, Steven. She'll make a terrific auntie for Eric and Hilary's baby. Anyway, back to what's going on here. Did Eric tell you that Beth's staying with me for awhile—quite awhile, actually? Everett's been transferred to Europe. It's a sort of once in a lifetime career opportunity. Doing this now could help him really move forward in the future. After a lot of planning, or as he told Beth, 'strategizing,' we came up with this plan. I just dropped her off for her first day of school."

"Bet that brought back memories."

"Pretty much everything I've done with her has brought back memories. Even going to the Washington Zoo felt like déjà vu from taking Eric and Emma there."

"That's a lot, my friend. How are you doing with it all?"

I'm touched by the reference to *friend*. We've only been navigating this unusual connection for a couple of years. More than once, I've felt he wants it to be a different connection, perhaps even like when we were married. I've successfully deflected most of his hints. I'm good with being friends, not so much anything else.

"I'm doing fine so far. She's a delightful kid. Interested in everything, boundless energy. But I'm also holding my breath for when she starts missing her father, her school, the only home she's known. It could get tough. She needs to get used to a new school, make friends. It's a lot for a little girl."

"For all of you, Larissa. And, Everett, wow, what an adjustment it will be for him as well."

There's a few more minutes of catching up before he needs to get off the call and back to work.

"Keep me posted. Call if you need to talk—I'm always here. Also, I'm thinking about coming that way in a few weeks, maybe we can get together. I'll visit Eric and Hilary either on my way down or back from seeing Nina's new apartment. I'm hoping to help her move."

Just as I think we're finished, Steven calls out, "Wait, Larissa, don't hang up. I totally forgot the other reason I called. I heard it last night. On my way home from a late work meeting, I heard the song—the one Monica wrote—come on the radio. I almost drove off the road!"

"It's amazing, isn't it? It happened to me in a car on my way to the airport not too long ago. Talk about being taken off guard. Then, Monica let me know she was going to be interviewed soon about the song. I was worried about a whole bunch of what-ifs in the event that it becomes more popular, so we met up when I was in New York. I'll have to find out if it's happened yet."

"Yeah—well, I didn't get to that part. After they played the song, the station played a short clip of the interview to get people interested, I guess. The whole thing airs soon, according to that clip. *Amazing* is the best word for the little bit I heard. Not only is she incredibly talented, she spoke with a quiet calmness that was almost hypnotic. She never mentions anything that could identify Emma, but her love and admiration for her comes through. Contact her—she can tell you how to hear the whole thing, I'm sure."

It's my turn to acknowledge the caring nature of Steven's comments. He truly is a good friend, wonderful father to Eric, and invested in our lives. "Thank you, Steven. I'll do that—I appreciate you letting me know."

Okay, so if my day isn't going to be emotional enough with all that's happening with Beth, now I've gotta see, or hear, or whatever is up with the interview. I've got a few hours till pick-up time for Beth, so let's see how I can get myself organized to accomplish more things on my list.

Contacting Monica jumps to the top of the to-dos.

She picks up on the first ring. "Hey, Larissa. What's up?"

Having only a small amount of patience for the niceties, I slip over them and get to the question. "Steven heard a small clip of your interview. Tell me about it—and how I can hear it?"

"Wow, news travels fast in your family! It was just recorded yesterday for the radio talk show here in New York. I planned to call you and let you know that the full interview is airing in a couple of days, on Emma's birthday, actually. Once you told me the date, I told my agent that I wanted to try to do something special, and she made it happen!"

She pauses for my reaction. It's silent because no words have come to me yet. When I don't reply, she continues, "Larissa,

I've been thinking about our last conversation. I know you have some worries, if this song becomes popular. I want you to know, my purpose in writing this was just to honor Emma. If it ever becomes a song that makes a lot of money, I want to share that benefit. I'd love to know about organizations or charities that are important to you, to Emma, and I could donate to them. It's a big 'if,' but please think about it."

Her thoughtfulness touches me. I've been so fearful about this whole thing, not trusting how it would unfold. But I hear Emma's message from the other day and find the words.

"Monica, that is such a generous gesture. I guess we really don't know what will happen with this tribute. I'd be honored to suggest recipients—if the song brings in a sizable income, I'd love for others to benefit." It's hard for me to believe that the song might actually do that, but I guess anything is possible.

"Do you have any ideas, or do you want to think about it more?"

"I've been giving small amounts of money in memory of Emma to three organizations. It would mean so much if we, guess I mean you, could do more."

"*We* is the correct word, Larissa. Without your support, I wouldn't be doing this. I would have kept it to myself if you'd asked me to. I knew you were hesitant at the beginning. However, it's out there and who knows what will happen? With a little help from our angel girl, it might be a big hit. So, tell me the three."

"They pertain to water—organizations that are working to save our valuable waterways—one in New York, one in Florida. Eric and Emma grew up going to the Finger Lakes almost every summer. Being by the water both in upstate New York and in coastal Florida brought me, then Eric and me, so much healing after Emma transitioned. And, in both places, we made discoveries and new connections that have changed our lives forever. So,

I have a favorite organization in each of those places. Then, I've recently found out about another project—started by a young man after his father died; he and his dad were very close and shared a love of surfing. He created the project to honor his father."

I share the name of the project so she can look it up when she has a chance.

"He takes donations to fund riding surf boards into the waves. The surf boards have the names of people engraved on them—names of people who have passed and their families want to honor them with one last ride into the waves. It resonated with me because Emma loved the beach so much, and I see so many signs of her every time I'm near the water. I just think his mission is special."

Monica responds, "Oh my gosh, what a beautiful image that conjures up. I'd love to help that project, and the others—thank you for the suggestions, I know Emma is somewhere smiling at us. When I get home, I'll send you the recording of the full interview. Let me know what you think—I hope it's something you can feel good about."

After listening twice to the recorded interview, I'm compelled to write down a few of the phrases she used while speaking. They're special and I want them handy whenever I need to hear them. And, they'll be perfect to share at our little celebration of Emma on her upcoming birthday.

Some people live till nearly a hundred but don't really live; not so for my friend. Then Monica spoke about Emma's smile, laugh, love of travel, and inspiration from music.

In the end, we only regret the chances we didn't take. And she described the vulnerability she experienced while taking the chance on something as deeply personal as writing this song, how risky it felt to make it public.

I wanted this song to be a bridge between my life here and wherever my friend is now. And next she spoke of the need for people to build bridges between worlds.

What? I remember how she spoke about bridges when we met, then there were the conversations that Beth and I exchanged on our way down here. Connections, bridges, they come up so often. People to people, world to world. Have they always? Or just since I've been looking for them, more open to their symbolism?

Steven is right, she's eloquent and very composed. I've got to hand it to her. Not only is the song a beautiful reminder of Emma, but Monica is handling the sensitivity of the subject matter far better than I expected. As a thank you for her generous offer today, I send Monica one of my favorite photos of Emma. She's standing in tree pose on a paddleboard—we'd taken a stand-up/paddleboard yoga class a few months before she died. It's as if she has mystically risen up from the calm water. The splattered, fiery colors of the sunset framing her slightly darkened frame, making it look like a black silhouette of her against the sky. Even though it's semi-dark, her enigmatic smile is visible. Something about that reminds me of Monica's song. And while it's not a surfboard, Monica will see Emma's love of being near the water and understand more about my dedication to the organizations I described earlier today.

Talking with Steven and listening to the interview made the day speed by. I want to quickly organize closets and make more space for Beth's prized possessions. I assemble the desk I'd ordered as well. She can arrange the other things in her room when she gets home.

Pulling up to the designated pick-up spot, I catch a glimpse of her. The long ponytail with little, loose ringlets sprung free over the six hours since I'd pulled it back. Watching her talk to the little girl who escorted her this morning without her knowing

I'm there is reassuring. As they walk to separate waiting cars, they wave goodbye to one another enthusiastically. My heart soars.

"So, how was your day? I hope it was a good one!"

"Yes, I like my teacher and I made two friends. I have homework to do."

"Great! Well, I put together the desk. You can decide where it should go and set it up for your homework. Also, it's pretty funny that it's your first day of school, and it's also your daddy's first day to land in a new country. He's six hours later than us. We agreed to talk at four o'clock our time so he can go to bed soon after. We have about an hour till we call him."

"I want to tell him about my day. Will we do video chat? I want to see him."

The phone rings right at four o'clock. Beth jumps up so quickly to grab it that little bits of her snack crumble onto the floor.

Her excitement is contagious. "Go ahead—you know my password. I'm sure it's the call you're waiting for. I'll pick up the snack."

"Daddy! It's you! How was your plane ride? Are you there yet? My day was good." She asks a dozen, rapid-fire questions, jumps to her own reports about her day, and Everett's deep chuckle is the constant background noise.

There's finally a break in her ramblings—just long enough for her to take a breath—and Everett jumps in.

He answers her questions about the plane, tells her about his hotel, then asks her to put me on the phone too.

"I'm here! I could hear most of what you said. Glad to hear your travel went uneventfully. What's up for the next few days?"

"Well, before I get to that, you need to know I'm in Rome, not London. Last night, totally last minute, they changed the order of things because my new boss has a convention in Rome this week to announce new initiatives in that region. She wants me to be here to assist her in the transition."

"Rome, well, that *is* a way different starting place. Beautiful country, so many different regions. I hope you get the chance to explore."

"Yeah, I hope so too. My boss and the other staff here seem to know their way around pretty well."

"So, your new boss is a woman. How's that seem to you?"

"I'm good with that, Lissa. I've spent my life with women who are driven to get things done—think about Harriett, and now my sister running that bait shop. She's taken it from a hole in the wall to a place where every fisherman on the Treasure Coast stops for equipment and local advice. My wife was the same way—always had a to-do list a mile long and always got it done. I'm beginning to think you are another one to add to the list."

"And I think your daughter might be the same!"

"Yeah, she might be. It sounds like she's happy at school."

After picking the next time to talk, Beth and I finish setting up her room. We agree that under the window is the place she likes her desk the best.

I ask her what she'd like for dinner.

"Mac 'n cheese, I think. Can I help?"

"Of course you can. What part do you want to do?"

"When we make it at home, Daddy lets me stir in the cheese, then--Gamma, can I listen to the 'Smile' song? The one about Emma?"

I'm confused by the sudden switch from stirring cheese to listening to the song, but more importantly, my heart is touched by her calling me 'Gamma.' So unexpected, but so dear. How do I process the intensity of my reaction? She could switch to any topic and my spirit would continue soaring.

The song comes through the speakers and both Beth and I sit quietly and listen. She is staring off into space, almost as if in a trance. I notice her eyes welling up midway through the song and reach for her hand.

"I like those words, Gamma."

"Which ones, honey?"

"When she goes:

Smiles say the words of the stories in your heart,
Mostly when we're feeling fine.

Beth stops for a minute, silently mouths words to herself as if trying to remember. She nods her head and continues,

Then, other days, when sad and apart,
They remind me—your stories are still mine."

Hypnotized by her little singing voice, I reply, "Mm, that is a nice section. What do you like about it?"

"Talking to Daddy made me really happy, but I also felt a little sad. I like it here, but I miss him. It reminds me of the words."

"I think I understand, Beth. Do you know what that part of the song is called? In music terms, it's a bridge. A part of the song that's a little bit different, connecting two sections that are similar. So many things can be bridges! Smiles, phones, songs—Monica told me that she wrote the song to be a bridge to the place where Emma is. Even though she misses her, the song is a way to reach out with happiness, to stay connected. It's like I told you a long time ago. Sometimes happy and sad can happen at the same time, or feeling apart but still together. It took me until I was pretty old to learn that."

"I do remember. You told me, then I told Daddy the same thing. But you know what about those words? I think the words mean that both smiles and tears tell stories from the heart."

Following her train of thought, I answer, "Yes, I think it does mean that. And maybe you can tell Daddy about how the song makes you feel—he might feel the same. You know, that's the magic of songs, of music. They can make you feel many things, and sometimes many things all at once."

"Talking to Daddy made me feel lots of things at once too. So did going to a new school. I'm tired and hungry. Can we make the dinner now?"

All I can do is nod my head and laugh.

17

You don't have to understand things for them to be.
MADELEINE L'ENGLE

At my next appointment with Marie, she asks, "How did you do this year on Emma's birthday? Any celebration or more low-key?"

The first one after she died, we invited all the people who'd stood by our sides as we attempted to negotiate our grief. We made tie-dye shirts and birdhouses and told Emma stories. The last two, much quieter.

"Lower-key for sure; Beth had only been here a few days. So, we baked a cake together, she wrote Emma's name on it in bright-pink frosting. We played the song of course and danced. After Beth was in bed, I shared Monica's interview about the song with Eric, Hilary, and my friends. It was quiet and sweet."

"How did you feel, Larissa?"

"You know, I guess I just feel like we deserved more Emma time, and she deserved more earth time. But then, what does 'deserve' have to do with anything, right? I was super grateful not to be alone. Don't feel like I have to do a big hoopla the way

I did the first year, but I need to recognize her special day. We ended up telling really cute, funny, bittersweet stories about her."

"Want to share a couple?"

The wistful nature of this whole thing is challenging, but I like the idea of Marie knowing Emma a little better. I nod my head and share a bit.

"We got going about her idiosyncrasies—aren't those the things that stay with us about people? Maybe weird and quirky, but the things that make them unique?"

"I think that's exactly what we remember. It helps to keep people alive in our hearts."

I wipe away the telltale tear, swallow the growing lump in my throat, and continue.

"Like she was so particular about some things, and others? Not at all. Her clothes were thrown all over her room. But then, those that actually made it into her dresser drawers were folded in absolutely perfect, tiny squares and lined up like folders in a file drawer. I didn't even know anyone could fold clothes like that! Or Renee added one in, Emma was kind of a germophobe—uh, sometimes. One time, Renee had to take her to Urgent Care for me because of an allergic reaction. Emma got really ticked off because she said the nurse hadn't washed her hands for a long enough time to really kill any bacteria. But, she'd happily grab your coffee, or whatever, and drink out of your cup."

I notice Marie smiling and continue.

"It felt good to laugh about Emma rather than cry. To love someone enough to know her quirks and be amused by them; to honor her for her individuality. Unconditional love at its finest."

I recall the final few minutes of the evening and tell her of Isabel's toast:

"Yes, a toast to our dear, sweet Emma. A young woman who only thought of others and was generous to everyone she met. We know you're flying high, flying free, beautiful angel—we miss you!"

Marie is quiet, then suggests, "I couldn't think of a more fitting tribute. Thank you for telling me those details—I almost feel like I got introduced to your special daughter in a more intimate way than ever. Between the song words and those little anecdotes, I find myself loving Emma."

I don't know why this moves me so deeply, but I reach over and hug Marie.

"Oh geez, I'm probably not supposed to do that, right?" pulling my arms away as quickly as I can.

"There's no rule about that, Larissa. We can be human here."

She pauses, takes a deep breath, then moves along in her usual professional manner.

"How're things going with Beth? It's been how long now?"

"They're good—it's taken a few weeks to settle into a routine, but we're on a roll now. We video chat with her father every couple of nights, she's making friends at school, and I'm figuring out how to get my stuff done for work while she's at school. Kinda like riding a bike—haven't forgotten how to juggle work and a kid."

"Sounds pretty good. What about your walks? And yoga? Finding time for those things? They seemed to save you back when you were struggling with Emma being gone and Eric missing?"

Her question makes me take pause for a moment.

"I did get to yoga once with Isabel. Eric and Hilary took Beth to a children's play at the library, so I was free. I do take plenty of walks with Beth, sometimes Is and her kids come along."

"Do you remember a couple of years ago when we talked about 'tending your own fire'? Doing the things that fuel your inner self? Keeping yourself warm and energized? The things that kept you going were far different than what kept Renee or Isabel at their best. Just because something is good for Beth, doesn't necessarily make it good for you."

"I confess I haven't done as many of those things lately. It's taken a bit of time to settle into our routine. Or, uh, I guess you'll probably now point out, Beth's routine. Okay, point taken. I'll figure out a way to carve out more time for myself. Old habits die hard. I always felt if my kids were happy, I was happy, and I'm carrying that over to Beth."

"There's some truth to that, but it's not the whole story. Your walks were a form of meditation. A quiet mind allowed you to see signs from nature and appreciate the beauty around you. That's tough to do when you're walking and talking with a chatty kid. And, I just remembered, there's going to be another little one in your family in a few months. You'd better get yourself a routine now, before that one grabs ahold of your heart as well. Speaking of that new family member, have you talked to Steven about it? Grandparenting might add a new dynamic to your relationship. You're still figuring out being parents together for Eric."

"Steven's doing well. He's coming to visit soon—wants to see Eric and Hilary, of course, and we'll also probably get the chance to catch up. He called me awhile back when he heard Monica's song, so we caught up then."

After telling her about Beth's reflection on the song lyrics, Marie remarks, "She's an observant kid. In touch with her feelings too. I can see why you're enjoying your time with her so much."

"One other thing I just have to tell you, Marie. Ever since we met, Beth has been calling me 'Lissa,' a sweet, shortened name—probably easier for her to say. But, this week, she started calling me 'Gamma.' It melted my heart. As if we weren't having a wonderful time already, that shift has been lovely."

"Oh goodness, I can see that you and she are becoming closer by the minute. Just remember what I said about a little time for yourself. Tend your own fire, Larissa."

Figuring I should act on Marie's reminder before it slips my mind, I call Isabel on my way home and leave a message to call me.

Before I even finish my message to her, she calls back.

"What's up, Larissa? Everything good?"

"All is well, my friend. Marie gently nudged me today— reminded me that I'm pretty absorbed in Beth and not doing enough for me. How about we do yoga or a walk and coffee later this week, and I'll get Eric or Hilary to watch her?"

"That sounds good. There is another possible alternative for Beth. I've twice let Lisa stay home and be the 'babysitter' for her brother when I run to the store. If you're comfortable, we could try that. It's during the day and yoga's only a little over an hour. Even if we get coffee, it's not very long."

I'm not sure what I think. Lisa's twelve, but I think I left Eric and Emma alone for short times when he was that age.

"Let me think about it, Is. I know she's a responsible girl, but Beth and Bobby? Isn't that a lot to ask? I don't know. Maybe I need to check with Everett on that one."

"I'm not trying to push you into it, but if we go on Saturday, Bobby will be at a game with his father. It would actually give Lisa something to do that day, so she doesn't feel as left out of the father-son thing."

"Isabel, change of subject, well kinda. It has to do with responsibility. I've been thinking about getting a phone for Beth. She's young, but pretty mature. I'm thinking I might feel better if she can call me no matter where she is. What do you think?"

She offers, "That's a hard one, but I know what you mean. I changed my mind about it a couple of years ago. I'd been really against kids having them till mid-teens. But then, there were times that Lisa was upset when at her dad's, and he didn't let her call me on his phone—really pissed me off. So, not only did I go against what I'd said for years, she and I have a pact that neither her dad nor Bobby can know she has one. It's in her backpack just in case. Do you think I'm a bad mom for making her complicit in a little deception?"

The thought of anyone describing Isabel as a bad mom is ludicrous, and I tell her so.

"Hey, Is, sometimes you gotta protect kids, do what you think is right, regardless. I actually did almost the same thing with Emma because of her dad. But I told him she had it and I put a tracker on it so I knew where it was, if it was off or on, all that stuff. And now, there are even more ways to restrict the apps, be assured of what they are accessing. I'm going to do it. I'll let Everett know—he might even be reassured that he can reach her or send her photos directly, or whatever."

Sitting at home later, I decide I'm just going to get Beth the phone in the morning, then talk to Everett about leaving her with Lisa before I do it. He'll have a sense of being involved in parenting decisions—I'm thinking that's no small thing when thousands of miles away. The fact that both girls have phones should make him more at ease with them being on their own for part of an afternoon.

The next day when Everett calls, Beth can't wait to tell him about her new friend Brittany and going to her house after school. She gives him a play-by-play rundown of everything from what snack they had, to a new board game she learned. Somehow, she also has details of Brittany's father's job, her mother's craft projects, her sister being in a play, and where her older brother has a part-time job. After reporting all her news and asking Everett a question or two about what he does after work, her interest has waned and she moves off the call to do her homework.

Before I ask him about letting Lisa stay with Beth, I fill him in on the playdate at Brittany's from my perspective.

"She's a sensitive girl, your daughter. She's been talking about Brittany for a couple of days and how some of the other kids were mean to her. I talked to Brittany's mother, and it turns out they live just a block away. When I dropped her off, I couldn't wait to tell you because you might feel relieved by this, her family is Vietnamese. Remember you were concerned about her being away from the diverse neighborhoods of New York? Well, anyway, they had a lot of fun and Brittany's going to come over here next week." I start to tell him about the phone and ask about leaving Beth alone with Lisa, but Everett interrupts me.

"Just a minute, I gotta tell you something. Remember when we talked about that COVID-19 thing a few weeks back, just before I left? Well, it's no damn joke here. Things are getting crazy. They're limiting flights from China and talking about a 'lock-down,' whatever the hell that is. Work is telling everybody to wear masks, that we must stay either in our office or at home, even discouraging going to restaurants or taking the bus. What the hell is going on? And what's a lock-down?"

The words 'lock-down' grab ahold of me and rattle the state of well-being and calm that surrounded us only moments ago. I'm searching my mind for an answer. Nothing comes to mind; just a tiny jolt of fear causing an unpleasant tingling down my spine.

"I don't know what that means, but it sure doesn't sound good. Maybe you need to just come home, back to the U.S.? I mean, we hear on the news about cases occasionally in New York and California, but nothing like what you're talking about. I don't want to tell you what to do, or overreact. Are they trying to scare people? Make them stay home? Lock-down sounds ominous."

I see him shaking his head and raking his hands through his hair. Clearly, he's confused, conflicted.

"I'll talk to my boss about all this craziness tomorrow. She's more on top of things from corporate. You might be right about trying to scare people into using the masks and staying out of crowded places. If people are careful, maybe this'll all go away. Can you get Beth to come blow me a kiss goodbye? I wanna see her sweet face one more time before I go to bed."

She comes running back to the phone with a big grin on her face. Ah, the innocence of seven-year-olds.

"'Night, Daddy, don't let the bedbugs bite!"

She skips back to her homework, and when I say my good-byes, Everett makes an attempt at humor, "Geez, bugs and viruses! What the hell else are we going to be dealing with, huh, Larissa?"

I laugh along, but it's a nervous laugh at best.

Later in the evening, I realize I'd forgotten to tell Everett about Lisa staying with Beth and my idea about a phone. His news about the virus impact on his daily life totally sidetracked the conversation.

Before school the next morning, Beth asks me to do her hair. I start to do her usual braids but then she points to a photo of a much more elaborate combination of several braids close to the head, and then two long ones down back. Totally out of my league for hairstyling.

"Beth, I have no clue how to make those beautiful, tight rows. I need to go to a stylist with you to learn how to do that! Want me to make an appointment?"

Her usual happy, sunshine morning face is darkened by a seldom-seen frown. "My mommy knew how." Followed by a heavy silence I'm struggling to fill.

Before my brain can kick into gear to send messages to my voice, she comes out with, "But, know what, Gamma? Brittany's mother is going to be a stylist. She said she's going to 'hair school.' Maybe she can do it or teach you, right?"

"Sure, if you want to wait for her to learn, or we can make an appointment, whatever you want!"

"I can wait. I like Brittany and her mother. What's 'China flu'?"

For the second time this morning, I am totally flummoxed by how to respond to her. What is she talking about?

"I don't know, Beth. Where did you hear that?"

"Those kids that were being mean to Brittany. They said she should go back to China, that nobody here wants her China flu. It made her really sad. She doesn't have a flu and she's not from China. Why did they say that?"

Anger rises instantly. That anyone would say such a thing to a little girl! It sends my heart racing, makes me want to call the school, and brings the same tingle of fear cascading down my spine that hit me last night on the phone.

But Beth and Brittany don't need my anger. They need information and compassion.

"I can see why you and Brittany are sad. That sounds hurtful. I don't know what those words even mean, but I'll find out, and then we'll figure out what to do next. I'm proud of you for being a good friend, Beth. Everyone needs good friends."

I finish her hair and make a quick decision.

"Speaking of friends, how about if Lisa comes over and takes care of you tomorrow? Her mother says she lets Lisa be in charge of Bobby sometimes when she has to go out. If we go to yoga, would you like it if Lisa came to stay with you?"

Beth nods her head, but takes her time to answer. What is she thinking about?

"She can come over and keep me company. I don't like being alone. But, if she's in charge, will she be the boss of me? What if I don't like what she says?"

"So, a couple of things—first, she doesn't need to be the boss. You said it better. You can each keep the other company while we're gone. Second, I got you a phone of your own today. We need to go over the rules for using a phone, like what apps, how much time, and where it belongs during school hours. But, I don't want you to worry about being alone. Finally—the two of you won't be here on your own very long. Maybe we can find a movie for you guys to watch? Before you know it, we'll be back!"

"Wait! What? You got me a phone?"

I spend the next half hour or so reviewing the rules with Beth. I fully expect we'll need to go over it again, but she starts figuring out all the phone's bells and whistles faster than I can even keep up. She even thinks of things that hadn't crossed my mind.

With a serious tone to her voice, she proposes, "So, Gamma, I want to be able to listen to music, like the song Monica wrote, whenever I want because it makes me feel happy. But, I know there's music that's not appropriate. Brittany's mother said she did settings so that Brittany and her brother can only listen to certain music. Should we do that on my phone?"

Nodding my head yes, a little research shows me how to set the phone to do just that. *Who knew? One more way I can reassure Everett when we have the conversation.*

On Saturday, Isabel and I are ready to go to yoga. We set the girls up with a movie and a snack, tell them how long we'll be gone, and to call us in case of an emergency. Before long, we set out for our class and our "adult time" as we told them.

The class and savasana have done their magic. Isabel and I are strolling home in a relaxed, almost dreamlike state when her ringing phone startles us back into reality.

I hear Lisa's voice yelling into the phone and feel immediate terror. *What is going on?* Isabel fires off questions and finishes with, "Don't open the door—we're almost home."

She grabs my hand and says, "We gotta hurry. Some kids are on your sidewalk yelling things that scared Lisa and Beth."

As we half-walk, half-run the rest of the way home, it feels like hours instead of minutes, with the voice in my head repeating, *I knew it was a bad idea to leave them alone.*

No one is out on the sidewalk when we get there. The story spills out in bits and pieces. The girls are scared, but fine.

Isabel asks, "So tell me again what happened, Lisa?"

"There was a knock at the door. I looked out the peephole and Beth saw from the window it was some boys from school. I told her we should just ignore them and go back to the movie. But they stayed up on the porch and yelled stuff."

"It was good you didn't open the door. What did they yell?"

Half sniffling, half trying to sound very confident, she reports. "One boy kept saying, if you hang out with that Brittany girl, you're gonna make us all sick, get the China flu. So just stay home. We don't want you at our school anyway."

I motion for Beth to come over. She looks hungry for reassurance, or a hug.

"I bet that made you guys sad. No wonder you wanted us to get home. I'm happy Lisa called us."

Beth's face crumbles and tears stream down her face. "I don't like those boys, Gamma. They're the ones that told Brittany to go back to China. They're mean. My new phone was in the kitchen. I was ready to call 9-1-1 if they didn't leave."

"Good to be prepared, Beth, but glad you didn't need to. The boys sure are mean. And they don't belong on our porch yelling things at you. We're going to talk to their parents and your school. Behavior like that is not acceptable."

I put on a good act until we convince the girls to go upstairs and finish an art project.

"I'm so pissed, I could throttle those kids. What the heck is going on? I guess they've been saying nasty things to Brittany at school as well. I'm calling that principal and getting to the bottom of this. No offense, Isabel, but I'm not sure it was a good idea to leave the girls. If something worse had happened, I can't even--"

"I know, I hear you. But the girls were smart and nothing worse did happen. Life is tough for kids, and maybe we can stop this crap before it gets any worse. You and I can make more of a ruckus at the school than just Brittany's parents alone."

18

Between what is said and not meant,
and what is meant but not said,
most of love is lost.
KAHLIL GIBRAN

Renee, Isabel, and I are taking a stroll, coffee to-go cups in hand. The kids are at school, and our agenda is to decompress, to rant about the meeting with the principal, the bad news on the television, and then bring one another back from the crescendo of emotion to a baseline that allows for enjoying everyday life.

My summary: "That was a series of weird encounters."

"What did you expect? Everyone's on the defensive. Once we all got our voices heard, the principal was pretty good about directing the boys' parents. They agreed that the kids need to apologize, so we'll see. It's the first time there's ever been an incident like this since my kids have gone there. I think that principal has her hands full right now."

I'm calmer than a few days ago, but not as ready to settle as Isabel.

"Hands full or not, first time or not, this could mess up Beth's whole time at this school. She was so happy till now. Just a damn shame people are being so hateful."

Renee jumps into the latest headlines.

"A few weeks ago, we had no clue what 'lock-down' even meant, 'China Flu' wasn't in the news, and the only time anyone ever wore a mask was if they were sick. Now it's all we hear. I'm tired of it all, you guys, sick and tired of it."

I drop my anger at the kids and follow her lead.

"Steven said the schools up in New York are all closing at the end of this week. The governor wanted to do it sooner, but they need to give people time to make plans for kids being home. Do you think the other states will close too? How can this be happening? How do we just close schools? And for how long?"

Isabel chimes in, "I've no clue what I'll do about work if the schools do close. I can't just start staying home, and their father certainly won't be any help. It just sucks, you guys."

Renee shakes her head and offers, "It won't be for long, Is. They just want to stop the huge crowds in emergency rooms, especially in bigger cities. Our administrators met with everyone at work yesterday and said we're going to divide things up—people with kids can work from home, the rest of us have to go in. So, now the ones like me without kids are complaining that it's unfair. No one's ever happy."

I hear myself volunteering, "Isabel, I work from home most of the time anyway. And that will probably be even more often if there's less travel and on-site training. If our schools do close, your kids can come to my house to do their schoolwork. Like Renee said, it's only gonna be a couple of weeks, anyway. Just till this is under control. And, maybe it'll stop this group of kids from picking on others."

"What's the scoop with Everett? I hear it's really bad in Italy and spreading like crazy there. Is he gonna come home?"

I've been avoiding talking about this. First, the unknowns of this virus terrify me; it makes me physically sick to think about it. Second, I want him to get out of there and come home. Third, I'm trying not to get outwardly alarmed and scare anyone, particularly Beth.

"It's not good. Right now, they're quarantined in their apartments. The company has a section of a hotel with apartments just for the U.S. staff. He's staying in his own space, working from there, only socializing with work friends, and wearing masks whenever he has to be out—like for groceries. I hate it, you guys. It almost feels like he's gone from my life again. I know he's not really gone, but knowing he can't come here, and I can't go there, is really messing with my sanity. The world feels totally out of whack."

As if to emphasize how out of whack everything is, as soon as I return home, I get a call from Everett well before Beth's pick-up time.

"What's up, Everett? How are you?"

"Just checking in to see how you guys are."

Before Beth gets out of school? Weird. Guess that's a sign—I should take advantage of a private call to tell him about the nasty school-kids incident.

"Things are fine, but I do need to tell you about something without Beth here."

"Uh, okay. I forgot it's too early for her to be home yet—sorry."

"Last time we talked, I planned to ask you what you thought about me having Lisa stay with Beth while Isabel and I went to yoga. But we ran out of time on the call."

"Aren't they a little young for that?"

"I think they're both pretty mature. Anyway, we tried it a few days ago and--"

He cuts me off and interjects, "You just went ahead and did it? Like how long did you leave them?"

The questions are not merely inquiring—and the emphasis on 'leave' is unmistakably an accusation—not a good start.

"I thought it was a good chance to try it out—only an hour or so, they had a movie to watch, and both Beth and Lisa had their phones in case of an emergency. Anyway, some kids from their school came up on the porch and started yelling things about her friend Brittany. We learned the hard way that a lot of people with Asian backgrounds are being targeted because of this whole COVID thing."

"Whoa, so Brittany was there, too?"

"No, no, she wasn't here. The kids were telling, I guess warning, Beth not to be Brittany's friend. It was scary for Lisa and Beth, but they did the right things. They didn't unlock the door, they called us. By the time we got home, the kids had run off. We calmed the girls down. Went and talked to the principal earlier today. The kids' parents came in and the boys are going to apologize at a meeting tomorrow. Seems like all is going to be well."

"What the hell? You think all is well? You decide to let one kid watch another kid and they get harassed, threatened? I can't freaking believe this, Larissa. I'm not cool with any of this."

I didn't exactly see this coming. Or, maybe I did and I feel guilty?

"I'm sorry. I'm sorry you see it that way, Everett. At the time, it seemed a reasonable thing to do, and honestly, as Isabel and the principal pointed out, the girls knew what to do."

"Okay, they knew what to do and everybody is now going to sit around and what? Shake hands? What about if those kids hadn't run away? What about if they broke in or worse? I can't shake this feeling, Larissa. What were you thinking?"

"I was thinking that it was a safe way for the girls to get practice at being alone with a safety net. It was a finite period of time and they know how to call if they need help."

"Since when does Beth have a phone? Do I get a say in that? She's only seven for Pete's sake. Now she has access to all the crap on the internet? Again—what were you thinking?"

"Everett, do you really think I'd get her a phone without restricting what she can access? I thought you'd be happy to have a direct line to her—literally. And, I was thinking you trusted me to use my own judgment. If I'm wrong in that--"

Guess I must be wrong—he interrupts again, "Trust and using judgment. And uh, how has that gone in the past? Your record as a parent isn't exactly without its issues. I should trust someone who discarded me? Oh shit! Wait, wait, I didn't mean--"

Too shocked to think it through, now it's my turn to fire off a response, "Maybe you need to come back home. You can't trust me; the world is a mess, we're in the middle of conditions we've never been in before—lockdown, quarantine, isolation. Kids are targeting other kids, and schools are about to close. Not sure whose judgment is in question, here. If you're not 'cool,' as you say, with my decisions, you should come home and try navigating this insanity yourself."

"What do you mean, schools are going to close? You didn't mention that, either. This is crazy—half the reason I decided to leave Beth with you was so she could be in school."

Trying to maintain a modicum of composure, I calmly repeat myself.

"Then, I guess you do need to come home. I can't control the schools. If this situation isn't what you want for Beth, come home."

"I'm sorry, Larissa. I shouldn't have said what I said; I got carried away. I can't come home, Larissa. Not now. Listen, it's complicated. I didn't mean . . ."

Something deep inside me, that I don't like, is stirring. It's the emotional equivalent of the sour taste of bile rising, about to spew out into our delicately constructed relationship.

"You can't, or you *won't*?"

The line goes dead. Did he hang up on me, or did we get cut off?

I'm still seething when Beth gets home. I can't let her know what happened. Luckily, Eric and Hilary are bringing Steven over for dinner. Not like I'm really fit to be around people right now, but at least they'll be a distraction from the shitshow of a phone call I experienced a couple of hours ago.

Beth's day must have been fine. She's excited about seeing Eric and Hilary later, so scoots right upstairs to get her homework done. I paste a smile on my face and tell her I'll let her know when they get here.

I replay the conversation in my head while peeling potatoes. Everett seemed off from the minute we got on the phone. Made me hesitant to tell him about the whole ordeal. Had he sensed that? Was something else going on? Why *can't* he come home? Did he actually hang up on me? Too many questions and absolutely no answers. All my insecurities about how he must regard a mother who gave him away at birth are making themselves known again—front and center. It feels like a damaging landslide has interrupted our lives, adding to the upheaval around us.

The routine of a family dinner is a welcome respite from the thoughts torturing me.

When Beth takes Hilary upstairs to show her the project she started, Eric and Steven come into the dining room to see if I need any help.

"Nothing really—just setting the table. Grab yourselves something to drink. Everything's in the oven and should be ready soon. How was your trip down, Steven?"

"Honestly, I was glad to get on the road. Everything is so crazy with shutdowns. Most of our clients in day programs live in group homes, and the state has quarantined them all. Guess they need to be safe, but it's sad to see our usually bustling centers with nothing going on. Everyone's gotta pivot and see if there's some way we can provide services online, but that's full of issues to figure out. It's exhausting. Then, they're talking about having checkpoints along the highways to get into New York. Every day it's something new to worry about."

"Tell me about it." Too late, I realize my comment was sarcastic at best, probably closer to morose.

Eric doesn't miss it.

"What, Mom? What's up? Trouble in paradise?"

How do I respond to this? He's kidding around while I'm miserable. "Let's just say there's no such place as paradise, my dear. I need to go check on the roast—don't want it to dry out."

I make the quickest escape that I can without running. Eric follows me into the kitchen.

"Mom, really, no joke. You're upset about something. Is it that whole thing with the kids yelling stuff at Beth? She's fine. Kids are just plain stupid. Mean and stupid. It's gonna blow over—especially because I doubt they'll be in school together much longer."

"Maybe. Or, maybe they'll have too much time on their hands and be even worse. I don't know, Eric. I wanted nothing more than to have Beth here, to help Everett out. But, maybe it's more than I can handle, especially if he doesn't trust me. Having her for vacation, taking a road trip—those were fun for us both, and let's face it, short term. This is, well, a bigger deal. Raising your own kids isn't easy; raising someone's else's—it ups the ante."

"What do you mean 'not trust'? She's here, isn't she? Come on, you love this. You haven't had so much fun doing art projects and teaching your little sayings in a really long time. Hilary couldn't believe how happy you both looked when we were over last week. You're letting that one thing get you down? A few goofballs are ruining this whole deal? That's not the Mom I know. Shake it off."

"I can't talk about it now, Eric. I don't want Beth to hear us. Let's just say, Everett was pretty pissed about the whole thing. I don't know what bothered him the most—the boys, the fact that I got her a phone, or that schools might close. He hung up on me."

"He what? That doesn't sound like him. What did he say? What did you say?"

"He basically said my judgment sucks. I told him if he didn't like how I was doing things, he should come home."

"So you gave him an ultimatum? Not like he can just pick up and hop on a plane, put his job in jeopardy. What did you really expect?"

"Whose side are you on, anyway?"

"Didn't know there *were* sides here. Just trying to, uh, see both sides, maybe."

"It was weird, Eric. He said he *can't* come home. Didn't say why, but used the word *can't*. First, it sounded more like he doesn't want to, then knew he went too far. He started to back-pedal. All I heard was 'I didn't mean,' but then the line cut out. I think he hung up on me. Enough for now. Let's get this dinner on the table. I need a break from this."

Hilary tells us about her latest doctor appointment and Steven can't wait to see the ultrasound image. Before long, Beth gets up to take our plates into the kitchen. I hear her calling to me.

"Lissa, your phone's in here and it's ringing. It's my daddy. We should tell him my new phone number so he can call right to me!"

Ugh—yeah, sure—he'll be so happy to have her new phone number. "Go ahead and pick it up, honey."

Eric glances up at me with a questioning look. I shake my head side to side ever so slightly.

Beth is occupied for a few minutes, then calls out, "Hey, everybody, come say hi to my daddy."

Hilary and Eric hurry into the kitchen. Steven starts to go, but when he sees I haven't moved, he begins to pull my chair out and says, "Come on. Everett's on the phone."

"Go ahead—take your turn, I spoke to him already today."

Eric calls me to come talk, but I tell him it's their turn. There's no way I can be part of some light-hearted phone call with him right now. Let them catch up and have a fun conversation without me.

When they all come back with dessert on their plates, the consensus is that he looks good and seems to like his job. The superficial stuff we always say about people after a video chat.

Steven reports further, "He says his boss is teaching him about the company, but also filling him in on travel in Italy. He's hoping as soon as this virus thing calms down, they can go on some side trips. Says it would be fun to travel with someone who knows the language."

Peeved that he and I didn't have an opportunity to talk about fun things like side trips, my two cents are, "Huh, didn't know she's Italian, or speaks the language."

Eric pipes up, "His boss is a she? Hey, maybe that's why he's looking so good."

As usual, his quick wit sparks laughter. I can't really join in—the thought running through my mind: *maybe she's why he can't come home.*

19

Forgiveness is the fragrance that the violet
sheds on the heel that has crushed it.
MARK TWAIN

Four months later, the unthinkable has happened. More unthinkables than I care to count, with too many unasked-for lessons learned.

I learned that while the death of my child three years ago defined *unthinkable* for me personally, the death of over one hundred thousand people in the U.S. alone is unthinkable for our country, our world.

I learned that even the joy of the birth of my new grandbaby, Benjamin, can be diminished by the shadow of a frightening, contagious illness.

We learned the consequences of "lockdown"—it's claustrophobic at best, deadly at worst.

We learned that rarely spoken words like *pandemic, unprecedented,* and *quarantine* have a sneaky way of becoming everyday vocabulary.

We learned that if a virus that lasts five to ten days isn't bad enough, there could be lingering brain fog and dozens of other health problems.

We learned that while virtual schooling, working remotely, and Zoom temporarily solve many problems, they can hijack the quality of life.

And while there's little I can do about the pitfalls of working from a distance, circumventing schooling issues has become a huge part of my life. I gave the kids an assignment with twenty minutes to work on it. They must find places, within the United States, to which they would love to travel. Rules—they need to find a place they've never been, and they need to pitch it to the rest of us.

Coming up with fun ways to keep these kids interested in learning is both exhilarating and damn exhausting. What I thought would be a two-week commitment to homeschool Beth, Lisa, and Bobby has already turned into months, with no end in sight. And at some point I can't even remember, we added the dear, little boy Renee is now fostering, Louis. Another unexpected consequence of a pandemic—more children need stable homes with available adults.

Caressing my cool cup of iced latte while they work on the assignment—they must be working because there is no talking or giggles coming from the kitchen counter (our makeshift schoolroom)—I daydream about renting an RV and traveling the country. I'm so caged in by this whole global health drama. When the national parks open up, I'm determined to hit the road.

Even the spur of the moment trip that Beth and I took to Florida a couple of weeks ago didn't help with the cooped-up feelings of the last few months. Kristy was thrilled to see both Beth and me. My dear friend Adele opened up her serene setting on Hutchinson Island for us to enjoy, to use as a retreat, in hopes that the waterside setting might work some magic. But it didn't get us far enough away from the news and the factions arguing about whether masks work or not, or about how long schools should be shut down. The island had its calming effect, but the chaos of the world somehow snuck across the bridges and crept in anyway. Maybe a remote park in Wyoming or Utah or someplace out West could ease this constant tension.

Before the time is up for the researchers inside, I reread the letter I'm getting ready to send Everett. After the difficult call at the start of his time in Italy, we took to writing letters. Bits and pieces of his story and my emotions slowly revealed themselves in a far less volatile tone than the phone call had taken. The extra time involved to use paper and pen, to choose words, to edit or rewrite, have served us well. An understanding of one another that previously did not have enough time or practice to take root has grown, even blossomed, with the lengthy spaces between letters. He calls Beth for their video chats, but he and I save our meaningful exchanges for this age-old method of communication—one of the better unexpected outcomes from being isolated.

The slowness of the communication was actually a benefit when Everett wrote me his latest news. He was contacted, through the DNA website, about his biological father. If I'd heard that message via phone call, I'm sure I would have said something stupid, something I'd regret. Instead, letter-writing gave me the time to mull over what I want to say. A real gift to rebuilding with Everett, rather than tearing down our carefully constructed bridges. *Read it once more to be sure you've got it right, Larissa.*

Dear Everett-

It must have been jolting to receive another surprise from an online DNA service; I'm guessing you didn't fathom being notified by them again years after learning of our connection.

What have you decided to do? I honestly have no opinion, no advice to offer. My time with your biological father was so minimal. Time tells me that it was no fault of our own. A charming exchange student at a party, underage drinking, my innocence, my parents' shame, and his planned return home before we even knew there was another life to consider. Add that momentary encounter to an era where such things were kept secret, and decisions were made to do what common wisdom thought was best. Perhaps not best as we look back, but my mother took charge.

One thing to consider—something led him to take the initiative to do a DNA test and search. Maybe when he read my bio on the high school reunion website, something churned within him. Maybe it sparked a recollection he'd never consciously experienced, and in turn, he felt responsibility.

I don't know how you make the decision to meet him or not. I can see why you've been struggling with it, though. The timing of his email was challenging. I take it he's in Europe, so it must be tempting to try to see him. When you first got there, you had so much to learn and absorb, not only about your job, but also a new country. Then, lockdown and restrictions on travel.

I see now why you might be torn between staying and coming back. I wish you'd trusted me to be honest with why you didn't want, or didn't feel you could, come back here when I suggested it. I'd like to think I would have been understanding, but we were both a bit on edge. I'm grateful you've shared it now and hope we can continue to be honest with one another, to trust. I'll support you whatever you decide. Trust is the crux of it all, isn't it? We've certainly had our share of complications in developing a relationship of trust. I'd like to think we're on the right path, though.

On another topic, we're doing okay here. The days are pretty full with keeping the kids busy. I'm still with them most of the time, with Isabel and Renee helping out when they can.

I might try another short trip with Beth. It was terrific to see Kristy and be by the water for a few days, but I think we need more distraction. Don't worry—I'm not talking about anything crazy or breaking rules, just depends on if the parks open up, and of course, if you are okay with us going. I don't need to tell you, it's hard to be at the mercy of this rotten virus.

Love you and am ready to talk when the time feels right,
Lissa

Beth, always the designated messenger from her fellow students, comes out onto the porch and asks, "Whatcha doin', Gamma? We finished. Can we have a snack before we do the pitches?"

I'm so lost in the letter that it takes me a minute to switch gears and jump back into my facilitator role. I'd almost forgotten that "pitch" was a word I'd used in making the assignment new, and hopefully, interesting enough to grab their attention.

"Yes, I can't wait to be convinced by what you have all found. What do you think we should have for a snack?"

Twenty minutes later, they're taking turns trying to impress one another and me with the destinations uncovered in their search assignment. I'm keeping a list and once they've all reported in, I tell them, "Great job so far. The next step—we're going to vote, by secret ballot, on our top favorites—the ones you'd like most to go see. We need to pick one from each of your work. Then, those who found those places are going to pitch one more time to Eric, Renee, and Isabel. They're all going to come over in an hour for pizza and to hear your presentations. You can make pictures, or maps, or whatever it takes to showcase these travel gems, convince them you've picked the best place. Maybe they will put one on their own travel wish list."

Our invited guests arrive on time and we decide to have the pizza first, do the presentations over coffee and dessert.

"Uncle Eric, how is baby Benjamin doing? When can I finally see him?" Beth asks to see the baby almost daily. Even though we are all being careful, it seems like too big of a risk. I've been to see him only once, the day he came home from the hospital.

"I think it's almost time, Beth. Hilary and I talked about it just this morning when we knew I was coming over here. We're thinking we'll check with the doctor at his next appointment."

The face that was pouting only a moment ago brightens up at his news.

"We'd like it as much as you, my favorite little girl! And Mom, haven't had a chance to tell you yet—unless Dad called you himself?"

"Not recently—last time I spoke to him was almost a month ago. He was pretty discouraged about when they might be able to open day programs back up for the people who live in group homes. He's had to lay off staff, he's bored just doing administrative stuff—he's such a people person! Sounds like it's just miserable all around."

Eric quickly nods in agreement.

"Miserable enough to decide he's going to retire and move south. I guess the whole slowdown has made him think. He's still trying to decide where—maybe here or closer to Nina, but he wants to be close to both of us, and he says with Benjamin now here, he just wants to move even sooner. Since his brother passed, he says everyone he wants to be near is too far from upstate New York."

I've been so absorbed in keeping all the plates spinning here, it never occurred to me how lonely Steven might be. Jimmy was a huge part of all Steven's decisions—where to live and work—over the years.

"When their mother died, Steven made caring for Jimmy his top priority—the center of his life. Makes total sense that with you and Benjamin here, Nina in Florida, he'd start thinking about moving and making the most of his time with you. I'm happy for him." How strange it would be to once again live in the same place as my ex-husband, my first love.

"Uh—earth to Mom, you look like you're staring into space. Listen, change of topic. Have you talked to Everett in the last couple of days? Oh man, I'm sorry, are you guys still only doing letters?"

Jolted back to Eric's next news flash, I reply, "We're writing letters. Don't be sorry—I'm not. It's been good. Let's see, he talked to Beth two, no wait, four nights ago. That's odd." Now, I'm concerned—he usually calls her every other day. Does Eric have news that I don't?

"What? What's going on with him, Eric?"

"One minute, Mom. Hey, kids, aren't you guys going to do some kind of presentation for the rest of us? We'll be ready in ten or fifteen minutes. Why don't you go get ready for that?"

Lisa is the first to protest, "We worked on it this afternoon, Eric. Our pitches and posters are all finished. Are you trying to get rid of us or somethin'?"

Isabel interjects, "Listen, young lady. As the oldest, you need to be the role model, respect your elders. Eric asked you nicely, now I'm telling you to rally your buddies and wait for us out on the enclosed porch."

The four students, four friends, four allies shuffle out with stooped postures and eyes toward the ground. I almost laugh at their dramatic exit, but I'm too concerned with Eric's whole demeanor regarding Everett.

"Spill the beans, Eric. What's up, is Everett all right?"

Eric stands up and begins to pace. "Yeah, yeah, he's fine. Just that, well, you already knew that Everett got an email through the DNA website. It was from a guy who said his DNA matched with

Everett's; Everett comes up with the closest possible match—like as his son."

Geez, I didn't have a clue that Eric was going to blurt this out. I'd told Renee, but not had a second alone with Isabel to tell her. As I glance her way, her face covers the range of shock to totally expressionless in under three seconds. Bless her—she'll be hurt in private, but never reveal it here.

The other heads around the table nod, so he continues.

"Everett was pretty shocked and not sure what to do. They'd emailed a couple of times, like the week before Everett went to Italy and his first weeks there. Anyway, not sure who knows what, and now I think I should have kept my big mouth shut."

I didn't know he'd heard from the father *before* he left for Italy, and I'm not too crazy about where this is going now. But Eric started down the path and might as well finish.

"It's okay, Eric. Everyone here is part of our family—blood or not. And, yes, he and I have chosen a slower way to communicate. It has some great advantages, but guess I'm about to learn also its pitfalls."

"Anyway, before he knew it, the lockdown came and meeting in person was out of the question. How weird, ironic, I guess, that once he got to Italy, he was so much closer, but couldn't go see him. The guy lives in Malta, like four hours away."

My mind wanders to that foreign exchange student. I didn't even remember what country he was from. *Hadn't I cared? Or had I blocked it from my mind?* My eyes must have closed with my musings—as I open them, everyone is looking at me.

Bringing myself back to the present, I mumble, "Um, what?"

It seems as if I'm the one they expect to speak next, but slowed down by his stops and starts, Eric still hasn't shared whatever the news is.

I make eye contact with Eric and nod that he should continue.

"Yeah, I'm rambling. To the point—Italy opened their borders end of last week and, well, Everett went to Malta. They met. The guy, his name is Joseph, Joe. And his story matches up. He was an exchange student in Mom's hometown. And guess I'll stop there. Some stuff is just Mom's business. Anyway, Everett stayed and visited a couple of days and just got back to Rome today. He sounds confused about his feelings, but okay. Man, it was strange enough finding out about my dad a couple of years ago. He's found out about both parents in the last few years. Okay, I'm talking too much again."

Now the obscure bits and pieces in my memory bank begin to add up into some semblance of the story—kids in high school called him Joey. His swarthy skin and dark, curly hair were legendary. Every girl in my school had a crush on him. He easily made it onto the soccer team and shined in the theater club. I admired him from afar most of the year—until the final production, and, well, especially the after-party.

Renee tries to fill the silence and reassure me all at once.

"That is a lot for one person to handle. These sure have been a strange few years. Strange because of loss, strange because of what's been found. You've all made the most of it so far; I have faith you'll do it again this time. And while we're talking about faith, please help me have faith that this leap into life with Louis is going to be a good one. Good one for him, mostly, me second. I need all the help I can get from you guys."

Renee's sincere pleading for our support brings me back from the past, into the here and now. Right now, she needs help in this new relationship more than I need to dissect one from the past.

"She's right. We've lost a lot, but we've found so much. Whether it's finding signs and ways to connect with Emma, finding relations we didn't know existed, or finding adorable Louis, discovering connections is opening up to new possibilities. They can be scary, but also our reasons to live. Speaking of which, a few of our 'reasons to live' are patiently waiting on the porch to show us their work. Ready?"

20

*There are years that ask questions
and years that answer.*
ZORA NEALE HURSTON

The kids have made good use of their time. The porch is set up like a miniature theater, with four chairs for them up front, and a small semi-circle of chairs for us to listen to them. Each chair has a colorful poster board propped up to aid in presenting their ideas. And they have changed out of their usual t-shirts and sweatpants. The boys have on real pants and polos, the girls skirts and blouses.

Scanning the titles, I'm delighted at the array of places they've discovered. In their planning meeting, they decided who would go first, who would introduce, and other details, but they've kept the rest to themselves. My spur-of-the-moment-urge to contemplate travel, while giving them something to do has ended up exceeding my goals. They totally immersed themselves in this!

Lisa stands up first to introduce the assignment and announce that they will be pitching in the order of oldest to youngest. As the oldest, she then launches into her pitch.

"I don't know about you, but I want to go mining for diamonds. Herkimer Diamonds, which are really quartz. If we go to Herkimer, NY—only about two hours from where Miss Lissa grew up, we can mine them ourselves and make jewelry." She continues on with an explanation of the powers of crystals, details of jewelry making, and even a campground to stay at. She may have gone on forever, but thankfully, an alarm sounds. They've even thought of setting timers for their presentations—brilliant.

Bobby is ready to go and tells the group all about Mesa Verde National Park. Most of it I already knew, but he ends with this tidbit, "Besides visiting the cliff dwellings of the Ancestral Pueblo people, this park is also an International Dark Sky Park. Anyone know what that is?"

Seeing us all shake our heads side to side, he offers, "Didn't think so. It's a place where the sky is so clear that you can almost always have beautiful starry nights for stargazing. That's why I want to go—there's something to do both day and night time!"

Up next, Beth pulls us in by telling us she wants to go someplace only about an hour away from here—Callaway Gardens in Pine Mountain, almost all the way to Georgia's western border by Alabama.

"It's a beautiful place to see butterflies. There's more than a thousand of them flying in the glass building. Butterflies are Gamma's favorite thing. They make her think of people she loves who aren't here anymore. I want to take her in September. September is Blue Morpho month. She likes monarchs very much, but these butterflies are much bigger and are shiny blue."

I'm touched. *She wants to take me*. Such a sweet sentiment.

All three of the kids are moving around behind Louis. It seems like he can't stand up. What's wrong with our littlest speaker? The girls each take one of his hands as Bobby whispers in his ear. Louis nods his head and whispers back.

Bobby points to Louis' poster and says, "He's not ready to talk yet, but said I should get his part started. He thinks we should travel to Dinosaur Monument. It's, um, in . . ."

Louis bolts up out of his chair and takes over. "Utah, it's in Utah. There are dinosaur footprints, bones, and drawings on the walls, I can't say the word. Can you say it, Bobby?"

His buddy helps with, "Petroglyph."

"Yeah, that. They're carvings in the wall that look like drawings. Anyway, people who lived there a thousand years ago made birds and lizards and snakes on the walls. I want to see them."

When they've finished, the adults clap enthusiastically. I'm clapping along thinking, what am I going to do? Each of them said they want to go as if this is a real trip we're planning right now. Did I say something to make them think this was going to happen like anytime soon?

It's gotten quiet, and I feel all eyes on me.

"Oh my gosh, you guys. Your pitches were amazing! I want to go to every single one. And the audience should know, they worked on this all afternoon just to give you ideas for travel someday. Aren't they terrific salespeople? One more round of applause before we dig into the brownies that Renee brought!"

"But, um, Gamma, so when can we go?" Beth's deep, dark eyes look bigger and rounder than ever.

Eric walks toward the kids and says, "Trips like these take a lot of planning, little one. We can make lists of where we would like to go—some call it a bucket list. And then we work towards checking them off the list slowly. Remember when you told us how many states you checked off while driving down here from New York? It's kind of the same. You can put any of the places you heard about tonight on your own bucket list and then start figuring out how to make them happen."

"I'm too little to start making them happen. I need you guys, please?"

He saved me a moment ago, now I need to step up and do my own share of explaining.

"Uncle Eric's right, Beth. It takes planning. But maybe that can be our next assignment. We'll put these four destinations on a map and start learning all we can about how to organize trips like these. Good things take time, sometimes more than we'd like."

Somehow, we make it past the travel crisis and on to the brownies. Everyone is gone and Beth's in bed, but Eric and I are sitting at the island in the kitchen. When he checked in with Hilary a bit ago, she and the baby were going to bed. The little bit of alone time with him is precious.

"Thanks for the help when Beth wanted to start the travel immediately. She took me totally off guard twice. First, when she said she wants to take me to the iridescent blue butterflies—my heart fluttered, actually, nearly exploded. Second, when she thought we were about to start the group road trip any day—didn't know what to do!"

He laughs and says, "They all thought that. What did you tell them, anyway?"

"I sure didn't say we could get up and go, that's for sure. But, you're right, I guess, I must have said something that planted the seed."

"They're a pretty cute bunch, Mom. COVID has sucked in so many ways, but it seems not so bad when you see these little kids so excited over a project."

"It's one small example of a silver lining to a dark, damn cloud."

But I can't let the earlier conversation go just yet.

"Can we get back to the Everett and Joey, I mean Joseph, thing?"

Eric's chin drops to his chest and he takes a deep breath before reaching for my shoulder.

"About that, Mom. I'm sorry—sometimes I have no damn filter. Once I started, I couldn't figure out where to stop."

His pitiful self-deprecation breaks down any defenses I had left.

"It's no big deal. I'm glad you stopped, though. You have no filter, and I struggle with controlling my own reactions to events from when I was fifteen. There are days I feel there's mutual responsibility for the whole encounter, and days when it seems I was seduced . . . or worse. But since Everett has been in our lives, I've told myself none of that really matters. I'm not going to focus on the parts I can't change. My energy is focused on how you and I, all of us, can be a family with Everett and Beth. If Joseph comes into Everett's life now, well, not sure it's my business. Not sure it changes anything about what I do, how I live my life."

He's quietly nodding his head, taking his time to respond.

"I might just get that. Ever since Benjamin came into our lives, I think of things so much differently than before—already. I've tried to imagine how it must have felt for you to surrender a baby, and well, I just can't. I wonder, though. What about if he, Joseph, is uh, mad that you didn't tell him about the baby? Didn't give him a chance to be a father back then?"

An immediate anger response, heat traveling up my neck, gives me pause. I guess my magnanimous speech of a few moments ago hadn't considered the possibility that I should have contacted the father. The older student who, as my mother so properly stated, 'had his way with me'? The possibility that I need to be contrite in some way? Better practice my response here and now with Eric, might serve me well if this comes up later, like with Everett.

"Same thing, Eric. I can't change what happened. By the time I knew I was pregnant, he'd gone back home from his exchange experience. I had no clue how to find him. There weren't internet searches back then, that's for sure; didn't seem to be any other choice."

"Couldn't the family he stayed with here have given you a way to reach him?"

I look down at trembling hands in my lap and attempt to fight back the mad, the sad, the guilt, and reply, "Eric, I was young, scared, made to feel ashamed, and your grandmother went into high gear to take care of things. I don't think I owe anyone any further explanation."

This time, he comes over next to me and pulls me into a hug against his chest; so close I can hear his heartbeat.

"You're right, Mom, you don't. I'm sorry and I'll shut up. It's none of my business. I think I'm just worried about you and Everett. It's been so good since we found him. I mean you guys got a little testy over Beth, but that seems better now. This new challenge scares me a little."

"Don't be sorry, don't be scared. Your questions have actually given me a chance to prepare, to think through what might possibly come up now that they have met. I have no idea how Everett or Joseph will react. Having time to process it on my own may be the best thing for us. Taken off guard, I'm not quite so measured. I don't want to mess up all the progress Everett and I have made by snail mail. When, or if, he does choose to bring it up, I'll have things more sorted out on my side."

I stop to gather my thoughts and ask, "Back to *your* dad. When did you say he's thinking about making this change? Anytime soon or waiting till a retirement-age birthday, or--?"

"Didn't say exactly, but I got the impression sooner than later. He even said he's meeting with a real estate agent about listing his house up there. He has that little apartment here he can use until he decides where he wants to settle. Says he wants to get his hands on his grandson as soon as he can."

"So, we're all ready for the same thing, then! Waiting for the pediatrician to give us the go signal. That masked-up snuggle a few weeks ago isn't exactly what I'd envisioned. I'd like to think I'm being as safe as possible. We're staying pretty isolated here, it's just that I can't totally control what Lisa, Bobby, and Louis do when they're home. Isabel and Renee are as careful as possible and make them wear their masks if they're near anyone else. How much more can we expect, right?"

After Eric leaves, I start thinking about sharing the new grandchild with Steven. It reminds me how many experiences we've shared over the years. A question pops into my mind that I cannot dismiss. A quick glance at the clock and I'm convinced it's not too late to call him.

"Larissa? What's up? Everything okay?"

"Yes, things are fine. Do you have a minute to talk? I have a question to ask that isn't urgent, it can wait if need be."

Steven laughs in reply and says, "I'm guessing it can wait, but you'll be up all night if you don't get it out now. Go for it—I'm all ears."

"You know me too well. So, as Eric probably told you, Everett has heard from Joseph, his biological father. In fact, I guess they met in person. I don't have all the details, just what Eric said before he started thinking he'd said too much."

"I did hear, Larissa, but just as you said, not many details. How are you doing with that?"

"Let's put it this way, I'm trying my damnedest to keep calm. There's a lot of baggage related to Joseph that I've never even tried to unpack. I'd never seen a reason to go there. Now, I'm painfully aware that I need to get to work on some of it."

"I'm no expert, Larissa, but what did you want to ask?"

"It's not at all the same, after all, you and I were married when Eric was conceived, but what is the same, or at least similar, is that you didn't know you were Eric's father until much later, and Joseph didn't know about Everett. When Eric and I were talking tonight, he made a comment that upset me, and I'm trying to understand it better. He asked me how I'll handle it if Joseph is angry that I never contacted him, never let him know about Everett. That thought had never crossed my mind, and quite frankly, shocked me. So, my question—were you angry at me when you figured out Eric is your son?"

The silence on the other end of the phone tells me that Steven is thinking, maybe choosing his words carefully?

"For one thing, Larissa, I don't really know when I figured it out. Questions came into my mind when I learned of your pregnancy, I had my doubts, but no facts. I know that I didn't want to rock your boat, and thought maybe the idea of him being my child was a case of wishful thinking. I loved you too much to risk hurting you. You were hurting when you left me, and I didn't want to make it worse."

"So, you wondered for years and were never tempted to approach me about it until we met up in New York two years ago? You weren't angry at the thought of missing out on your child's life?"

"That makes me sound like I didn't want my own child—that wasn't it. I put it out of my mind because when we connected the few times at conferences or whatever, you were happy, seemed like you and Roger, and your kids were doing great. Like I said, I cared too much about you to be the one to force an answer and start some kind of family upheaval over a half-baked hunch."

Now I'm the one that needs to consider my words before I speak them aloud. Steven cared so much for me, loved me enough to let my happiness come before his own possible connection to a child. There's a lesson or two in that course of action, or inaction.

He continues. "But, once we reconnected after Emma died and while Eric was missing, my questions re-emerged. Even though they might have caused an upheaval, I felt like maybe there was a chance it would be a relief for you to share some of your angst with someone else who cared. I'd like to think that's what's happened since that time."

"Yes, it was a crazy realization for me, but it all made sense once you voiced it out loud. No doubt it's been very good for Eric for you to be in his life. I thought it would be way harder to get through than it has been. And I'm happy you weren't angry at me. Not so sure if Joseph will be as gracious if and when we meet someday. Do you think he has a right to be mad?"

"I have no clue. From the recollections that you've shared with me, I don't think he has a right, but who knows what he'll think from where he sits."

The rest of our conversation shifts to our grandchild and Steven's timetable for retiring and moving.

As he says goodnight, I reply, "Thank you for listening, for answering, and most of all, for the love and care you've shown me over the years. Not sure I always deserved it, but thank you."

21

The moon is a friend for the lonesome to talk to.
CARL SANDBURG

A few days of working with the kids helps them understand why we can't just pick up and go hundreds, even thousands of miles in different directions. It turns into a map-reading lesson, a national parks lesson, and we bring in math when we calculate miles per hour and how long the driving would take. With her additional skills, Lisa even does price comparisons between airfare and renting and fueling an RV.

"For your hard work on this, how about if I promise you a trip to the Callaway Gardens to see blue butterflies in September? I'm pretty sure you'll be back to usual school, so we'll go on a weekend. Does that sound like a plan?"

After the others go home for the evening, Beth and I have a quiet dinner on the porch.

She brings up the travel wishes again.

"You know, the other kids think you picked the butterfly trip because you like me best, Gamma. I didn't like when they said that. Is it true?"

Leave it to kids. "No, I didn't pick the butterfly trip for that reason. I picked it because it's something realistic to do as a group without needing to make a huge trip. If I could wave a magic wand and get us all to those other places without the cost and the schedule craziness, I'd do it tomorrow. It just doesn't work that way, little miss sunshine."

Her face drops, but she stays silent.

"The other part, though? I love all these kids—I love their mamas, so I love them. But, are you my favorite? Absolutely, positively, no doubt! I told you on our zoo trip that you're my favorite—that's always and forever."

She smiles and scoots over onto my lap.

"But what about baby Benjamin? Isn't he your favorite too?"

Man, nothing gets by her.

"You and Benjamin each hold a very special place in my heart. Just like your daddy, Uncle Eric, and Auntie Emma. Hearts can expand—that means get bigger—to hold all the special people in your life. And all of you keep making my heart grow."

"My heart grew lots, Gamma. When I was five, I didn't even know you yet. Now, all the same people you just said are in my heart too. I like that hearts have room for everybody."

Her body noticeably softens and sinks into mine. I slowly lie back against the sofa, and our bodies accommodate to one another's rhythm, until our breathing is perfectly synchronized. My eyes are drawn to distant specks of starlight and I feel Emma's brightness shining down upon us, giving me hope that we will get through the latest developments.

I have no idea how long we've been reclined into this blissful, relaxed place when the ringing of my phone startles me. *How dare anyone break this spell?*

The sleepy voice in my lap says it another way, "Why is your phone ringing so late, Lissa?"

"Is it late? I don't even know what time it is, little one. Feels like we've only been sitting here a few minutes. Let me get the phone and we'll see."

It's not really very late for us, but it sure is for the caller.

"It's your daddy, Beth. Let me see what's going on." It's the first time he's dialed my phone directly rather than Beth's in quite some time.

"Hello, Everett—what's the matter? You're up late. I mean, is everything okay there?"

"Yes, yes, all fine. It's not late for you, though, right? Beth is still up?"

"She is. Well, kind of. We fell asleep together out on the porch looking at the stars—such a peaceful evening. I was about to tell her that you might be looking up at the same stars from across the ocean. I used to tell Eric and Emma that when I traveled for work—look out at the window and we'll be seeing the same thing. It always made them feel better. At least, I think it did—I know it made me feel better."

"Aww, that's cute. I'll tell her that now. Listen, after I talk to her for a few minutes, can we then send her up to get herself ready for bed so I can talk to you alone? It's been awhile. Actually, too long—since I've heard your voice anyway. I like our letters, but I don't like not talking to you, you know?"

The way his voice softens at the end of his question melts my heart. "I do know. I didn't want to push our luck—just figured we'd talk when the time is right. Maybe it's right now. Yes, here she is. Go near a window and tell her you're looking up."

He smiles in anticipation.

I busy myself picking up the dinner dishes so Beth can talk without me in her space. As I come back out to the porch, I hear her describing the travel project to Everett.

"Everybody had good ideas. Mine really surprised Lissa, it

was the most special. I wish you heard me, Daddy. We did lots of research."

Time to interrupt them to tell her my surprise.

"Guess what, Beth? I asked Uncle Eric to videotape your travel pitches. They're all in a movie. We can send Daddy the clip and it'll be just like he was here for the whole thing."

"Can we play it now? I want to watch it along with him."

Everett jumps in, "Beth, my little sunshine, it's late. Uncle Eric will send me the video. If you want to watch it with me, let's do it tomorrow or the next night? You need to sleep and I need to talk with Lissa."

The smile fades from her face, but she slowly rises, says goodnight, and starts shuffling toward the stairs.

Trying to soften her disappointment, I offer, "I'll be along in about ten minutes. Get yourself ready and pick a story for us." She nods her heads and gives us the time he requested.

"So, what's up? Why are you calling so late?"

"A couple of things are going on. First, there's talk here of some restrictions being lifted soon. Rumor has it we might be able to start talking about when to return stateside. My boss dropped some hints in a meeting today, but she needs corporate approval or some other nonsense. Don't tell Beth yet, there's still too much up in the air. But I wanted you to know. You've been awesome about this whole thing, going on and on for like seven months, so much longer than expected. It won't be forever, I promise."

"I don't need a promise for when you'll be back. I miss you, and I know she does, but we're doing fine and we'll continue to do fine. I'm sorry I worried you before by leaving her alone with

Lisa, but I assure you, it hasn't, and won't happen again."

"I can let that whole thing go, Mom, if you can. I shouldn't have gotten angry about the phone and the boys, it just hit me . . ."

I don't hear any of the words he's saying. All I can hear is that he called me *Mom*. I need to look at the date and write it down! When Beth called me *Gamma*, my heart melted. Now he's calling me *Mom*, in spite of our misunderstandings? What more could I ask for? The rest is unimportant. I've become real to them. Real as a grandmother, real as a mother.

"Hello? Are you still there?"

"Yes, yes, I'm here. Must have just had a quick break in the connection. Anyway, yes, I can let it go—happily. I did get mad, mostly because I was hurt. Hurt because I want so badly for our relationship to be a good one, to grow into the beautiful one it should have been for decades. I'm more than ready to write it off as growing pains, learning how to make the best of an unusual situation. What else? You said a couple of things?"

"Yes, growing pains for sure. This second thing is harder to tell you, so I'm hoping we can get through this as well. In my letter, you saw that Joe, uh, Joseph contacted me through the DNA site. I answered him, we wrote a few letters, and then well, I went to see him. To go see Joe. I just had to do it while I'm here, before I return to the U.S.—he's so close. I don't know how you feel about it, but . . ."

I lose his words again. Even though Eric prepared me, hearing it from Everett makes it real. I don't know how I feel either.

22

One good thing about music,
when it hits you, you feel no pain.
BOB MARLEY

I've talked about it with Renee, with Isabel, even with Steven, and I still don't know how I feel. Time to talk to Marie. I need her to help me sort it out before Everett comes home. I want to be happy when he gets here, not in some funk because of how he got on this earth.

"Everett went to see Joseph, his father, and how does that feel?"

"Marie, I'm a mixed-up mess of reactions. I'm happy for Everett, from the perspective that it must help him to have some answers. My own recollections are so sketchy. At least about the things he'd want to know—like his father's looks or personality or whatever. Other things—that he doesn't need to know—are too vivid. Like the feelings of embarrassment, shame, guilt. I told Eric that I want to put all that aside and just be happy for Everett, just be in the moment, but I'm not doing so well at that. Not as well as I'd hoped, anyway."

"Maybe that's not a realistic expectation right now, Larissa. You went through something awful. Back then it was characterized as a girl getting drunk, flirting, and a boy taking advantage. Reality is that you endured trauma. Trauma can't be dismissed by vowing to put it aside for some greater good. There's at least two parts to this. You processing the trauma, and then figuring out how to deal with Joseph coming into Everett's, and maybe Beth's lives. You and Eric and other loved ones are already a huge part of their lives, so now what will you do as this moves forward, if it does?"

"Oh, it's moving forward. Everett spent time in Malta—four or five days. He met Joseph's family, traveled around the country a bit, went to the place Joseph was raised. He says enough to let me, and sometimes Beth, know what he's doing, but doesn't go into details. I can tell he's trying to walk a fine line. I'm curious—waiting with bated breath—what will happen when Everett comes back here? Will there be a plan for more contact, visits? My gut tells me it's not going to be a case of only seeing one another once every six or seven years on a vacation."

Later that day, I'm debriefing with Renee while Isabel takes the kids to a new playground that opened up this week.

"After talking awhile, Marie had me think about what I'd say to Joseph if we met. She made me role play—with her acting as Joseph. It was damn hard, Renee. I thought I was going to pass out. Then, after a break, she walked me through the whole thing again. It was torture while I was there, but I gotta tell you—right now, I somehow feel lighter, less anxious. I hope it lasts!"

"Sounds rough, but maybe what you need. Hell, if I know. These complications from adoption—damn."

I keep forgetting that these discussions of biological and adoptive relations now have a deeper, more personal meaning for her.

"Are you thinking about Louis? How's he doing?"

"He's doing very well, I think. And so does his social worker. It's me—all the what-ifs. I'm attached to him, Larissa. It may have taken me a long time to decide to do this, but now we're bonded. In my mind, in my heart, he's my son. What if someone from his biological family comes along and messes up what we have? I couldn't take it."

"I don't know what to say, Renee. Can't pat your back and say everything will be fine, cuz we don't know. The new presence of Joseph is the perfect example. A few years ago, I didn't know if I'd ever even find Everett. Once I did, I only wanted us to build the loving relationship I'd wished for since my pregnancy. Now the father we never knew is in the picture. Like we've said so many times, have to keep ourselves in the moment and enjoy what we've got. We need to hang in and work at this more."

At that moment, music starts coming out of my pocket. *What the heck?* Trying to scramble to turn it down or off or something, I realize it's "Smiles from Her Heart." How is this possible? As I turn the screen on, it's playing from a streaming app. I open the phone and see that somehow, a link to the song is in a text from Steven. I must have pocket dialed, or pressed the link, or connected in some other crazy way to that text. Or, don't the articles about communicating with the spirit world say that spirits try to reach us by messing with technology in inexplicable ways?

"Stop trying to explain it, Larissa. Let's just listen." I didn't realize I'd said any of that out loud. I'm grateful that Renee quiets my racing thoughts to make room for the song.

Monica's joyful melody and the soothing lyrics inspired by Emma fill the air, causing us to fall silent and appreciate. As the final refrain repeats, "love that does not die," my heart rate and breathing slow. The message is clear—crystal clear. We love our children, and regardless of what happens, that will not change. It's truly unconditional.

Later in the evening, I call Steven not only to find out about his text, but also, tell him about how we heard it.

"Oh, wow, Larissa, that's awesome. I texted you because I was listening to music while I was working on this house. I went to some app on my phone and shuffled songs under a playlist titled something about 'making your soul soar.' Thought that was a cool-sounding mix worth playing; an assortment of songs that would get me through my least favorite remodeling tasks. About five or six songs into the shuffle, it came up. Guess she's really made an impact. No doubt that it's reaching people if it's on some playlist compiled for a music platform."

"Testimony, right? Another lesson from the pandemic—a message from a song can transcend the misery surrounding us. As the playlist title says, make our souls, our spirits soar. Maybe people everywhere need their spirits to soar."

So much has happened in the last few weeks. Steven is still mid-transition to retirement. He found a house about two miles from Eric and Hilary and is remodeling it when he visits. Everett is planning his return home from Italy, awaiting approval from his supervisor. The kids are getting ready to go back to school. Public schools are opening up for a regular fall schedule pretty soon. I'll be babysitting one or two days a week for Benjamin when Hilary goes back to work. No opportunity to think much about the song recently until I heard it from Steven—at exactly the time I needed to, evidently.

"That's amazing, Steven, thanks for sharing it right then. I don't know how it came on in my pocket, but it did, and it absolutely made my soul soar. It had been getting kinda bogged down."

"Your pocket or your soul?" He pauses, then, "Yeah, that was a dumb joke. What's getting you bogged down?"

"Uh, the usual. Worrying too much about things I can't control. Does that sound like I just went to counseling, or what? I was letting the possibility, the unanswered questions, of Joseph being part of Everett's life get to me—derail me, basically. Stupid, but true."

"Stupid's a bit harsh. Maybe Marie has a bunch of fancy ways to try to get you to focus on other things, but I think I get it. It's not easy to think about letting someone you blocked out of your life, for totally justifiable reasons, back in. Everett and Beth are a huge part of your world now. It's unsettling at best, scary at worst, to think about another parent coming into their lives. Hell, you've barely gotten over me coming into Eric's. You must feel like it's one more test, right? How resilient can you be?"

His question makes me consider further. "You know, I think my strategy, ever since Emma passed, is partly resilience and partly, maybe even mostly, distraction. Distraction from the things that hurt. But it's even more than that. Resilience gives me the energy to keep going, but distraction—finding things to do, places to visit, people to enjoy—gives me the direction to go in. Does that make sense?"

"It makes as much sense as anything, Larissa. For your situation, but also for mine. I had so many things to focus on with caring for Jimmy for years, and a demanding job. With those responsibilities gone, I need my own distractions. That's part of why I'm looking forward to this move. So many people I care about are there. I'm looking forward to being closer to Eric, Hilary, little baby Ben, and even Nina and Kristy in Florida, but also to you. You've taken on a lot with schooling these kids. Maybe I can help."

"Well, that's a generous offer. Seems like it's going to get easier, though, with schools opening back up, Everett coming back. It's great he's finally coming home, but I don't even want to think about how I'll feel when Beth's not with me full time anymore. That strategy is flat-out denial! When they head back to New York, I'll definitely be losing my main distraction. I'm hoping to watch Ben a couple of days a week, though—gaining a chubby, new distraction!"

I swirl the wine in my glass, fluff the pillows back up behind me and a thought comes to mind. "You know what, Steven? I'm taking the kids to Callaway Gardens in a couple of weeks. Back when they did the travel pitches, I promised them we'd go in September when the blue morphos emerge from their chrysalids. Renee and Isabel are both busy that weekend, so I could use some help. I don't want to be totally outnumbered by kids. Want to go?"

"I don't know what the heck a blue morpho is, but I'm up for an adventure. Which kid pitched it? I'll ask to be filled in so that I'm as ready as the rest of you."

"It was Beth. She picked it because of my affinity to butterflies. The morpho is a stunning blue color, brown on the underside with a prominent round spot. Because that spot looks like an eye, they say that when the morphos flap their wings, it looks like they're winking at you. She's got all sorts of information that she collected and I'm sure she'd love to share it with you. Come over when you're ready for a break from that house reno and chat with her."

"Doubt I can take a break tomorrow, I have materials being delivered. But, why don't you two stop over here? I can show you the house and maybe you can give me some decorating tips. You always said I was color-blind, diagnosed or not. You'd better stop by before I select any paint colors."

The memory of that god-awful combination of colors he chose for our living room decades ago makes me chuckle.

"Sure, Beth and I will stop over. She'll get a kick out of telling you about the butterflies. It will be fun to have you along for the trip!"

23

*It is strange, but true, that the most important turning
points of life often come at the most unexpected times
and in the most unexpected ways.*
NAPOLEON HILL

The first couple of days that the kids are back to school, the silence in the house is positively deafening. Everyone else seemed to think I'd be happy to have my days back to myself, to be able to accomplish my own work without taking frequent breaks to guide the kids in their lessons. They're way wrong. By noon each day, I've checked in with my office, replied to all my emails, even had a couple of Zoom conference calls, and I freakin' miss those kids.

Time to do some mundane household chores like organize drawers or clean closets. Damn, I hate to resort to that to occupy my days. Countdown to when Hilary goes back to work and I can enjoy Benjamin on my own. Maybe I'll set up a play area for him—that's way more fun than closets.

Catalog shopping for toddler toys and wall hangings makes a couple of hours fly by. I get up to make an after-school snack for Beth and am startled by the phone ringing.

"Mom?" It's Everett's voice with a lot of noise in the background. Strange—it doesn't sound like an overseas call. I've come to expect that ever so slight delay before hearing someone speak, almost as if the connection is going under the water and coming back up again.

"Guess what? I just landed in DC. Crazy, right? I'm uh, going to be in Atlanta by tonight."

My hands start to shake, I need to sit down. I'm overjoyed, I'm scared, I'm maybe in shock.

"Great—I just don't know what to say. How?"

"It's crazy, but they made the decision yesterday to send us back before some surge or uptick or whatever with the virus. Said we needed to get everything cleaned up in the makeshift office, packed up, and that our electronic tickets already had us checked in. In no time, we were off to the airport."

"I'm so surprised, I just don't know . . ."

"Right? Like I said, it's totally crazy. Listen—I still need to go through customs and get rechecked in and all that stuff, so let's make this quick. Please don't tell Beth, I want to surprise her. Even if it's a little late, keep her up—I'll text you when we depart or you can track it online, or whatever. Honestly, I can't believe I'm actually here, either. There were days I was afraid, well, I'll tell you later. See ya!"

Just like that, he's off the line. *What just happened?*

It registers with me that Beth is in the room. "Gamma, why are you sitting like that? Are you okay?"

I'm sitting on the edge of a countertop chair, feeling like I'm half off, half on. I don't think I've moved a muscle since Everett hung up.

"Nothing to worry about, honey. I just had a weird phone call that surprised me. But nothing bad, I promise." I left a lot out, but at least I didn't lie to her. How am I going to fake my way all afternoon and evening until he walks through the door?

I need some moral support. Even if I don't tell anyone else that Everett is on his way back, I need to have a distraction. Or maybe if Renee comes over with Louis for dinner, she and I can sneak a few minutes while the kids play?

I phone Renee and she agrees immediately. I don't know if she sensed something in my voice, or she really wanted pizza, or she needs an adult conversation not related to work, but it doesn't matter. I'll have someone else here so that I'm not pacing while trying to keep the news from Beth. Thank God for Renee.

Eating and listening to the kids retell their school-day activities takes up about an hour and a half. Okay, but he's not even boarded his flight yet. Who knows if he's even through customs and all that pandemonium?

"Beth, why don't you and Louis go into the toybox in the basement and see if there are any toys down there that baby Benjamin might like? He's going to start coming here soon."

"Where? I didn't even know there's a toybox down there. How come you didn't tell me?"

"It's all baby stuff, Beth. Nothing you would have liked. It's behind the bookshelves I showed you. Maybe you guys can put everything you think he'd like in one pile and we'll wash them all tomorrow."

They scoot off down the stairs, and I reach for wine glasses.

"Red or white, my friend?" I pick out my favorite glasses, ones with butterflies etched in the glass. Maybe wine and butterflies will calm my nerves to a tolerable level.

"Um, white, I guess? What's the occasion, Larissa? Is there something going on I don't know about? A new job or--?"

The shaking in my hand returns as I pour. "No, nothing like that. Everett called me from DC. He's back in the U.S. and on his way here, now. I just got the text that he's boarding for Atlanta in twenty minutes."

"Holy shit! I mean, why are you just telling me now? We should have planned a welcome back or something, don't you think?"

"Shhh—I didn't tell you, didn't plan anything, because I just found out myself. Like just before Beth got home from school."

"Isn't she excited? She seemed, well, normal, not like anything is up."

"She doesn't know. He wants to surprise her. I'm just so shocked, so unprepared. I know I should be totally overjoyed, but for some reason, I'm scared. I'm scared of how, geez, Renee, what's going to happen now? He stays a couple of days and then the two of them just fly merrily back to New York and resume their lives? And I'm here? Alone?" My resolve dissolves and I'm crying—literally on her shoulder.

My friend wraps her arms around me and holds me, as she's done so many times before.

"I better get myself together. That dumb task of sorting through the toys downstairs won't occupy them very long; I don't even remember if there are any toys worth the effort. I don't want Beth to see me crying. I can barely explain it to myself or to you. I haven't got the energy to help her understand. Time for my happy face. Damn, and I need to get a room ready for him. Can you take the kids for a walk while I do that? I can't have her seeing me getting ready for company, she'll figure that something's up."

"If that's what you want me to do, sure. I'll take them for a walk. Then when we get back, they can watch a movie and we can have a refill. I think we're going to need it."

Another hour or so passes. He's in the air and scheduled to land, only a few minutes later than scheduled. Renee's right. Time to set them up with popcorn and a movie and give us time to wait, to have a few peaceful moments outside on the porch under the stars. Maybe I can breathe more deeply, get myself centered.

"Yeah, I think I'm just scared of another damn change in my life. It's been a joy having Beth here. Even though I knew it was temporary, some part of me believed it was our new way of life. And I love this way of life."

"It's kinda how I feel about my life with Louis. I'm reveling in every minute, he's such a sweet, smart little guy. We have so much fun. But I'm always waiting for the other shoe to drop. The shoe that means we're no longer a pair. It sucks to feel so vulnerable. Loving this little guy is such a privilege, but I'm scared too. Scared to lose him. I don't need to tell you about losing someone you love. The thought of it makes me sick, nauseous, and a nervous wreck."

"It is too damn hard, Renee. We've got to think with our heads, not our hearts. You know there are safeguards against that happening with Louis. And I've got to keep reminding myself that Everett's not going to take her away for good. They visited before this, they'll visit again. And way back when he made this commitment to go abroad, he thought it would give him more opportunity to be mobile in his job. The whole world works from a distance now. Maybe he can come here to work? Maybe he'd want to? Or even if he goes back to Florida instead of New York? That's only a day's drive. I can't be so doom and gloom. Beth will see right through me—she always does."

For a little while, staring at the stars does its magic. We are calmer and talking about something other than loss of our beloved kids. Then, the sound of the front door makes Renee and I shoot out of our chairs as if a rocket has launched. By the time we are inside, Everett has found the kids in the den in front of the TV and Beth is shrieking at the top of her lungs, "Daddy! Daddy, it's really you!"

He picks her up and spins her around while answering, "Yes, little one, it really is. And, who's this little guy?"

Louis runs over to Renee for reassurance. When she nods, he replies in a barely audible voice, "My name is Louis. I'm this many." He holds up four fingers and then moves back closer to Renee.

With Beth still wrapped around him like a clinging baby monkey, Everett walks over to me and pulls me in for a hug with his other arm.

All I can manage in return is an arm and a whisper in his ear, "Welcome home. We missed you."

Everett pushes Beth and me out in front of him and replies, "And I missed you two like crazy! It feels like I've been gone a hundred years."

Assuming he must be hungry, I head to the kitchen to warm up the leftovers. Renee and Louis come along, letting Everett and Beth have some time alone together.

The smell of pizza and hunger pangs lead Everett and Beth into the kitchen only a few minutes later. Everett tells us all a bit about the sudden decision to come back to the U.S. sooner than later. Beth has a dozen questions about the trip back and he patiently answers each one. He asks Beth and Louis about school, cuddling Beth in his lap the whole time.

I glance at the clock a couple of times because it's getting late and tomorrow will come early for these kids. Who knows if I'll even be able to get her to go to school with her daddy here. And how long is he, are they, staying? I don't want to ask, but I want to know.

Beth takes that plunge.

"Daddy, do I, do we have to go home, to New York, I mean?"

Everett glances at me, then back at her and answers in a way that I never expected.

"Well, that depends on a few things. A few decisions the adults need to make. We'll need to talk more before I can really answer that."

She looks puzzled, then replies, "Okay, so you mean, we need to *strategize*?"

Laughing at her reference to the term he used when this whole thing started, he replies, "Yes, I guess so. First, I need to get Gamma and a few others up to speed on some things that might be happening soon, then we can strategize. I'll be sure to let you know when we're ready to get your ideas on the whole thing."

What in the world are the things he's talking about, and who are the few others?

24

There is a crack, a crack in everything.
That's how the light gets in.
LEONARD COHEN

I cannot fall asleep. This is the second time Everett has shown up with short notice and sprung information on me that I'm not expecting. Not that he actually provided much information this time. His answer to Beth's question was more than a little enigmatic. I waited and waited for him to come back downstairs after he put Beth to bed, anticipating that I would hear more once she was out of earshot. However, after an hour of waiting, I checked and found him sound asleep next to her. Guess the time change and travel was too much for him to carry on any adult conversation tonight. So, I'm left to wrestle with the myriad of possibilities that spring into my mind at every hour between midnight and four in the morning.

The alarm goes off at the usual time for a weekday morning. I always set it a half hour early to lounge over a cup of coffee before it's time to wake up Beth for school. No lounging this morning, though. I hear voices down the hallway.

As I approach Beth's room, Everett is speaking quietly to her, "I need to talk to Gamma first, Beth. By the time you get home from school, we'll be ready to all talk together, I promise."

"I don't like secrets, Daddy. It makes me scared. Can I just stay home and watch a movie till you guys are done talking? I promise I'll wait patiently. Then, as soon as you finish, we can all talk."

I'm guessing he's forgotten how persuasive she can be. Wise beyond her years, that one.

"Listen, little miss sunshine, waiting in front of the TV is not a good use of your time. Go to school and exercise your brain. We'll come pick you up together the minute you get out of school. Then we'll talk strategy. I'm surprised you remembered that word from before I left for Europe. Go learn a new impressive word today and we'll get ice cream to celebrate."

The promise of ice cream must have had an impact. I hear her move into action and recognize the opening and closing of dresser drawers as a sign that she's agreed to cooperate.

Everett is walking Beth to school and I'm pretending to get work done on my computer. In reality, I'm continuing the list of what-ifs in my brain that I left off with at four this morning. Is he going to move here? Oh, God, is he going to move to Italy and take Beth with him? Move to Italy where her previously unknown grandfather is only four hours away in Maltawhile I'm across the ocean? Or, much less dramatic, maybe he's going back to New York and just wants to leave her here till a long school break, like Christmas. That one works for me.

I'm deep in thought when his voice resonates through the house, "I'm back. Where arc you? I brought pastry. We gotta talk."

"Coming." I rise slowly, steady myself with two hands against the desk, and try to walk out of my office. I stop twice for deep breaths and then quietly recite a mantra, "Some things are out of your control, but you can control your reaction."

He's sitting at the dining room table, not in comfy chairs in the living room. Maybe because we have food to share? Or maybe to be more like a conference table, an official meeting?

"Okay, well, there's a few things, Lissa. A few things I need to talk about."

Hmm . . . not *Mom* this time—damn, we're back to *Lissa.* Geez—am I reading into things or what?

"I'm all ears. Tell me about the adult decisions we need to make. Unless, well, unless they're already made?"

He shakes his head, looks up at me, and smiles.

"No, I meant it when I said 'we' need to talk. There's some stuff that happened while in Italy that I never expected, but it did, and now I have to figure things out. You and I may still be fairly new at this, but you're the only mom I have, well, at least now you are. And you've been Beth's caretaker for more than half a year. I want you to hear me out and, well, I know I need to be the one to make the decision, but I want to know what you think."

I'm relieved but still more than a little skeptical.

"Like I said, all ears."

"And, like I said, I never expected this, but, um, well, my boss and I . . ."

He's hemming and hawing so long that I think I get the picture. "I'll take a shot at this—let me make this part easier. You and your boss are romantically involved, is that one of the things?"

The look on his face is actually laughable. Totally photoworthy. Before I know it, I do start laughing because he is so shocked at my hypothesis.

"How did you? Why are you laughing? It's not a joke . . ." then he starts laughing too.

When the laughter dies down, and we've each had a few bites of pastry, he continues, "Well, I don't know if that's mother's intuition or a lucky guess, but, yes. Gabriella and I went out casually a few times, then with the lockdown, it got so we mostly only saw the people we worked with, formed a 'tribe' like people started to say. Anyway, soon it was clear there was an attraction—more than just co-workers. It was great, but it also got more and more difficult as the relationship developed, for a few reasons. For one, her being my boss and all. So, that's kinda why I came back without much notice. There was an opening back over here in another marketing division of the company that was a good fit for me. I wouldn't report to her any longer, and it meant that returning home was possible. So, here I am."

"It's going to be a long-distance relationship? How do you think that will be? Or are you cutting it off?"

"No—not cutting it off; and hopefully, not apart for long. So many companies have made allowances for location because of the virus that she's trying to get back here as well. She has family in both the U.S. and in Italy, so thinks she can be comfortable any-where. Except, now, actually, she wants to be back here because of me, us. She's pretty influential in the company, so thinks it will be only about six to eight weeks before she can relocate. I'm keeping my fingers crossed. Gabby is a really fabulous person. I think you'll love her, and I hope Beth will too."

So far, I've not heard anything on which to offer an opinion. This is his life. I fiddle with the spoon resting by my coffee mug and decide to dive right in and break the suspense.

"I don't really hear anything for me to weigh in on. Your love life, is just that—yours. Am I missing something? You've said 'here' a couple of times. When she gets to the U.S., where will you be? Are you both going to be based in New York or . . .?"

Now my fingers are crossed under the table as I silently perform my internal version of a prayer.

"There's the big question. We haven't figured that part out yet. There's a pretty good chance that I can be located anywhere. What we don't know is if the company will be as flexible for her, since New York is headquarters. So, I was thinking of figuring out a way to stay put here in Atlanta until there are more answers. With Beth in school and all, why move her without some idea of whether this will be where we're ending up in the long run?"

Why, indeed. I let out the breath I'd been unconsciously holding. At least they're not leaving right away.

"Why don't you and Beth just stay with me till you have more information? There are two empty bedrooms. You can use one for sleeping and the other as your office. Might not be ideal to live under your mom's roof in your thirties, but if you want to, it's good with me."

"Are you kidding? Really? I wanted to ask, but you've done so much already. I thought maybe you could give me leads on apartments close by, but if you really mean that?"

This is as good as I could have possibly wished.

"I wouldn't have offered if I didn't mean it. I didn't know if it's something you'd want at this stage of your life. This big old house could use more activity. Whenever everyone leaves, I rattle around in here waiting for the next time. I'd love having you here. And it makes total sense for Beth—less disruption."

"Like I said, it should only be a couple of months. And I'll pay rent."

"No rent—just grab groceries or take-out dinner now and then. No promises about length of time necessary. After all, we only thought your Europe trip would be a couple of months. I made the offer and it stands. When Gabby knows her details, we'll regroup."

I'm so relieved I'd like to stand up and dance. But I notice that he's still looking a bit tense and decide to save my happy pirouettes till he's truly finished.

"What else is on your mind, Everett? You still look concerned, weighed down."

"There is something else. You know already that I went to visit Joseph, and we spent a few days together. He's a really nice man, Mom. At least from the time we spent and our conversations since. I'm guessing that's hard for you, or awkward, or whatever, but it's better than him being an asshole, right?"

I almost chuckle again. Almost.

"Uh, yes, that is better, Everett. I've always preferred nice to, well, not nice. But, I'm having a hard time processing how the whole thing about Joseph feels to me, actually. I've talked with my friends, talked with Marie, and I keep resolving to let things be, that I can't control them, but it's hard in ways I've been at a loss to explain very well. I can agree that I'm grateful he isn't a jerk, and I'm happy for you that your visit went well. I never expected him to come into your life, but life is full of the unexpected."

"The last thing I want to do is make anything hard for you. You've done so much for me, for Beth. I love you, Mom, and don't want to do anything that hurts you. Yet, I feel like I need to give him a chance, too. Get to know him better."

I can deal with this, I've dealt with far worse. What's the harm in Everett getting to know him, really? Doesn't mean I have to spend time with him.

"I don't want to control your life, Everett. I love you, too, and I remember telling you once, awhile back, that loving someone new doesn't diminish the love you have for those already in your life. Or like I told Beth, the heart expands for new people, there's always room for more. So, if you want to let Joseph into your life, I need to respect that and determine what, if anything, it means to me. I already told you I can't put my feelings about him into words very well, but I vow to do my best to stay on the sidelines on this one."

He nods his head and reaches for my hands. He rubs his thumbs over my fingers as he keeps nodding.

"And I respect that. That's as much as I can ask for right now. There's just one more thing. Papa Joe, uh that's what he asked me to call him, honestly, I'm still trying to get used to that, Joseph wants to come to the U.S. He wants to meet Beth."

"That's understandable, I guess. But, like when? Travel still isn't fully open. Sometime in the future, when things open back up, maybe?"

"And, well, Joseph wants to see you. Wants to talk with you in person. And I don't think he wants to wait very long. He's pretty determined."

For the second time today, I need to steady myself against furniture when I rise. I feel compelled to move, to pace, to do something other than sit here stirring coffee and picking up pastry crumbs during every lapse in our conversation.

"I don't know what to say, Everett. I think I need to get some air, take a walk."

I'm searching for my sneakers when Everett asks, "Can I walk with you? Can you show me that park where you take Beth, to the bench and the spot where you see butterflies? She talks about it all the time, says it's magical."

Looking in his eyes, I see the love he professed a few moments ago. I nod my head, grab my coat, and say, "Yes, but please don't talk for awhile. I need the peace and the repetitive rhythm of walking. But I also want you near me. So, yes, let's walk to the park.

25

What counts is not the things that happen,
but what we do with them.
ANNIE ERNAUX

*E*verett keeps his promise and doesn't say a word the whole way. We walk side by side, our steps becoming synchronized, drawing us close in spite of the silence. The arched gate is in front of us before I know it. I point toward the benches among flowers that the butterflies cannot resist.

"Welcome to the spot Beth called magical. We've had many talks here over the last few months. And the butterflies never fail us. In fact, look right there." A trellis covered in orange, trumpet-shaped honeysuckle blossoms is the current place for two butterflies and a hummingbird to hover while they sip the nectar. Three precious flying creatures.

"Wow, they're beautiful. I want to get a photo."

"Tougher than it looks to capture them. If you move quickly, you startle them. Be patient—if you wait, they often come back, so just have your camera ready. Beth's gotten to be a pro. Not long ago, she even got a video of the hummingbirds."

He stares at the blossoms, looks up at the sky, then grabs my hands just as he'd done back at the house.

"This is why I don't want to move Beth until we have a solid plan. You've shown her so many beautiful things, made so many special memories. Sure, the trip to DC was a time she won't forget, but these everyday opportunities are meaningful as well. You've been able to spend so much time with her. The gift of your time is irreplaceable. If I'd ever decided to take her along to Europe, she would have been cooped up in a hotel room converted to a mini apartment for months. There's no way to thank you enough."

"That goes both ways, Everett. I'm beyond thankful, eternally grateful for the time I've had with her. When Eric and Emma were her age, I tried to spend as much time with them as possible, but as you know, a single working parent can only rearrange a schedule a few ways. The last seven months have restored my soul, brought me a sense of fulfillment and purpose that I never expected to have. None of us expected to be restricted by this damn virus, but there have been some unexpected benefits. I was able to help all the kids with school. And, wow, you may have found your special person. I hope so."

He smiles, gets out his phone, and begins scrolling.

"I hope so, too. I forgot to show you pictures of her. Start with this one of Gabby and swipe. There's a few of us together sightseeing in Rome."

"These are great. You both look really happy. See, the whole virus thing was not all bad."

"Heck, no. I traveled out of the U.S. for the first time, learned a ton for my job, and met Gabby. Lots of good stuff."

As the next image comes up on the screen, I stop swiping and stare at a face that brings back a tangled web of memories. Trying to get it out of my sight without making a fuss, I swipe again and see Everett and Joseph. I'd never noticed Everett's resemblance to Joe before. Guess I never wanted to. Now, it's undeniable. I'll never unsee it. They are indisputedly father and son.

"Oh man, I forgot those were on there. I'm sorry—should have prepared you, but too late. I guess you know who . . ."

My head nods and nothing comes out of my mouth.

Everett gently takes the phone out of my hands, looks at it briefly, and sets in on the bench next to us.

"Are you okay? Want to go home? I'm so sorry."

After a few minutes, I turn to him and try again to make a pledge to him.

"You cannot spend any more time apologizing to me. You did nothing wrong. I, we, if anybody did anything wrong, it's Joseph and me. I don't want to hear you say you're sorry about this again. Not from this moment forward. And I'm going to work very hard at forgiving myself, forgiving him. There were wrongs done, but we were young and you are the gift. Only one of many reminders that we humans don't always make the best choices. In this case, the so-called lapse in judgment resulted in a beautiful person. A person I never dreamed I'd have the privilege of finding, of seeing again. I didn't want to share you with the father I barely knew or deal with Joseph in our lives, but I will. I will find a way. Might take some time, can you be patient with me?"

"No one could ask for more than that, Mom. Thank you for saying all that and for letting me off the hook. I don't know how to do this either."

He glances at his phone again and stands up. He pulls my hand and says, "Someone is going to be very ready for her ice-cream cone soon. We'd better make our way back. She won't let us off the hook, I'm sure of that!"

We pick up the pace going back to the house. We'd walked out of the house without thinking about wallets or ice cream.

"One more thing. I need your advice about what we tell Beth. This is a lot for her, don't you think?"

"A lot for Beth? Hell, it's a lot for me! My opinion, and I'm probably biased, is to tell her about Gabby. The decision to stay here for awhile is driven by you and Gabby wanting to be together. It directly impacts Beth and her feelings of being settled. Joseph? Well, guess it depends on how often you'll be in contact with him, if he's going to want to make contact with her sooner than later, and how much you think she can handle about, uh, why she's just now learning about him."

"Yeah, I think I start with telling her today about Gabby and staying in Atlanta. Put Joseph on the back burner for a little bit."

We pull into the school parking lot right at dismissal time. Beth and Brittany walk toward the car, hand in hand, talking nonstop.

Beth speeds up, pulling Brittany along.

"Daddy, this is my friend, Brittany. Can she come for ice cream, too? Gamma, can you text her mommy? Brittany was supposed to walk straight home and meet her mother there."

I text her mother and get the thumbs up. I'm relieved that Everett and I won't need to jump right back into a conversation about the things we talked about most of the day. The girls are excited about ice cream, and I'm grateful for the frivolous intermission. I expect Beth will be all ready to "strategize" when we get home.

Once Brittany is dropped off at home with chocolate and sprinkles all down the front of her school dress, Beth comes out with, "So, have you two made those decisions for mature audiences only? Are you ready to talk about a blueprint?"

Everett gives me a sideward glance and I burst out laughing. Before either one of us can reply, Beth continues.

"You guys told me I needed to learn a new vocabulary word today. So, our teacher was teaching us about synonyms. After she explained it, she asked if any of us had a word we needed to find a synonym for—I said I had one. I asked about *strategy* and we found 'blueprint' in the synonym chart online."

"And, where did you come up with 'mature audiences only'?"

"Oh, Daddy, I knew that already from movies. Gamma taught me what the letters mean on movie advertisements. We ran out of cartoons during COVID, so we had to look up other movies, but we could only watch ones that were 'G,' right?"

"Absolutely correct. Glad you remembered that, and glad you learned a new word. And for the record, yes, we did discuss a plan, though it's not quite as detailed as a blueprint. Let's get home and get in comfy clothes and then we can talk."

I want to show my respect for the father-daughter relationship, especially over the next several weeks, or however long they're under this roof. I decide to lay that groundwork with this discussion.

"You two go ahead and get started. I need to do a couple of things in the kitchen to be ready for dinner later. I'll be there in a few minutes."

After dinner is all prepped, I pile some snacks on a tray, and clear my throat to announce my arrival in the living room.

Beth's head swivels toward me as she bursts out with an excited report.

"Daddy wants us to stay here, in Atlanta, for awhile. He wants to wait for a friend he made in Italy to come back to the U.S. too. He says her name is Gabby and that he thinks I can be her friend too. Is she gonna be your girlfriend, Daddy? Are you in love or in like? If she's your girlfriend, can she be my friend, too?"

"Whoa, that's a bunch of questions, Beth. One thing at a time. Gabby and I went on dates in Italy, so I think that does make her my girlfriend. We enjoy one another and like doing things together. I think we'll know more about your other questions when we're all in the same place. She can definitely be your friend too."

"But, what if you like her and I don't? Then what happens?"

Everett and I make eye contact, and I decide to try to help with that one.

"In my experience, little one, if a person is nice and kind to someone I love, then I like them. First, I like them because they are good to my person. That makes me want to give them a chance and get to know them better. I'm guessing that might be how it goes for you too. You can probably talk to Gabby on video chat before she gets here. That might help you get to know her as well, little by little."

It's clear Beth is thinking this over by the head nod that she slowly shares.

"I'm very happy that this plan means we're not moving back to New York right now. I miss some friends there, but I think I'd miss everyone here more. Daddy said he made some other friends while he was away. Some people who work in his company and a man in a country called Malta. He said I might get to meet them someday."

I paste a smile on my face to squelch any reaction to the information Everett shared about Joseph. So much for my advice about waiting. What he shared is relatively innocuous anyway.

"He said the man in Malta is Joseph and that he knew you a very long time ago. Did you know him, Gamma?"

It was innocuous, until that little piece of information.

Okay, I can play along. I think I can.

"It was a long time ago, but he came to my high school. Daddy knows more about him than I do. I'm going to go check on dinner, you guys. Beth, maybe you can help Daddy make a list of what we need to get to make his room homier."

Thankfully, the conversation at dinner is directed by Beth recounting her day and Everett telling her about going to the park. I can roll along with those topics. No problem, no emotion.

It's another gorgeous evening, so I go out to the porch to enjoy the sounds of crickets and birds. Their stories, their noises are constant and reassuring. Nothing settles me more than blocking out difficult human conversations with the calm delivered by Mother Nature. Always different, but always the same. I don't hear Everett come out until he clears his throat. His voice is hushed, barely audible.

"I should have prepared you. I'm sorry. I started telling her about making friends while I was gone and Joseph tumbled out with the rest. It seemed natural, but I could see it took you off guard. Guess it was all on my mind, and I lost my way in the moment. But I think it went all right, don't you?"

It's clear I have done a bad job of my own self-talk. I keep saying I should be able to let things go and focus on the moment, but damn, it is freakin' hard.

"Everett, Beth is your child and you need to do things your way. You asked my opinion; you didn't promise to go with whatever I said. I tried to make my reaction as neutral as I could in front of her. You're right, it was fine. But she'll come up with more questions. Better be ready."

"I hear you loud and clear. It's striking the right balance, isn't it? Giving her the information she needs and can understand, without overwhelming her—I think I'm out of practice."

"Yeah, in parenting, even practice doesn't make perfect. I swear we screw up more than we succeed. But, can't give up. Gotta show up and move forward with love and purpose."

26

True friendship withstands time, distance, and silence.
ISABEL ALLENDE

"Attention, you guys. This isn't just an after-school snack gathering. It's a planning party. Planning for our trip to Callaway Gardens on Saturday. Let's figure out our strategy. Guess who else is going with us?"

Before any guesses are shouted out, Steven pops into the kitchen wearing a t-shirt that says, "I Got Away at Callaway." I can't help but laugh, as well as wonder, where the heck did he get that?

Sounding a little whiney, Beth asks, "Did you already go there, Steven? Without us?"

He picks her up, spins her around, and says, "No way—wouldn't think of going without you! I told my friend that I was going and he offered me this shirt. I thought it would get us in the mood."

Beth's pouting mouth quickly becomes a beaming smile. "It'll be fun having you along. I think Gamma could use the company. Did you do any research about the gardens?"

Lisa interjects before Steven can reply. "I read on the website that if kids dress up like a butterfly or a bug, they get in free. Can we do that? Make our own costumes?"

"Good to know, Lisa! We've some time, but we better get started. What about if you all decide how you want to dress, we'll make a list of materials we need, and tomorrow, we'll go to the craft store after school."

Now Louis is the one who is pouting. He's often reluctant to share his feelings, so I move over close to see if he'll tell me what's wrong without the others hearing.

"I don't know how to do it."

"Don't know how to do what, Louis? Can I help you with something?"

"I want to be a furry caterpillar. I want to be something that starts off crawly and ugly, then changes."

Lisa hears his request in spite of my efforts at being nonchalant. She's been protective of him since the moment Renee brought Louis into her life. Without a moment of hesitation, she offers, "Louis, I know how to sew on a real sewing machine. My mom taught me. Lissa can help you find furry fabric and I'll sew you a tube to put over your clothes. We can make antennae and googly eyes."

Not sure if he's jealous or just practical, Bobby comments, "Won't he be hot in some furry fabric?"

Lisa gives her brother a shove, then quickly puts her arm around him and offers to help him too. Before long, they're busily drawing pictures of what they want to look like for our day at the gardens. Steven is scrolling through the website and comments, "There's more to do there than I thought. Hiking trails, a display of giant bugs, a lake with a beach, even a show about birds of prey. We're going to have a full day!"

The week flies by. The kids come home from school each day ready to work on their costumes. Today, we're having a butterfly/

bug fashion show, so that Renee, Isabel, Everett, Eric, and Hilary can get a little sneak preview of the bunch of insects that Steven and I will be escorting on the day trip.

I'm making a butterfly-shaped cake for dessert and realize I don't have the correct food coloring to get the effect that I want. I yell up to Everett to ask if there's anything he wants from the grocery store. The reply that I get sounds too serious for my question. He responds desperately, "Wait!"

Everett comes down from his office looking like he's seen a ghost.

"I'm waiting—is something wrong?"

"Just got off the phone with Gabby. She says the company isn't ready for her to return to the U.S. And uh, she wants me to go back there. She isn't sure if they can get me back into Italy or not with the travel restrictions, but she wants to try it, to say I'm essential to the business or something."

"And you said?"

"I said that I'm not so sure, even if I get clearance, whether that's a good idea. Mom, this is tough. I don't want to have to choose between her and Beth, between my family here and a job, between a long-distance romance or being near someone I'm beginning to love. This sucks, totally sucks."

He looks miserable, forlorn. Too forlorn for me to outright tell him that I think it would be stupid for him to go back. Things are still too unpredictable with the virus, to say nothing of how Beth might take it if he left again. And I can't judge anything about his relationship with Gabby. Maybe she simply wants him back in Italy because she's lonely. I walk over to put my arm around him and reply, "It sure does suck. When does she want, or need an answer?"

"I don't know. I couldn't take the stress of the call, and well, I told her I'd call back later, I need some time. If the world wasn't so crazy, maybe I'd try to take Beth and go for a few months. She's gotten pretty mature. But with the rules changing almost daily from country to country, it's too risky. My head is spinning. I think I need to take a cue from you and go for a walk."

"You do that. Let your mind wander, or let it simply go blank for a couple of miles. I'm going to pick up food coloring for the cake and snacks for the road trip. You need to be back for the kids' fashion show at six o'clock. They're so excited—I'm not sure how they're going to wait a couple of more days."

"What? Oh hell, I forgot all about the trip. Can't you guys go another--no, not fair, that's selfish."

Was he really going to suggest we change the plan?

"Right you are—selfish. Maybe the time alone will be good for you. Or you could go over and help Eric with Benjamin, enjoy a guy day. He's giving Hilary a mom's day out."

I don't wait for a reply. I've somehow managed to keep my mouth shut so far and don't want to blow it now. He needs to make a decision without my opinions interfering.

After shopping, I stop for coffee, taking a few minutes to reflect on the conversation with Everett. The little heart the barista made with the topping on my latte reminds me that regardless of what he decides, I'll stand by him. I loved him when I didn't even know where he was or anything about his life, I'll love him through this stage. Stay by his side when he needs support. Letting the sentiment wash over me, I feel calmer. Calm, but then uneasy when I sense someone standing next to me. I turn to see a familiar face, relieved that it's Steven.

He asks, "Hey, can I sit with you, or am I intruding?" He looks around as if to determine if I'm with someone else or alone.

"You're not intruding. Just taking a break before our fashion show tonight. Are you ready to make the drive with four kids?"

"I'm looking forward to it—it's a break from this house renovation. You looked pretty deep in thought. Seems like you were pondering something more than the butterfly costumes."

"You're right, I was. Just thinking about Everett and Beth."

"It must be amazing for you to think about how your life has changed in the last few years, Larissa. I mean, mine has, too, but nothing like what you've experienced."

"No kidding. But actually, I wasn't really going down that path—for a change. I was replaying a conversation Everett and I just had, and wrestling with whether to offer my opinion, or whether to stay neutral. He has yet another decision to make. While it'll have an impact on me either way, it's far more of a dilemma for him, and more impact on Beth—again. So, do I shut up or weigh in?"

One side of his mouth turns up as he gently offers, "Ain't that always the million-dollar question? I don't have anywhere near the parenting experience that you do, but it seems like that's the key to parenting as the kids get older. How to gracefully stand by their side, giving space, being available when they need you."

His words sink in and remind me yet again of how easily we once talked about almost anything. It strikes me that the implications of his words are wise ones.

"Isn't that the key to any relationship, Steven? Balancing being available, even consoling, without violating space? Loving but letting people choose their path?"

He nods his head and smiles, fully this time.

I continue to share my ideas, "It reminds me of us, years ago. I was totally broken, hurting to my core over our pregnancy loss. Looking back, now I see that you were trying to comfort me, trying to be supportive. My grief was too big for comfort, too raw.

The doctor made light of it, said miscarriages are common, told you to take me home, and that we could try again."

"Lissa, I didn't know what to do, say, how to deal."

I put my hand up, then gently touch the back of his.

"I know that now. Then—not so much. It was all about *my* pain, and my feeling that no one, especially you or the doctor, knew how I felt. So, I bailed. I made an impetuous decision that changed many lives. Yours, mine, and totally unknowingly, Eric's. We talked about it a few weeks ago, but it still astounds me to think about how lives are altered immeasurably by one choice, one action. That's not exactly like pondering the what-ifs, it's more of a realization of the power of a single decision. A decision can change one's path dramatically—often, for life."

"It's true—and immense to contemplate. Some might say things turn out the way they're supposed to, but I'm not so sure."

"Me neither. Who knows why I thought it had to be one way or the other—right then and there? I either had to be married and with you every second, or walk out the door? There may have been a compromise that I couldn't think of in my haste."

Silence settles and emphasizes the impact of all that was just said.

I pull myself out of the booth, standing so quickly that Steven startles and spills his coffee.

With an urgency inspired by our conversation, I explain, "I need to tell Everett to take his time. He doesn't need to decide today, tomorrow, or even next week whether to go back to Italy to be with Gabby, or whether to stay in contact with his father, or any of the other things that seem so dire to him right now. I can't change our past, but I can share what I've learned. Only taken me close to thirty years to appreciate the value of slowing down and allowing myself time to marinate before taking action."

"He'll listen. He *wants* you to guide him at the same time as he is seeking independence."

I give him a thumbs up and add, "Don't forget the costume debut and dinner—six o'clock."

There's about a half hour until Beth gets home. If Everett's back, we'll have a few minutes while I frost the cake. If not, I need to find time to talk later.

Finding no one at the house, I start mixing colors to get this butterfly just right. Something about cooking, especially baking, is meditative. It's good that Everett's still out walking. As I think more about my own rush to make a move of some kind after Steven and I lost our baby, I recall keeping diaries during those years. I can almost picture the one I was using at the time because once I lost the pregnancy, I alternated between writing my entries to myself or writing to the child that never had a chance. I wrote daily, or sometimes hourly. I'd stare at the journal and look for signs in the delicate cover illustration. Pastel-shaded butterflies, hummingbirds, and flowers invited me to pour out my feelings, and I readily complied. I had no close friends to talk to at the time. That journal became my sounding board, my counselor, my confidante. And the entries addressed to my child, the one who I'm sure was my first daughter, they were my lifeline, my bridge to her.

I drop the knife I'm using to decorate the cake and exclaim out loud to no one but myself, "I know where that journal is!"

I clean up the kitchen, carefully cover the cake for its unveiling later, hurry up the stairs, and pull down the ladder-like steps to the attic. I remember seeing the journal when I was looking for my mother's old letters a couple of years ago.

The box isn't hard to find. There are several journals in here, more than I recall. I wrote in them on and off over the years.

Stroking my hand over the cover of the one I was looking for brings back memories stowed away in the far recesses of my mind. Memories of feeling like I was on a roller coaster, waiting to plunge even further down. The words are sometimes harsh and self-judging, others sad and full of lonely remorse. Once in awhile, a passage emerges with understanding and resolution. The pages beckon me, the swirly, purple ink makes me want to write like this again, put my feelings out into the universe. So many times I've started diaries, then stopped.

"Mom! Where are you? Does this rickety ladder even hold an adult? Come on down here, I can't fit up there."

The concern in Everett's voice breaks the spell of the paper, ink, and words strung carefully together, but is also pleasing. In spite of the little bumps in our journey so far, he is concerned, protective.

"Yes, I'm up here; coming down now. What time is it?"

"Beth got home a few minutes before I got back from walking. She was looking for you out back, but hadn't gotten up this far. She wants your help getting the last-minute costume details fixed. Need me to do anything?"

I want to ask him about his walk, share my revelations from the past, but no time for that now.

27

When a child gives you a gift, even if it is a rock
they just picked up, exude gratitude.
It may be the only thing they have to give,
and they have chosen to give it to you.
DEAN JACKSON

The cake is a hit, the costumes adorable, the excitement contagious. After shooing everyone out the door, it's past Beth's bedtime. Everett's muffled voice behind his closed door signals he's on the phone, so I lay down next to Beth to talk quietly for a few minutes before she turns out her light.

I grasp her fingers gently and share, "I'm so happy that you found out about this butterfly sanctuary so nearby. I'd heard of Callaway for years, but just thought they had beautiful plants to look at—never knew the details we've learned since you started telling us. I'm excited."

She squeezes my hand a little tighter and says, "It was a hard choice, Gamma. I wanted to find a special place for you, and couldn't decide between going to a beach where we could find new special signs like the sand dollars and heart stones in Florida, or to go someplace to see butterflies. Most of the butterfly places were far—like Mexico and Costa Rica. Then, I saw this one only an hour away. I think that's a sign, don't you?"

Touched by her wish to connect with me and my passion for signs, I reply, "Oh, most definitely. It is a great choice."

Everett comes in, whispers in her ear, then turns out her light. "Sorry I missed your bedtime story. Time to get some shut-eye, little one."

Everett closes her door and gestures silently, as if she's already sleeping. He points at himself, at me, and then downstairs. Accepting the quiet invitation, I nod my head and descend, heading toward the kitchen.

Unable to keep a straight face, I inquire, "Are we on a secret mission?"

"Huh? No, no, I know you want to get to bed, but I just want to talk for a few minutes. I thought about Gabby's request while I walked, and I'm not going back to Italy. Timing isn't right, you know?"

"I came back from the store hoping you'd be back here already, so we could have spoken then. I wanted to tell you not to rush, you don't need to decide today, tomorrow, or on any artificial timeline. I did that too often in my younger years, Everett. I saw things as either/or, and almost always as if everything was a critical decision. Steven and I might have stayed together if I hadn't made the snap decision to leave in the midst of emotional moments. I don't know if Gabby wanted a quick answer, but my advice, if you want it, is to take your time."

"Thank you for that, for sharing. You're right, and I kind of did what you're saying. I told her I'm not coming—at least, not right now. I didn't rule it out totally. I suggested we wait a few more weeks to see if the company considers her request to come stateside. Something makes her think it needs to happen right now. Maybe she's getting impatient with how long it will take, and well, this is weird to say, but I guess she misses me more than either of us anticipated." He's blushing and his voice becomes barely audible.

"That's really sweet, Everett. I'm happy that you two have this budding relationship. Give it a few weeks and see what happens. You and Beth are still welcome to stay here until it gets sorted out."

"That was my next question. I don't want to take advantage. I started to get worried about our apartment in New York, but called the guy I sublet to, and he's relieved. He needs to stay there a little longer. We decided to check in again in a month. So, I guess it's all good for now. Feels strange to be thinking about a living situation month by month at this stage of my life, but like you said, maybe that's not urgent at this moment."

"Waiting seems to be the best option for now. Maybe you'll have much more information in a month. The kids were cute tonight, weren't they? So full of energy! Thank heavens Steven is coming along."

He offers again, "I'll come along if you need, you know."

I pause before answering and then reply, "I think you need some time to yourself, or as I said earlier, time with Eric. Give yourself some space while we take charge of the action-packed agenda."

On the big day, we're on the road by eight-thirty. Not bad for a planned eight o'clock departure. Only had to go back once— Bobby forgot his glasses, and I forgot my phone. Both essential and worth the extra ten minutes. The guidebook says the best time to see the blue morphos is around ten in the morning, so we'll still make it in plenty of time.

Gate entry is smooth. Our assortment of butterfly and caterpillar costumed kids are delighted at earning free admission with their colorful creations. Steven and I take dozens of photos of them together, while the costumes are still intact, before we set out to the butterfly center for the much-anticipated, unique, shimmery spectacle.

I am mesmerized, right alongside the kids, with the sparkling blue iridescence of these amazing butterflies. It is as if the humming of their synchronous flutter is being led by a conductor hidden in the rafters above them. Photos can't capture it, words can't describe it. Only the precious image embedded in my brain, a memory postcard, will ever come close to capturing and recalling the spectacular display.

During the lunch break, we plan the sequence for the rest of the day. See the birds of prey, the giant bug exhibit, and try the zipline before heading to the lake for our last stop—to cool off and relax.

The activities unfold with surprising ease, in precisely the order we laid out ahead of time. That is, until I hear a yelp ahead of me on the path. Then there's crying, and voices calling my name and Steven's alternately, louder and louder.

He and I look at one another and pick up our leisurely pace. "We're coming, we're right here!"

Beth is lying on the gravel walk. Her knees and palms are bloodied; she's crying and pointing toward her foot.

Lisa takes charge of reporting, "Beth was skipping and her foot went off the walk. I think she twisted her ankle."

I'm no diagnostician, but the ankle is swelling quickly and Beth winces when I touch it. I reassure her, then the concerned others, that this will be okay.

Steven stoops down to pat Beth's shoulder, glances at her, then me, and says, "I saw one of the center's employees on the path with a golf cart. Let me see if I can go flag him down and get this girl a ride."

Beth nods her head with a solemn look on her face and says, "It hurts so bad, Gamma. I was skipping along and then I saw these pennies."

She slowly opens her bloody, sweaty, little fist and shows me three pennies she'd retrieved. Three pennies once again. I'm taking them as a sign that she's going to be okay. Someone is watching over her.

Leaving a dirty trail on her cheek as she wipes off a stray tear, she asks, "Hold these for me, please?"

I take the firmly clenched coins and put them carefully in my pants pocket, buttoning it closed for safe-keeping.

"Thank you, Gamma. Do you think I broke it? My ankle or whatever? It hurts. I'm sorry I wrecked our day."

"No apologies, little one. No one intends for accidents to happen. You haven't wrecked our day—no one can take away the good time we've had so far. Let's just get this looked at as soon as we can."

Steven and the worker pull up, and gently load her in the cart. The young man even has sacks of mulch that he uses to carefully elevate her leg for the ride back to the car.

The other kids and I walk back. Louis comes close and reaches for my hand while we walk.

He looks up at me with his eyes like saucers and asks, "Is Beth okay, Miss Lissa? Are we going to the hospital?"

"I'm looking on my phone right now, Louis, for the closest place to take her. It's not a hospital, but the Urgent Care has doctors and nurses who can help Beth. I think we can find one pretty close."

The kind worker offers to take her to the office for a first aid kit, but I think it's better we just head to the clinic. It's about fifteen minutes away and the online registry says the wait is thirty minutes—better to just get there. They gently lift Beth into the SUV and the other kids pile in around her.

I warn the others, "Be careful not to touch her leg or bump into her. Sudden movements hurt really badly when you're already in pain." Steven drives while I use tissues and water from the drinking bottles to clean off the superficial dirt from her scrapes. She quietly winces again as I dab at the open areas, and I decide to just let it be until she's in a treatment room. It looks like there may be tiny pieces of gravel in there that only a tweezer can reach—no sense in possibly pushing them in further.

I call Everett to let him know what's happening, but there's no answer. I leave a message, trying not to alarm him. I'm relieved to remember that I still carry all of the permissions that he gave me when he was out of the country, so we'll have no trouble if any decisions need to be made—hopefully, that's not the case.

By the time we're done in the exam room, x-rays have been taken, and we're all back in the car, not certain of our next move, my phone rings. It's Everett calling back.

I don't bother with asking what took him so long, but launch into a summary of our last couple of hours.

I finish up with, "The physician assistant cleaned up her scrapes, taking a few pieces of gravel out. They took x-rays, splinted her ankle to keep it immobilized, and recommend an orthopedic consult on Monday. They gave her ibuprofen as well. We just got back to the car. We've got a whole pile of hungry, hot, tired kids here."

I listen a moment and then say, "No, no, you don't need to drive down here—not necessary."

Steven taps my shoulder and gestures for me to hand him the phone. He listens to Everett for a short time, then informs him, "Listen, Everett, while your mother was in with Beth, the other kids and I made a decision. We still need to eat, and it's getting late. It's foolish to drive back now. We found a hotel nearby with a restaurant and a pool. I reserved two rooms—one for the boys and me, one for the ladies. We're going there now, having a swim to cool off, eat dinner, and get them all to bed. We'll be home in the morning. They will be fine." Evidently, Everett has more to say, but Steven doesn't leave room for argument.

I'm tempted to protest. After all, no one consulted me on this whole plan. But then I realize it feels really good. I didn't need to make the decision, find a room, or arrange a doggone thing. Every once in awhile, it's nice to relinquish all of that responsibility. I'm thankful Steven came on this little trip, and pleased at the prospect of relaxing rather than driving back in the dark.

My feelings must not be clear on my face because Steven gives me a questioning look while first pointing his thumb up, then down. I reply with a smile and both thumbs up. He hands the phone back to me.

"Yeah, Everett, so that's what we're doing. Can you call Renee and Isabel and let them know? I'll have the kids call them once we're settled in the room. Yeah, sure, you can speak to Beth."

Steven looks at his phone one more time, enters the address into the car's GPS, and before I know it, we've got the kids in two adjoining hotel rooms. They're super excited when they see that the rooms are adjoining and when we open it up, they have all kinds of space to stretch out and watch TV later. Glad that they each brought their bathing suits for the lake, everyone is changed and ready to head to the pool, except of course, Beth.

"Beth, do you want to try to use the crutches and come down to watch the kids, or shall I stay up here with you while they swim? Either way is fine with me, you just have to keep your leg raised."

Bobby leads the group in encouraging her, "Come on down, Beth. I'm sad you can't swim, but we don't want to leave you alone up here. You can be the starter and judge us while we have swimming races."

His idea makes a small smile return to her face as she answers, "I'll try the crutches, Gamma. Will you stand next to me?"

Pool time and dinner proceed, with the kids looking sleepier and sleepier throughout the meal. We take that as a definite signal we need to get them to the rooms and settled down.

Once the girls and I are all changed into the t-shirts we'd bought as souvenirs, I call into the attached room, "Everyone dressed in here? We can watch one short show before all going to bed."

No one is in the other room. Hmm—where are they? Just then, the door bursts open and they come through with bags of cookies and drinks.

Steven is leading the group. "We brought dessert, ladies. Let's turn something silly on TV and enjoy!"

The kids begin grabbing the snacks. It's as if they hadn't eaten all day, rather than finishing dinner less than an hour ago. Lisa is playing the little mother to Beth. She asks what snacks she'd like and hands her the remote so that she can have control from her pillow-dominated perch on the bed. The boys move in to watch whatever she has preselected.

Steven holds another bag up for me to see, and says, "Would the lady enjoy some wine for dessert, rather than the other choices?"

After this long day of fun, sun, stress, and emergency reactions, wine never sounded so good.

"That's the best thing I've heard since the free garden admission almost twelve hours ago. I think if we go out on this balcony, the TV won't be quite as loud, but I can still hear Beth if she needs anything. Shall we?"

The balcony is nothing fancy—a couple of lawn chairs and a plastic table, just big enough for two glasses and the wine bottle sitting in the ice bucket—however, a table for two with a linen covering and candlelight could not have been any more welcome than this. I can even prop my swollen feet up on the table!

"Steven, getting these rooms was brilliant. The kids are content, even Beth looks happy, almost like a princess on a throne. I think it would have been very difficult for her to get, or to stay, comfortable for the ride home. Ice, ibuprofen, and snacks are all she needs right now. Did Everett sound perturbed when you told him your plan?"

Steven smiles and shakes his head, while enjoying his first sip.

"Perturbed is probably a little strong. Mildly surprised, maybe. He started to say something about being on the phone for most of the day and waiting for another call. Perhaps he was distracted, or even a little relieved. Not that he'd say that."

On the phone for the night—odd. Unless, of course, something came up at work in Italy, or more likely, continuing the conversation with Gabby.

"No, he wouldn't, for sure. But thanks for taking the phone, and well, taking charge of the whole scenario. I was tired and more concerned about Beth than anything or anyone else. Your plan was perfect. I wouldn't have thought of doing this, but I'm grateful that you did."

We sip in silence and then recap some of the most enjoyable moments of the day. Everyone really did have a wonderful time until the mishap. The fall, the Urgent Care, and the hotel will make the stories even better when shared later.

"Oh gosh, I just remembered that I should have Lisa and Bobby call Isabel and help Louis call Renee. I'm sure they're waiting to hear the kids' voices."

It does my heart good to hear the excitement in the kids' voices as they talk about their day with the moms. Bobby talks nonstop about the raptors, especially the red-tailed hawk. Lisa tells Isabel about the butterflies, then recounts every moment of the injury sequence as if she is a news reporter. Louis shares his fascination with an exhibit of caterpillars. While they're all talking, I sit with Beth for a few minutes.

"Thank you so much for finding this place for us to enjoy, Beth. I never knew of it, and the minute I saw the blue morphos, I felt the special connection with Emma that I've told you about so many times. And the sound of the wings—I can't describe it, but I hope I'll always hear it in my memory. A spell-binding, musical experience."

She shakes her head and replies, "Yeah, everything was good till I fell. I scared everybody, my dad, and even myself. I ruined it."

"No, no, you didn't ruin it. A not-so-good thing doesn't wipe out our enjoyable time before that. And, your daddy being scared, well, that's part of being a parent. Eric and Emma's doctor once told me that he'd rather see a kid come in his office with a broken arm than a kid that never climbed a tree. Adventure means risk, and we did have a good adventure. Not fun for you to get hurt, but would you have rather been home and skipped the gardens?"

She smiles and quickly responds, "No, I didn't like getting hurt, but I don't wish I'd stayed home."

Beth's little forehead wrinkles, she squints her eyes and asks, "Hey, do you have those pennies? Remember when we found some under our picnic blanket over Christmas vacation? There were three back then, and three today. When I saw something shiny on the ground, I tried to stop fast to grab them. That's when I fell. Does that mean they're bad luck pennies, instead of the good ones we found that other time?"

Hmm. What am I going to say to this? Giving myself some time to think, I slowly reach into my pocket and pull them out.

"I don't know, Beth, let's take a look. This really old one, I can't even read the date. But these other two, the shiny ones—this one is 1982—the year your daddy was born."

The smile on her face lets me know she's relieved.

"And this one, well, it's 1993—when Uncle Eric was born. Those can't be bad—maybe it means you wanted to share this trip with them?"

She stares intensely at them for a few seconds, then looks straight into my eyes.

"Gamma, when I was skipping, I was wishing that Daddy, Uncle Eric, and Baby Benjamin could be with us. For real, I was. I was humming 'Smiles from Her Heart' and thinking that."

How do I explain to her that I absolutely believe her—that I've come to think there really are almost no coincidences and that I've had enough proof of things coming in threes as blessings?

"Oh, honey, I'm sure you were thinking of them. I don't think it was bad luck at all. You might have fallen anyway. But, just maybe, you would have been hurt worse if you weren't being watched over by pennies sent from heaven with a message, signs that angels above as well as Daddy and Uncle Eric are always around for you."

She smiles again and says, "There's another reason I don't wish I'd stayed home. I wanted to come to the park to see your face be happy, and that wish came true, Gamma. You looked really happy."

I lean over to give her a big hug and notice her eyes are drooping. Lisa has already crawled in next to her and the boys must have gone to bed. The television is still on, with no little viewers. I take a deep breath, lightly tuck Beth's hair behind her ear, and turn off the TV. An aura of peace settles over me, over them, bringing the action-filled day to a much-needed conclusion.

28

Let us be grateful to the people who make us happy;
they are the charming gardeners who make our souls bloom.
Marcel Proust

Tiptoeing out to the balcony, I half expect to see Steven's head bobbing and to hear the sound of snoring, but I'm pleasantly surprised. He looks up just as I come through the door and finishes pouring my second glass of wine.

"Good timing, Steven. The kids are all sound asleep."

"I could hear little bits and pieces of your conversation with Beth and then it got really quiet, so I took a guess that you might be ready for a refill. If you hadn't come out, I was going to check to see if you'd fallen asleep as well."

I laugh and offer, "I can see why you'd want to check, but you know how sometimes, although you're exhausted, you just can't calm down right away? That's my current situation. Let's enjoy these few sips before calling it a night."

This little balcony is an unexpected bonus. There's a welcome respite here, in spite of the quiet rumble of traffic noise in the distance. An oasis in the midst of touristy road stops.

"I probably said this several times already, but I'm so grateful that you came along on this outing. When Renee and Isabel were both busy, I thought I'd be fine alone with the kids for just a day trip. Little did I know, right? You saved me, Steven." It's not the first time in our long history that he's been there when I needed someone. I didn't always accept his help gracefully, but it was offered pretty darn consistently.

Our eyes meet; almost as if he is thinking the very same thing.

"You've always been important to me, Larissa. Together or not, I've felt the connection and wanted to help. And recently, the way you jump in and give these kids all your energy—it's contagious. I literally wanted to be along for the ride. We make a decent team, don't you think?"

Is he asking about more than today? More than the current topic of conversation? And if so, it's true. We've made a good team multiple times since we met decades ago—at work, our marriage, as dear friends, and the last couple of years, Eric's parents.

"Steven, I think--"

His index finger gently taps on my upper lip, silencing my reply.

"Don't overthink it, Larissa. We did, and do, make a good team in many ways. I cherished it then, I cherish it now. Do I wish we could figure out a way to be a couple? Guilty as charged—I confess, I do wish that. I also know it's futile to push, and I can be content with things as they are. But if you ever think it could be more, well, I'm here."

He leans forward, kisses my right cheek, then my left, stops to make eye contact.

My eyes meet his, surprised, but not.

He comes close again and his lips lightly brush mine. I'm startled, but pleased by the sensation, the undeniable arousal, and the familiarity. I remain still, absorbing my own reactions.

Steven settles back into his chair, rubs both his thumbs over my clenched knuckles, and smiles.

I return the smile and reply, "Yes, you're definitely here. Right next to me and it's comfortable. Can we leave it at that? There are four kids in there that need transporting home early in the morning so their parents aren't flipping out, and who knows if Beth will rest easy through the night."

Steven glances toward the rooms, nods his head, and tells me, "I've never stopped loving you, Larissa."

I know he wants me to return the emotion. Maybe there's some part of me that wants to hear myself repeat those words back. But, I can't. It may even be true, but I don't have the energy to spare. Navigating a rekindled romance would require effort, and I'm not sure I can make that happen right now. Personal energy is at a premium these days.

I stand up to give myself time to put some words together, then say as much as I can at the moment.

"Yes, Steven, I know. I do know that and feel it."

He rises to meet me and I lean my head against his chest. His hand comes under my hairline and caresses my neck, pulling me ever so slightly closer. I linger for a few seconds longer and hear him whisper, "Thank you, sweet Larissa. Sleep well."

We each step back as if on a coordinated cue and walk into our designated rooms. Sounds of deep breathing emanate from beds on both sides of the wall. He heads into the boys' room, pulling the door within a half inch of being closed. That half inch is our connection, and it feels good. I'm ever so grateful.

When light peeps around the not-so-effective blackout curtain, I awaken to Beth's breath on my shoulder. How the heck did she hobble into my bed during the night? I didn't hear or feel her until now. I reach to stroke her hair and a raspy whisper responds with, "Good morning, Gamma. My leg hurts. Can I have more medicine?"

I hop up to get ice, prop her foot on a pillow, grabbing the ibuprofen and water.

"Yes, of course, little one. Did it hurt during the night? Wake you up?"

"Just a little. Daddy texted me on my phone to see how I was feeling, then I couldn't fall back to sleep. I wanted to be next to you instead of Lisa. I held on to the nightstand and the bed and hopped over—it was only one or two hops. Once I laid back down next to you, guess I fell back to sleep fast."

A snarky thought comes to mind. I'll keep it to myself but can't help thinking: *Bet now he's happy that I got a phone for her.*

"I think we were all very tired from our busy day yesterday. I'm sorry I didn't even hear you move. I'm not the best nurse, huh?"

She giggles and says, "Good enough for me. I don't want to be in a place with a real nurse. Are we going home soon? I want to see Daddy and be in my bed with my animals. I'll heal better there."

"I'm sure that you will. Lay here a few minutes with the ice. Even though it's early, I bet the others will start to wake up soon. We can even help that along. I'll pull the curtains open a little more in both rooms and maybe that will wake everybody else up." She smiles and nods her head.

I quietly tiptoe into the boys' room to make daylight more obvious. As I'm walking back to my own side of the accommodations, Steven's voice, quite raspy, but playful nonetheless, says, "Just can't keep you away, huh?"

I put my finger up to my lips, but whisper back, "Very funny."

Yup, definitely time to get this group back to Atlanta, back to reality and away from this unexpected oasis. Our short day trip has evolved into much more than seeing butterflies. And Everett will be waiting to hear from us, I'm sure.

Steven takes the wheel so that I can contact the parents awaiting news of our return. After texting that we are on the road, I receive quick responses from Isabel and Renee that they can't wait to see us, but Everett asks by text, "Can you tell me your ETA," followed almost immediately by, "I'm taking care of some things." *Is it me, or are these weird responses?* I don't want to read them out loud to Steven when little ears behind me might hear, so I ask him to stop for me to use the restroom.

He looks at me questioningly, and I reply, "Guess I had too much coffee. Anyone else need to go?"

While we wait for Bobby to finish, I show Steven the texts, and ask what he thinks.

"Geez, I don't know. Last night he said he'd be on the phone all night, but didn't exactly say why, now these. Yeah, maybe a little cryptic."

"He didn't 'exactly' say why? Did he offer anything?"

"Just that he had to talk with colleagues from Italy and wasn't sure how long it would take, implied it would take awhile. Something about confirming travel plans? I don't know. I guess we'll find out soon enough when we get back. Not more than forty-five minutes."

My mom radar tells me something is up that Everett doesn't want to talk about. My brain starts circling around the various possibilities of who he's talking to abroad and who is traveling. None of the options that occur to me are particularly appealing. Like Steven said, we'll know soon—if he's ready to talk about it. First priority, though, is getting Beth comfortably settled. Comfort for her is something I may be able to control, or at least influence. Not so sure about anything going on with her father.

The first face I pick out in our driveway is Renee. At the very same moment, Louis must see her as well, because he yells out, "She's here, she's waiting for me!"

"Of course she is, honey. She wants to see you!"

"I didn't know that. Sometimes mommies get mad and don't come back." Oh my goodness, his little brain and heart have experienced way too much for a little guy his age.

Lisa, Bobby, and Louis tumble out of the back of the car in a jumble of arms, legs, and backpacks, while Beth, foot still propped, waits patiently.

Everett is still standing in the doorway, I guess waiting for the others to clear a path for him to get to Beth. I'm reaching for her hand when Everett walks slowly out of the garage entry and offers, "I'll get her. I'm coming." Then he turns back toward the house and holds one hand up with the palm open, like a school crossing guard halting the homebound kids on a Friday afternoon.

Beth yells, "Gamma, can you take the ice off so I can get out? Daddy's coming!"

I turn quickly to do as she asks and watch Everett gently lift her out, while snuggling his head down against hers. Both relieved to be close again. Sweet.

I grab the ice and everything else in the back seat that I can possibly load in my arms. How did these kids make such a disaster of their space in only an hour? Arms full of a ridiculous assortment of belongings, I can barely see over the top of my load.

All I hear is, "Whoa, watch out, there!" before I realize I'm bumping into someone and everything in my arms lands on top of me as I sprawl in the driveway. Not at all hurt, I start laughing at the silliness of the whole scene. Relieved, so does everyone else.

Just then it registers that I didn't recognize the voice that warned me to be careful. I look up to see the unmistakable sphere of an expectant belly. A hand is reaching out from the same body—I'm not sure if it's offering assistance or a handshake.

"Uh, Mom, uh, meet Gabby, Gabriella."

29

*One day she finally grasped that unexpected things
were always going to happen in life.
And with that, she realized the only control she had
was how she was going to handle them.
So she made the decision to survive using courage,
humor, and grace.*

KATHY KINNEY

*E*ric springs to my side. "Here, Mom, let me help you."

I grab his arm to hoist myself up, brush off, then start
to pick up the clothes and snack wrappers strewn on the driveway
and blowing onto the lawn. I'm grateful for something to occupy
me while I collect myself. My body and thoughts are as much
in a disarray as the car contents. Manners return to me as I step
toward the young woman, with her long, dark hair and stunning
eyes that serve to keep my own eyes off her midsection. One not-
so-minor detail about Everett's girlfriend that's a total surprise.
Guess he forgot to share?

"Gabriella, hello. That was quite the way to meet."

"I'm so sorry you fell." Her face breaks into a luminous smile as she takes my face in both hands and kisses each cheek. I have no choice but to wrap my arms around her and give the hug I'm sure that she and Everett are expecting from me.

A round of "Awws" replaces the laughter, but once we let go of one another, an awkward absence of any sound settles in.

Until Renee strides over, arms spread wide and exclaims, "Well, Larissa, see what happens when you stay away half a day too long? Visitors arrive, then everyone you love takes over your house and starts cooking. Imagine what will happen when you finally take one of the trips you're longing for and stay away a week or two?"

In unison, laughter returns to the crowd, Hilary claps her hand and announces, "Indeed, we did take over the kitchen! There's plenty for everyone, come on in the house."

Everett helps Beth move off to the side. They linger until Gabriella joins them. It looks like they're having a mini, private introduction. I'm guessing Beth is as surprised as I am—unless that's why he contacted her during the night?

With Steven on one side of me and Eric on the other, we make our way into the house, dumping the trip paraphernalia on the sofa as we pass by. There's plenty of chattering in the other rooms. It sounds like it's all happy chattering—I'm pleased to hear the enthusiasm—in spite of the unexpected end to our outing.

The recounting of our expedition continues throughout the first and second helpings, then silence settles over the group when brownies are brought out. Sideways glances seem to be all that is happening.

Isabel gracefully eases conversation back into the group with, "Gabby, how was your travel? Did it seem strange to be flying again?"

Gabby first glances at Everett, then replies, "It certainly was strange. Everyone is wearing masks, of course. I felt a little anxious about it all, well, with this one to look out for." She strokes her abdomen protectively. Then, she stops abruptly, as if realizing she may not want to bring attention to the as yet unspoken topic.

"Anyway, flights were smooth and I am relieved to finally be here."

I'm more than a little confused by the 'finally' but am not going to say one word. How, when, and why she got here are questions I'll wait for Everett to share—if he chooses to do so.

I'm not sure if Isabel is tuning into the awkwardness that is hovering over this whole conversation, or if she simply wants to get her kids back home, but she rises from her place and says, "Lisa and Bobby, say thank you to Larissa and Steven for your adventure. We need to get home, unpack, and walk Valentino. He hasn't gotten much exercise with you guys gone."

Renee rises as well, and Louis says thank you without a prompt, "I had a really good time, even though I don't like that Beth got hurt. The butterflies were pretty and the raptors were fierce!"

The collective laugh at his expressive declaration is a welcome tension reliever. After they're all gone, Hilary suggests, "Larissa, how about if you feed and snuggle with Benjamin in the living room while Eric and I clean up?"

Grateful for the chance to hold my precious grandson and retreat to a comfy sofa, I reach for Benjamin and make my exit.

I hear Beth's voice from another part of the house as she asks, "Daddy, can I show Gabby my room and my animals?"

I can't help cautioning, "Everett—wait—she doesn't know how to use the stairs with those crutches."

Everett walks into the room and kneels next to Benjamin and me. He pats my arm in what I'm guessing is supposed to be reassurance and says, "I've got her; I'll carry her up. Gabby's right behind me with ibuprofen and ice. Thanks for taking good care of her. And we can talk later about, well, everything else."

I nod my head. Best not to say anything else at this point and shift my attention to Benjamin. Peering into this little guy's eyes while he enjoys his bottle grounds me. The calmness after the last day and a half is simply heavenly. No matter what is going on in the rest of the house, the rest of the world, I'm where I want to be.

When he's finished, Benjamin is content on my chest and snuggles his head into the space between my chin and collarbone. A space that is perfectly designed to accommodate that precious, tiny human. Chest to chest, heartbeat to heartbeat. My eyes close along with his.

The feeling of Benjamin against me becomes Eric, then Emma. My body responds the same way it did with two little ones before, and relaxes—all except for the arms securely around him. The unmistakable bond between an adult and a child who are connected. And, although I only held Everett once as an infant, and never had the chance with Beth, my feeling encompasses all of them.

An ever-so-gentle hand on my shoulder precedes Eric's whisper, "Mom, we need to get little Ben home, and it looks like you need to sleep. The kitchen is cleaned up and everyone else left."

The gentleness of his touch did not prepare me for the jolt back into the present from those cuddle times years ago. I look at Eric, down at the baby, and reply, "Oh my goodness, how long were we here? I must have been dreaming." I'm not about to share all that my dream included, it's too confusing even for me.

"Long enough to miss clean up! Now, get some rest, you crazy travel guide."

After they close the front door, I flop back into the chair and more fully return to present day. It happened again—my three children together, as if they'd always been with me and still are. Disorienting on one level, comforting on the other.

I hear quiet footsteps on the stairway, quite possibly to keep from waking me. I'm expecting Everett, but am confused that it's an unfamiliar woman. No, wait, the dream really did muddle my brain. It's Gabby, putting her finger to her lips to emphasize being quiet.

She whispers, "Do you need anything from the kitchen? Water? Tea?"

Still unsure of the time or how I feel, I respond, "I guess herbal tea would be nice. Here, let me get it. How about you?"

The rote steps to making tea in my own kitchen help me settle further and provide time to gather my thoughts. I barely know this woman, now we're sharing tea in the middle of the night. Already exhausted, am I really ready to do this?

Seated across from one another with hands encircling steaming mugs, a hundred questions pop into my mind. I'm not asking, though. I'm just going to sip the warm drink and wait.

"Thank you for letting me stay here, Mrs. Whitcomb. I appreciate it."

I didn't have a choice in this, I didn't even know about it.

Stifling that thought, I reply, "Larissa is fine, Gabby. And you're welcome. Friends of my children are always welcome." Safe, honest answer.

The kitchen is silent, except for ice cubes dropping into the bin and the droning of the dishwasher.

Gabby begins again. "Once Everett and I decided I would come here, my reservation was for a few weeks from now. But at my appointment early this week, the doctor said that was not going to be possible; I had to travel right away. So, everything got changed. I'm sorry about the early arrival."

Early? How about unexpected? I'm confused. How long has Everett known she was coming? When was he going to share that with the rest of us? When was he going to mention that she is pregnant? As these questions swirl around in my mind, Gabby seems to be expecting some kind of reply from me. I can't shake the feeling that it should be Everett speaking to me, filling me in.

"It sounds like you didn't have a choice. Or maybe the choice was to come right away or wait until after the baby?"

Gabby is staring into her teacup, so I just wait.

She starts once again, "Let me go back. There were many things to consider. Everett was not sure what he wanted to do when I told him about the baby. After many late night discussions, we decided it was most important for him to come back here. To see Beth, to see you, and to settle back into work in this country when the opportunity arose. Decisions about me and where I would be didn't really start until he moved home." She stops again. Her eyes flickering side to side tell me that she is searching for words. "Maybe it's too late to talk now. Maybe we should go to bed and wait for morning, wait for Everett."

As much as I want to know more, she's right. I'm exhausted from traveling and tending to Beth's injury. Besides, it should be Everett telling me about Gabby, the baby, and whatever other news they have.

"Thank you for trying to fill me in, dear, but I agree. It's too late for an important conversation, and one very important person is missing. Let's get some sleep and talk tomorrow. Are you comfortable enough in the room? Did he get you extra pillows? There are some in the closet—please help yourself."

Just as she rises, another set of footsteps descends the stairs. This time it's Everett.

"Gabby, Mom, what are you doing? Gabby, I know the time change makes it hard, but you need to try to get some sleep. And,

Mom, you too. You must be exhausted. Thank you so much for taking such good care of Beth. She seems to be good. I just checked, and she's sleeping soundly. I thanked Steven before he left too. In spite of the drama, it sounds like everyone had a good time."

"Yes, thankfully, it was almost at the end of the day, so plenty of nice memories were made before her fall. I'm grateful to Steven—it would have been far more challenging if I'd been alone with the kids."

"Look, there's quite a bit I need to fill you in on. Things kinda blew up in the last day and a half. When you called with the news that Beth got hurt, I was talking to Gabby on her layover in London. I didn't know anything about her trip till then."

He stops for a minute and looks at Gabby. "Hey, Gabby, why don't you go get comfortable and give me a minute to talk. I'll be up soon."

She nods her head toward me, then leans over and kisses his cheek before heading back upstairs.

I watch her pull herself up the steps with more than a little effort and surmise that she must be quite close to her due date. The profile says it all.

"I'm more than a little confused. Gabby told me there was a plan for her to come in a few weeks. You didn't know until last night?"

"Yes and no. I knew about the travel date coming up in a few weeks. But even that was only recently determined. I didn't know things changed until she called me while en route. I guess her doctor gave her a now-or-never travel order a couple of days ago, so she jumped on the planning. I admit, it is confusing. Has been all along. Even for me." He shakes his head, then cradles it in his hands.

When he looks back up at me, his face is difficult to read. I expect to see emotion, but he appears impassive.

"I heard you and Gabby saying that maybe this conversation should wait until we all get some rest. And honestly, if you can be patient just a little bit longer, I want to talk more with her myself. We've not had much of a chance to talk since she arrived, and there's too much going on. I can't think straight. Once again, I'm asking you a big favor. Can you give me a little time, please?"

The pleading tone of his voice and the face that now looks like it may crumble into tears convince me that what he needs most from me is compassion, regardless of the details of this sequence of events. As much as I'd like my questions answered, rushing this won't make one bit of difference in the long run. Like the old saying, "what will be, will be." Regardless of when I get the rest of the information.

"Yes, take all the time you need. We're all exhausted. Let's tackle this tomorrow, or whenever. I'm not going anywhere."

30

*One form of loving is when you
just want the best for someone,
whether it includes you or not.*
UNATTRIBUTED

The "not going anywhere" doesn't turn out to be exactly true.
Before going to bed, I'd entered the information about Beth's
accident into her pediatrician's online portal. When I looked at
my emails this morning, there was a message to be at his office
at 9:15. Beth was already up, so off we went, letting her father
and Gabby sleep in. Thankfully, the doctor felt everything was in
order and that if she felt like it, she could go to school. After texting with her father, he agreed I should drop her off, but tell her
to go straight to the nurse's office if she starts having any pain.

As I'm driving home, I'm thinking about Everett and me
having the conversation we started last evening. I hope we get to
it, but it sounded like he and Gabby need their own time before
the agenda includes me. When Renee texted me about the surprise arrival, all I replied was, "It's a puzzling situation—tell you
more when I know more."

A text from Steven comes over my car audio, "Hey, any chance you can meet for coffee? Not urgent, but I'd like to chat for a few minutes."

I use the car's response option, and after a couple of exchanges, decide on an hour from now. No use heading home, so I do the grocery shopping, then go meet Steven.

He's waiting in a booth at the back of the shop and waves me over.

"I wasn't sure what you wanted to drink, but these cookies looked irresistible, so I grabbed a few."

"Yes, they do look darn scrumptious. I'll be right back."

Carefully balancing my hot beverage, I slide in across from him and settle myself into the cozy booth.

"Feels good to sit down. I'm not sure at what point you left, but I fell asleep holding Benjamin last night, and after Eric woke me to leave, I had nighttime visits from Gabby and Everett. Up way too late after our eventful two days."

I share a little bit of the mysterious chats. He'd heard Everett's reference to travel plans during the call about Beth getting hurt, so I figured he might be interested in the next installment of the story, as brief and superficial as it was.

"Not really any of my business, but did you know about Gabby? I mean did you know she's having a baby?"

"Total surprise! He told me about their relationship, told me they were trying to figure things out and hoped to be in the same place, but no, that detail was omitted. And last night, he said something about it being confusing from the beginning. It's certainly confusing for me."

"Sounds like there are more nuances to the decision for Gabby to come here than you've heard so far. Probably wise to postpone the rest of the details until you all had some rest. I slept like a rock, more tired than I realized—how about you?"

"Not great—I tossed and turned a bunch and think I was subconsciously listening for Beth."

After filling him in on her doctor appointment, I ask, "So, what else is up? You said you wanted to chat. I'm happy to pause during the day for latte and cookies, but is something else on your mind?"

He takes a couple of bites of the giant cookie and replies, "You've got a lot on your plate, Larissa. I don't want to add to it."

"I do, but you know what? It feels like I've had a lot on my plate for as long as I can remember. Maybe other people's lives roll along uneventfully, but my experience hasn't been quite like that. Whenever the road seems to be smoothing out, there's another bump ahead. The only difference is whether it's a little bump or a giant pothole."

When I laugh at the end of my observation, he joins in. It's fun to laugh with someone else, especially someone I've known most of my life.

He lightly taps the back of my hand with two of his fingers.

"You know, Larissa, it wasn't the wine speaking or the hotel setting the other night that sparked my comments. I care deeply for you. And since you brought up 'as long as you can remember' a moment ago, that's about how long I've cared. Even when we were far apart all those years, you were close to my heart in one way or another."

I let out a long, slow breath before looking up at him.

"I do know all of that, Steven, I really do. And I didn't intentionally wipe you out of my life, either. I was dealing with those bumps, sometimes craters, in the road, and didn't have much time to think about relationships. At least not romantic ones. Relationships with kids, with friends, even co-workers have been center stage for quite some time now."

Silence settles in again for what seems like a long while, but likely only a minute.

"But is that all you want? Isn't there a place for something more? A place for companionship, closeness, loving arms on cold nights? I miss all that. It was a lot of bumpy roads for me, too, taking care of my parents, then Jimmy, while working. Then, realizing that I've been a father and not known it? So not only bumps, but twists and turns in my road as well. I think having a companion, having you by my side, would make it more enjoyable."

I feel my heart race. Is it excitement? Is it anxiety and dread? Or are they all divergent parts of the same response?

Thinking I need to choose my words carefully, I attempt to let him in on how I'm feeling about this.

"It sounds wonderful, doesn't it? A partner to help face the world when obstacles are thrown in the way? Someone to share joys and sorrows, to warm the chilly, lonely nights. And it will be wonderful for awhile, maybe even a long while. Yet, somewhere along the way, romantic partners begin to find petty disturbances, then expectations creep in; expectations that seem to cause those early, wonderful notions to fade away. Before long, someone in the relationship wants to write to an advice columnist with the latest complaint about the partner. Why doesn't she pick up after herself? How often do happy couples make love? Why can't he stop spending money on stupid things? Expectations that derail the amorous ride they'd embarked upon together. I don't think I have the energy for doing that again. Besides, I love you too much to let a cherished connection disintegrate into that place."

Unconsciously, my mini-rant came with an admission. An admission that I do love Steven. *Well, hell yes, of course I do.* We had a young, loving marriage. We went through the trauma of a miscarriage. It split us up, but he's right, we did stay connected. Sometimes through other people, sometimes through work. Then, we figured out that Eric is our son together. Ever since that time, he's been nothing but supportive, considerate, and helpful. To say nothing of a lifesaver this past weekend. Yes, he's all that, but I still meant what I said about expectations. I'm emotionally overcommitted and can't do that. I don't want to have to live up to anyone's expectations.

He's sitting back in the booth, arms by his side, waiting for more, or hoping there is no more? I can't tell.

He leans forward and asks, "Isn't there something that honors the best of what we can be together and lets the petty expectations go? Some in between that comes with being older and wiser, or maybe simply more patient?"

"I'm not sure I'm more patient—older, yes, but not more patient. Sometimes I think there are aspects of life for which I can't accept compromise, for which I don't want to be questioned or have to explain myself. But relationships require compromise. So, that doesn't bode well, does it?"

"I don't see you that way, Larissa. I see someone who accepts others for who they are; the good and the not-so-good. I'd like a chance at figuring out something different than what you describe. Something where we respect and enjoy one another, yet know when to back off and allow the wiggle room we'll both inevitably need. We've both lived without partners for a long time. Partners doesn't mean we must be in one another's space 24/7. Can we agree to keep talking about it? To spend some fun, alone time together occasionally and see how it goes?"

His eyes find mine and take hold of them. I see both how he looked at me decades ago and how he's looking at me now. Different, but still filled with openness and understanding.

"I guess maybe. That sounds pretty lame, doesn't it? But when we first reconnected, I didn't think I would ever see any of my three children again. Now, Everett and Eric are a huge part of my life, and I'm open enough to see signs, finding connection with Emma nearly every day. I had no grandchildren, now I have two, and apparently, if my eyes don't deceive me, I'm having a third pretty damn soon. My life went from empty to brimming over. It's a lot. I'm grateful, I feel blessed, but the emotional swings take their toll. Maybe there is space for you and I to have some kind of relationship beyond an amazing friendship, but maybe not. And I don't want to lose that friendship while taking the risk."

He nods his head and pulls his hand away.

"It is an amazing friendship, and we're family. We share a son, a grandson, and a whole bunch of friends who are family. I don't want to risk losing any of that either. Guess we just see how it goes next time we share some wine, okay?"

As he stands to go, I look up and smile, "Yes, that's a deal I can agree to. I appreciate you making time to explain more. I'll be in touch when I know more about Everett's situation."

I stay seated and watch Steven walk toward the door. Not sure if I'm feeling regret or relief, I go to the counter for a refill to go.

When I get back home, I head straight to the kitchen with the bags of groceries. A note on the counter from Everett says that he's taking Gabby for a walk in the "magic butterfly garden." How can I do anything but smile at that? Ever since I first felt Emma there, it has become a refuge for me, Renee, Beth, Everett, now maybe Gabby. I hope they figure out whatever they need to.

I go outside to plant the bag of wildflower seeds I'd been meaning to spread in the backyard since the kids returned to school. Daily life seems to rip me away from the simple pleasures. I found this particular mix because it supposedly attracts birds and butterflies. Don't want to unseat the local park as the place we go for butterflies, but I'd like to have more right here, right where I can look out any day and find comfort in the colorful flowers and the winged creatures feeding from them. My own little piece of magic.

"Yoo-hoo! Where are you?" comes through the porch door and then so does Renee. "What are you doing out here?"

"I'm planting seeds. What are you doing here in the middle of the day? Don't you have work until kid pick-up today?"

"I do, but kid pick-up is in just forty-five minutes and I got out of a meeting this side of town. No sense in going back to the office. Can I bring you out some ice tea?"

She returns into the house without waiting for my reply, so I put down my rake and walk up to the porch for a much-needed drink.

Renee hands me a glass and says, "I saw the note on the counter. What are those two up to? I mean, wow, right? Surprises again!"

I start to answer her and she bursts out laughing.

"Oh my God, Larissa! If you could have observed that whole scene from where I stood! You're on the ground looking up at the gigundous belly . . ." She's laughing so hard that she can't finish her sentence.

Unable to help myself, I start laughing along with her. I can't stop laughing. Every time I look at her doubled over, I start again. Now tears are streaming down my face.

Renee says, "Damn, I'm going to pee my pants. I can't even . . ."

Gradually, the hilarity of it all fades and we try again to have a conversation.

"I can see why it would seem funny, but I don't know, Renee. He still hasn't told me much at all. Just that the travel plan was very sudden. Then we decided that sleep was sorely needed by all of us, and we'd wait until today—or whenever."

"That's probably better."

"Yup, that's what Steven said as well."

"You've talked with Steven today?"

Oh, here we go. She's always trying to insinuate there's much more going on with us. "We met for coffee a little while ago. He wanted to catch up after our trip with the kids."

"Catch up? You shared the whole damn trip, right? How was that anyway? Did you lock the kids in the rooms and go grab an adult beverage at the bar? Little alone time?"

I laugh, half-heartedly this time. She's not really that far off.

"No—lock the kids in the room? Are you nuts? No. But, we did have some wine out on the balcony while they watched TV."

"Aha! Now, we're talking! How was it?"

"Honestly, it was sweet. I was so grateful that he'd made the plan for us to stay the night. And over wine, he did profess his love for me and his desire for there to be more between us."

Her head jerks upward and she grabs my wrist.

"Wait—what? Something actually did happen? Geez, finally, you two! Tell me more!"

I recap our conversation on the balcony as best I can remember, then tell her about today's at the coffee shop.

"Wow, so how did you leave it? The poor guy—I never knew you had gotten so cynical about love. I mean, come on. Give the guy a chance. Hasn't he proven over and over that he's your forever person?"

"Cynical? I don't think so. I just hate the implied expectation in romantic relationships that you need to sacrifice everything for the other person. That seems like an unrealistic fairytale notion to me. The same with 'forever.' No such thing."

"I beg to differ, my friend. It sounds like you're assuming that his idea of romance is wrapped up in some immature notion you're holding on to about expectations. Is it possible he wouldn't ask any of those things from you? Wouldn't have expectations about money, or sex, or housekeeping? Didn't you go through that stage once at a young age? You've put it out there as your concern. He might agree with you. He's got his head on pretty straight, Larissa. And if you ask me, his heart is genuine. And he ain't so hard on the eyes either."

She puts one arm around me and I can't help but soften and grin at her predictable reference about his appearance.

"I don't know, Renee. It's all a big 'maybe' for me. I told him we can share wine now and then and see what happens. That's about the only commitment that I'm willing to make right now. And I'm making no promises about 'forever'—there's no such thing."

"You know what, Larissa. I call bullshit. You talk a big game about not believing in forever. But from where I sit, that's exactly what you believe in. What is it when you see signs of Emma or your mother on the beach, at the park, on your porch? That's believing that they can and will always be with you—no matter what form they are in. Body or soul, they will connect with you no matter what. Believing that Monica and Emma are connected by that beautiful song? That's believing they'll always be able to continue the relationship they started. Believing that a rainbow is a bridge to another world or an afterlife or whatever? Maybe you have trouble with the word *forever*, but I think it's exactly what you believe in. You show me every day that you believe love can last beyond when everyone is here on earth in the form we understand the best. You absolutely believe that love does not die, that it's enduring."

31

You cannot swim for new horizons
until you have the courage to lose sight of the shore.
WILLIAM FAULKNER

Four days have passed and the much-anticipated conversation still hasn't happened. Everett and I have not exactly avoided it, there just hasn't seemed to be the right time. Maybe waiting for the perfectly right time is precisely why it hasn't happened. Perfect timing is rare.

I'm answering emails on my computer at the kitchen counter. My office is now transformed into Everett's office, and sometimes lately, it's Gabby's as well. I always thought this was a big house, but the way it's going, we may run out of rooms pretty soon. Guess the finished basement could be repurposed, it even has its own bathroom.

A louder than usual voice steals my attention from the email list. The office door opens and I hear Everett exclaim, "Damn, Kristy, all right. Yes, I admit you were right. I did as you suggested. I'm all in now; Gabriella is here. How about you let me do the rest my way?"

While I'm wondering at the raised voice, it becomes apparent that Gabby is the one who came out of the office, leaving the door ajar. She goes to the closet, grabs her coat, and walks out. She doesn't slam the door, but she makes it clear by her silence and determined walk that she's not interested in conversation as she leaves.

A few minutes later, Everett calls down the stairs, "Gabby, I'm off the phone. Come on back up here—please."

I call up, "She left."

At a pace somewhere between walk and run, he comes down the stairs asking, "Left? Like where'd she go?"

I hunch my shoulders, turn my hands upward, and tell him, "No clue—got her coat and out the front door she went."

He goes to the door, steps out, looks up and down the street. He puts his hand to his forehead, turns around and comes inside.

"She didn't say anything when she came down?"

"Not a thing."

He begins to pace along with his words. "Damn! Well, I'm sure she's fine. Gabby's learned her way around the neighborhood on our walks the last few days. And she loves the park. This is my fault. I should have known better—it took me too long to wrap my head around this whole thing. I get why she was mad, or hurt at first, but we've been good since she got here. Arguing with Kristy is too much negativity for Gabby right now."

"Do you want to tell me enough so I can understand what you're talking about, or isn't this a good time? I'm not trying to pry into your life. I just can't help you if I don't know what's been going on."

He sits next to me and offers, "Geez—I know. Time has gotten away from me since she got here, since you guys got back. You're not prying. I've been ready to tell you several times. I guess I'm annoyed or ashamed at myself. Not proud of my reactions, my inactions, whatever."

All I can do now is show him I'm listening and wait for something that makes sense.

"When Gabby first told me she was pregnant, I guess I was kind of a jerk. I was totally caught off guard, blurted out that I didn't know if I was ready for another kid right now. The middle of the pandemic, Beth across the ocean, just finding out about Joseph—how much more could I process? Then, while I was still trying to figure out how I felt about the baby, she told me she wasn't sure if I'm the father. It was only a few weeks into our relationship. I didn't deal with any of that very well. I was already falling for her, and the thought of her being with someone else threw me for a loop."

He pauses and pours himself a cup of coffee.

He raises the pot in my direction, "Want some?"

I shake my head and wait for him to return to the story. There must be more to this.

"Everything about that time made me feel trapped. Trapped by COVID, trapped by my job, trapped by the pregnancy. It was a lousy feeling. If it was my responsibility, my child, I knew what I should do, regardless of whether I felt ready or trapped, but the thought that it might not be mine took over. I finally told her I needed a break. I took some time off work, I went to see Joseph in Malta, and while away, I realized that I really did love her and didn't want to run away from her. But, at the same time, I wanted to come home, come here, be close to my family. I wanted to be with you, Beth, Eric. Totally torn between staying there or returning, I called my sister one night. Kristy read me the riot act. You know her, she never minces words."

"I do know her, so I guess I'm not surprised. What did she say?"

"She thought I was way off base—called me selfish and too proud for my own good. She not so gently reminded me that family and love for kids isn't dependent on DNA. She told me that if Gabby and I truly loved one another, couldn't I love her child—mine or not? I didn't have an answer and it pissed Kristy off. I think she said something like, 'Well, then maybe Gabby is better off without your sorry ass anyway' and hung up on me. I felt so damn alone and more confused than ever."

I wish he'd contacted me, shared some of this then, but cannot, will not say that. "I bet. New relationships, unexpected pregnancies are tough under the best circumstances, and this was far from the best."

"Anyway, thinking things would be better if we answered the question of fatherhood, Gabby scheduled a DNA test. I hadn't pressured her, but she thought it was best. Then, things changed again. The opening of the borders made me focus on a decision about getting home. As you already know, a position opened up stateside at our company, so Gabby and I decided together that I'd come back. We'd figure out the rest later. It became clear to me a little late that I didn't want to split up, I wanted us to be together. Just when I got my head together, her doubts kicked in. Like did she really want to live in the U.S.? Leave her family and friends there to be with my family?"

He looks down at his phone.

"That's her texting me to tell me she's at the park and will be back soon. Let me finish the story before she gets back."

"Everett, it's not necessary. This sounds so personal; I don't need to know every detail."

He puts his phone back on the counter and continues.

"I know it's not necessary, but I want to tell you. It hasn't made a lot of sense to me sometimes, so maybe saying it aloud will help. When she voiced those doubts, I told her to forget the DNA test, that it didn't matter to me. Just like Kristy had said— of all people, I should know that family can be those with whom we share biological origins, or those who care for us, or both. Family is about heartfelt connections, not DNA."

A moment of pride kicks in when he voices his realization. Hearing my child speak about family connections softens the rough edges of his story, at least for a moment.

"When we got the news that I should leave, I pretty much begged her to come to the U.S. She still wasn't sure, but urged me to get home while I could. Once I got here, we really missed one another. As you know, she even asked me to come back. It was like ping-pong there for a bit. When I told her I just could not leave again, she decided to come and got a ticket."

He's distracted by another text coming in on his phone, but he turns it off and continues.

"Next thing I knew, she called me on her way here. She'd gone to the doctor and he gave her two choices—leave immediately or not until after she delivered. I was in shock for many reasons, not the least of which was because I hadn't had the chance to tell you or Beth about the baby or Gabby coming."

"It must have thrown you way off to have her plans change so suddenly. I get why you wanted to have some time to talk with her when she first arrived. What was the reason for the doctor's order? Just being cautious?"

"She says things are good. He just thought maybe she's a little further along or going to go early, or I don't know. I'll feel better once we get to a doctor here and figure out our next steps—work, place to live, it's overwhelming."

"I'm sure it is. You sounded distraught when you were on the phone with Kristy a little bit ago. What was that all about?"

"She thinks I'm being too cautious about making plans, more commitments. She thinks it should all be so easy. I should ask Gabby to marry me, we should get a house together, Beth needs a regular family and routine. Basically, she wants to tell me how to live my life. It made me mad and I snapped at her. Gabby heard some of it and got upset. She doesn't like disagreements, and I think she wants things to settle down and be calm. She's also very worried about what you think of her. We probably need to all talk together when she gets back, no more putting it off. It's stressing her out thinking that you may disapprove."

I shake my head and look him straight in the eye, "Everett, whether we have the chance to talk tonight or not, feel free to tell her my story. Reassure her—I'm the last one to weigh in on other people's private lives. I don't have any right to approve or disapprove of this. Like I told her the other night—anyone who's important to one of my kids is important to me. We'll figure the rest out as it comes."

"She does know your story, our story. That's exactly why she's worried about your opinion. She feels badly that you had a baby so young with so little support, and that she is much older and should know better than to be in the position of not being sure of the father. She's ashamed."

"Then you need to help her shake that off. No one other than you two needs to know that there was ever any doubt about paternity—it's no one's business. And guess what? I know, deep in my heart, that the minute you see that little person, your doubt will disappear. You'll do this together, in whatever way works out best for the four of you. Beth is super excited about being a big sister. She asks me a new question about it every day."

The sound of the front door causes us both to stand up and head to the other room just in time to see Gabby and Beth come through. Beth is using a crutch in one hand and her other arm is leaning on Gabby.

"Gamma, Daddy, look who I found when Brittany's mother dropped me off. Gabby coming back from the magic butterfly garden. She said that three butterflies sat on the bench next to her!"

The smiles on both their faces tell me all I need to know.

"Guess what I told her? I said those butterflies were Auntie Emma telling her 'Welcome to the family!'"

With that declaration, Everett puts his arms out and pulls the two of them in close. I feel tears welling up in my eyes and walk over to stand nearby and wait. If Beth and Emma can welcome Gabby with open hearts, so can I. When he releases them, I place my hand on Gabby's shoulders and say, "Yes, dear, welcome. I'm happy Emma's spirit appeared to you today."

"It was beautiful—I'm honored. Everett and Beth told me about her. It's a sad thing that she went to the other place too soon, too young. A mother should never have to say goodbye to her child that way."

"You are so very right. It's harder some days than others. Signs from her make it just slightly more tolerable."

Beth nudges Gabby and points toward the bookshelves.

"I want to show you pictures of her. She's very pretty."

Gabby looks at me, asking permission with her eyes.

"Yes, please, go ahead and show her, Beth. I need to finish an email that is still open on my laptop. Maybe I'll join you after that."

They head to the sofa to look at photos and Everett follows me into the kitchen.

He puts his cup in the sink, rummages around in the pantry closet, then rubs his hands together. I'm still learning about my son—the hand rubbing is a sure signal that there is something he needs to say.

"There's one more thing, Mom. Probably also falls in the category of me waiting futilely for the perfect time when there is no such thing. Joseph wants to visit when the baby is born. Says he wants to do things right from now on and be involved with his grandchild from the beginning. I haven't answered him yet, but can't put him off much longer."

"That's up to you—you and Gabby. The two of you need to figure out if you're ready for a visitor and when. Better start now, because that will be self-preservation once the little one is here. It's kind of you to consider his wishes to be more connected to you and your growing family, but early on is tough with a baby. In case you don't remember, your life will be in an upheaval. Sure, it's a happy event, but it takes work to adjust. If you two want him to visit, I'll support you however I can. My opinion—you have many more important things to consider before this little one makes his or her arrival."

The list of those things goes on and on in my mind—where are they going to live, what about Gabby's job, all kinds of baby-related decisions, to name a few. I think Joseph visiting is low priority.

"Thanks for that. I do need to learn to prioritize some of this stuff, and pretty darn quickly. What did we call that when we planned for Beth to come here? A strategy meeting? Guess we need one."

"Exactly. And none too soon!"

32

Fill your paper with the breathings of your heart.
WILLIAM WORDSWORTH

As it turns out, it's Beth's questions after dinner that actually get the conversation going sooner than later. She suddenly asks, "Where is the baby going to sleep? I think there's room for a crib in my room. And is this baby a he or she? Am I having a brother or a sister?"

In all the fuss, I hadn't even thought to ask if they had any gender information. Leave it to Beth. Now, I'm curious.

Gabby looks at Everett and he gives her an almost imperceptible nod.

"Those are good questions, Beth. The answer to both is that we don't know. We didn't ask to find out if it's a boy or girl because we will love this new little person regardless. And we still don't know about bedrooms. We need to talk more to each other, to you, to your grandma about where we will be located when he or she comes."

Beth scrunches her forehead, purses her lips and turns her head toward me.

"Can't we all live here, Gamma? I think there's plenty of room, and you like babies, right?"

In spite of being put on the spot, all I can come out with is a burst of laughter. I've been wondering, Everett's been waiting for the perfect time to reveal or ask things, but leave it to this kid to just spit it out with unabashed curiosity.

Everett looks like he just sucked on a grapefruit peel, which makes me laugh harder.

"Mom, don't laugh at her. Beth, this is Gamma's house, not ours. She's been nice enough to let us stay, but it was never going to be our permanent house."

The scolding from Everett aids in my effort to stop laughing at her innocent boldness. "Beth, come here, little sunshine. This certainly is your home right now, and for as long as you need it to be. Daddy and Gabby have more to think about before they can answer. They need to figure out jobs, as well as what is best for you and the new addition. Actually, Daddy and I said earlier that we need to have a strategy meeting about all of this. We figured out a good solution last time we had a housing dilemma, right? I'm sure we can do it again."

Her wrinkled brow straightens out some as she explains to Gabby, "We needed to make plans when Daddy was leaving for Italy because we used to live in New York City. Wait, Daddy, are we going back to our old apartment? I'm not sure what I think about that."

Since Everett seems tongue-tied yet again, Gabby offers, "I saw pictures of when you used to live in New York. It looked nice, but I'm not sure if we want to be in such a big city. That's why talking about a plan is a good thing. What do you think we should do, Beth?"

Now, Everett jumps off his chair and speaks up. "Whoa, wait, everybody. I feel outnumbered by you three, or at least, out-talked. We're still waiting to get more information about what is realistic for work, especially Gabby's job. Once we know that, we'll be able to come up with answers about living arrangements."

He's right on one hand, but they really don't have a lot of time to wait. After all, babies rarely come right on time, and her doctor in Italy thought she might be early. As hard as I'm trying to keep my opinions to myself, I'm compelled to interject. "This decision is honestly none of my business, except I want to let you know that you can stay as long as you need to. I'm sure you want to get out on your own at some point, but making housing decisions quickly is rarely a smart thing to do. So, use this house as a base to keep you from doing something rash. If it's a few months, Beth's right, we'll be fine. If it has to be longer, you can renovate the basement into an apartment if you want!"

Everett finally relaxes and his face softens. "That's very generous. I don't want to take advantage, and I need to figure out the New York apartment. But if this baby gets impatient, we may not have enough time to consider things carefully. Thank you, Mom."

Gabby leans over as best she can to put an arm around me. "I'm so grateful. We do want to have our own place, but I do not think there's time before there's one more of us. My mother always said to trust your body and mine is saying some things I've never heard from it before. Not that I have any experience with how I'm feeling right now. And, about that, I'm very tired. I don't want to be rude, but I need to go to bed."

She kisses Everett, blows a kiss to Beth, and makes her slow walk to the stairs.

I look at the clock and realize she isn't the only one.

"Beth, you need to skedaddle yourself. I'll finish in the kitchen, Everett, so you can be with your ladies."

Kitchen chores allow my mind to settle. It seems like a very long time since I've had the time to be alone with my thoughts. I dreaded my alone thoughts while Eric was away and after Emma died, but every now and then, solitary time can be self-healing time. It's gotten quiet upstairs, and I savor these moments.

Reflecting on our last few conversations, it strikes me that during those times, I've been so focused on what Everett has to say, what he has done so far, and what he intends to do next, that I may not have been listening enough to Gabby. She has expressed genuine emotions, been considerate of me and my feelings, and even revealed some of her uncertainty. Damn, I've been insensitive. This woman is pregnant, for what I think is the first time, she's away from her parents and whatever other family she has in Italy, and she's about to start living in another country. She's been reaching out and I've not reached back. I wonder if Hilary has talked to her at all? Maybe helped her with the doctor search or shopping? I need to text Hilary in the morning. And geez, we should plan a shower for her, make her and this baby feel welcome, let them know we're excited and willing to support her.

I grab paper and pen and begin a list. The very act of writing, then contemplating, then writing again reminds me of my pledge, what, almost a year ago? A pledge to myself to start journaling again. What's that old phrase about "paved with good intentions"? It was before all this pandemic crap set in. Somewhere along the road of the last year, my intentions went down the tubes. *All right then, Larissa, find that journal pledge and write something this minute.*

I rummage through several drawers that totally deserve the title my mother used to use, *junk drawers*. They are repositories for everything from batteries to playing cards to rubber bands. In the third one, under an eleven-month-old power bill and my refrigerator warranty, I find two journals. The one I dug out recently from the time of my first pregnancy is on top. Right below it is the one from, let's see, also eleven months ago. They must have gotten tossed in this heap at the same time.

Flipping open the first page to read my pledge, my eyes fall on the list of family members. Reading the list, my eyes mist over. At that time, we didn't yet have Benjamin, of course Gabby wasn't in our lives, and so there was one grandchild, only Beth. The count is about to go to three. This should be motivation to write, to write so that someday, if they choose, my family will know about me, my thoughts. More importantly, maybe I can help them know of my profound love for them, give them a window into my soul. That's what this quiet time does—gives my soul time to rejuvenate, to come to the surface and quiet the thoughts. Those thoughts that are always scrambling around for attention. In the quiet, they take a back seat and the power of my inner essence can prevail.

My hand and the pen in it become the conduit for my soul. It's as if the physical motions necessary to get words on the paper come from somewhere above and beyond my conscious mind. Is this how Monica felt when writing the words and melody for the song? Is this how artists feel when they are creating something that comes from a place deep inside?

An awareness of hand cramping prompts me to glance at the clock. Well over an hour has passed during this outpouring. I tilt my head back, blink my eyes open and shut a few times, grasp and ungrasp my fingers. I smile to myself as a feeling of ease sets in at the same time as a sense of accomplishment. I didn't consciously seek out these quiet moments, they sought out me. They taught me, reminded me how important alone time can be. I've been surrounding myself with people and activity to keep busy, to distract myself, at the cost of depriving my soul of vital nourishment.

I'm tired, but I skim the words on the pages. Yes, this was a needed outpouring. Feelings about Steven, Eric, Emma, Beth,

Everett fill the lines of the pastel pages. Ideas I must share with Monica are woven in between, and even future wishes for all these loved ones emerge. I close the precious book and tap the cover.

Halfway up the stairs to go to bed, I go back down and grab the journal. It is not going to be relegated to the junk drawer this time. It's coming upstairs to my nightstand. The first thing I see in the morning, the last thing I see at night, and I'll probably get glimpses many times during the day. I'm taking an action that will solidify my intention.

I awake feeling exhilarated and calm at the same time. Whatever soul-feeding happened last night, the effects carry over until morning. In short, I'm ready for whatever the day brings. The journal on the nightstand jolts the memory of a dream. A dream of a young woman. Her facial features are not fully visible, but the hair is unmistakable. The thick curls could only belong to Beth, but the figure is definitely an adult. It must be her, many years from now. She's sitting on a window seat reading, with water behind her. It looks like the lagoon on Hutchinson Island. Her finger is moving along horizontally, following a line in the book. No, it's *this* journal. Oh my gosh, I need to write the dream down right this moment. It's a sign of what's to come, and I need to remember it. I finish scribbling and say out loud to myself, "All right, Larissa. You're committed to writing for your grandchildren's future. No lame excuses, no unfulfilled intentions."

The smell of nutmeg and cinnamon urges me to get dressed. Something, someone must be baking, maybe apple muffins? I haven't awakened to the smell of someone else's baked goods, since—must be since my mother baked for me. A long time to go without that pleasure.

The closer I get to the kitchen, the more luscious the smell. Another of my senses fills with warmth as I see Gabby and Beth turning on the oven light to peek.

"Something smells delicious down here!"

When she hears me, Beth squeals, "Surprise! We were up early and decided to make breakfast for you and Daddy. Gabby says she always has sweet things for breakfast in Italy, so we decided muffins instead of eggs."

I pour coffee and watch them take the muffins out to cool, Gabby gently guarding Beth from getting burned while allowing her to help. She's going to make a good mamma.

Gabby and Everett walk Beth to school and I take the opportunity to call Hilary.

She answers on the fourth ring, sounding breathless.

"Can you talk, Hilary? Just for a few minutes?"

"Yes, definitely. I was playing with Benjamin on the floor and heard my phone ringing in the other room. I ran so I didn't leave him long. What's up?"

I share my musings about Gabby and ask what she thinks.

"Oh, I don't think you've been insensitive. After all, it's been kind of a whirlwind. I did call my OB and they agreed to take her even though they're not officially taking new patients. I think she's going in sometime soon."

"Oh, good, that's sweet of you. What do you think about a baby shower? Shall we plan one? A lot of countries outside the U.S. don't traditionally do them, but it could be a nice way to welcome her."

"It's not like she's real old-school, she's a worldly woman. I think she'd like it. Plus, an all-ladies gathering might be fun for her. I have two friends I've been thinking she might like to get to know—one just had a baby a month ago and one is due a few weeks after her. Let's do it. Want me to ask her about dates?"

We talk a few more minutes, assigning tasks and brainstorming a guest list. I don't want to overwhelm Gabby, but it's a loving way to welcome her to this country and to show we are excited for them.

Happy to have that decided, I move on to clear up my work emails. I spot Monica's address in the *From* column and click on it. Her message is short, "Maybe I'll be writing those checks soon," and the link below it goes to the Billboard website. Really? What? I click on the link and see that "Smiles from Her Heart" is in the top one hundred.

33

When I truly care for someone,
their mistakes never change my feelings,
because it's the mind that gets angry,
but the heart still cares.

UNATTRIBUTED

Looking to share the success of "Smiles," it dawns on me that no one is around—Everett and Gabby have been gone a long while. I expected them to come right back after dropping Beth off. This news is too awesome to keep to myself and I don't want to interrupt Eric at work. Without even thinking, I dial Steven's number.

Steven is as enthusiastic about the song news as I am. He asks me to forward the email and link so he can see it himself.

He receives it quickly and I hear a whistle of admiration on his end. "I can't believe that Billboard is still the gold standard. We grew up thinking Billboard was the authority on all things in pop music. What does Monica's comment about charity donations mean?"

"Oh, Steven, back when I shared a bunch of my concerns with her, Monica made a lovely offer. She said that if the song ever really earned substantial revenue, that she'd like to make donations to a charity in Emma's honor. It was a touching thought, and I suggested possible recipients."

After I give him the run-down of what the three non-profits are all about, he wonders out loud, "Those would be touching tributes for sure. With a little publicity, maybe others would want to donate to them, too. The song could have a big impact in yet another way—let's hope!"

He switches topics and asks about the growing number of houseguests under my roof. "Is everyone settled in, finding their space? Or tripping over one another?"

I fill him in on our last couple of days and some of what has transpired, carefully leaving out the questions around paternity. Steven is as close to us as anyone, but those details are only their business.

"I don't know why I was having a hard time with their situation. Maybe because initially, it didn't seem like they were being totally forthcoming. Anyway, once the story finally came out, I put myself in Gabby's shoes for the first time. I'd been thinking more about myself and Beth, than her perspective. There's a lot to navigate in the next month or whenever the baby comes, not the least of which is the living situation. They want to get out on their own, but the time frame makes it nearly impossible. She, they, don't need any more stress. Thankfully, Hilary got her an appointment with her doctor, so they may know more after that."

There's a brief pause in the conversation before Steven clears his throat and responds.

"Please don't read anything into this. It's a practical offer, nothing else. I have a ton of extra space in this house. I've finished renovating three of the four bedrooms—one is even a kid's room, for when Benjamin visits. Those bedrooms are all on the opposite side of the house from mine, like a suite of rooms. My point is, if either they need to spread out, or if you want to give them private space at your house and come stay here temporarily, it's an open offer."

My reply is immediate.

"It's too generous, Steven. It's kind of you, but we'll figure it out."

"You're pushing me away, Larissa. I hear it in your voice. I said it's practical, nothing more. I can even go visit Nina for a few weeks or go up to New York and see friends. Don't shut me down before you consider it, or let Everett consider it. Friends and family help each other, right? Isn't that part of the deal?"

Scribbling circles over and over on the note pad next to me, I consider his words. There's some truth to what he says.

"I apologize. I did shut you down, maybe afraid to accept your kindness because it might come with strings attached. That's not fair of me. If anyone is going to make a short-term move, I might be able to stay with Eric and Hilary, or even Renee, and give them the house for the first few weeks. I should be thanking you for making me think of other possibilities."

The call ends on a good note in spite of my overreaction to his offer. Steven means well. But moving into his house? Not me, not now. Not even for a temporary fix. Fix one thing and complicate another.

I glance at the time on my phone again and wonder about Everett. Here's the problem, right? When we're all under the same roof, I worry about every part of their lives. Do they really need a hovering mother while they're trying to get used to the four of them as a family? If we live in separate places, I only know what they want me to know. Steven's right, they're going to need their space. For now, I'm unable to help myself; I text Everett.

He responds right away with, "Can't talk right now, seeing the doctor." Huh—guess I don't know as much as I thought. Had no clue the appointment was today. He follows it up with, "Eric picked us up after we left Beth at school; see you later." Well, good, I can put the worrying aside and accomplish a few things on my to-do list.

When I get back home later, there's an unfamiliar car in the driveway. As I walk in the door, Eric's somewhat muffled voice comes from the kitchen, "What do you think of Everett's new ride, Mom? Think it's big enough for--"

As they stumble into the living room, I see Eric and Everett engaged in a playful, rather fake-looking sparring match, both laughing and swatting at each other.

Everett jokingly admonishes, "Can't you keep quiet about anything?"

Eric's comeback is, "What about you? Can't you *tell* anybody anything? Everything is all top secret with you!"

A few more swats and playful barbs go back and forth before they straighten up a bit. Their tussling and teasing episode is like that of two brothers who've spent their lives together. And, although it's obviously in good fun, there's truth in each obser-vation. I hadn't thought about the contrast before, but it's real. Brothers raised in totally different environments, in households dealing with life in totally disparate ways. One an open book, the other a closed clam.

"I took Everett and Gabby to see my friend who sells used cars. Arnie hooked them up with that SUV—a real grocery getter, that one." He gets in another jab at Everett's upper arm.

I can't help but laugh at the apt nickname, the same one Eric and Emma gave to my various cars over the years. They constantly lobbied for something cooler, and I always made the same functional choice.

Unruffled, Everett retorts, "Might be time for you to get something more practical, little brother. Benjamin should be in a safe car when Hilary drives him around town. Admit it, you guys need a family vehicle too. No more sleek wheels for you."

I don't want to interrupt their banter, it's fun to watch. I'm happy that they have one another, happier than I dare express right now. I'd likely start a sob fest and change the whole mood.

I smile and reach for Everett.

"Good for you. I'm sure it's been a pain borrowing cars or walking everywhere. How was the doctor appointment? Where are Gabby and Beth?"

"Beth went over to Isabel's to play with Lisa. Gabby's napping. The appointment was good, she liked the doctor. And, uh, there is some news to share. I'd wait for Gabby, but, well, like I learned the other day—no such thing as perfect timing. This doctor confirmed why the other one in Italy wanted her to travel sooner than later."

Eric prods, "Come on, Ev, you can do better than that. Spill the whole story at once, not the little tidbits—it's like you leave breadcrumbs for everyone to figure out your stories."

Everett chuckles, shakes his head, and follows Eric's lead.

"Looks like we're having two, she's having twins."

Do the surprises ever stop? My voice rises an octave. "You're just hearing this now, at this late point in her pregnancy? Didn't they do ultrasounds before this?"

"Well, there was some confusion. Remember when I said that I was having my doubts?"

A voice from halfway up the stairs interrupts the conversation. "Stop, Everett, stop protecting me. I'll tell your mother and your brother. I'm the one who wasn't entirely truthful, let me tell them and stop blaming yourself."

Eric starts to interject, "Just like I said--"

"Not now, Eric. Let her speak." I wave Gabby the rest of the way down the stairs and meet her at the bottom one.

Her dark eyes focus on me with the same intensity they'd had the other day. "I haven't been entirely truthful, with you or Everett. I hope you can forgive me. I think Everett told you that at first, he was not happy about the pregnancy. It was a surprise to both of us, and we had some arguments about it. Things were even harder because of our work situation. It was not a happy time. There were days when I was ready to cut off our relationship and just do it on my own. So, I didn't always tell him about the appointments, about my progress. I even skipped a couple of doctor appointments. Stupid, but I felt everything was spinning outside my control. If I didn't go to the doctor, it wasn't real."

Everett walks up behind her and reassuringly puts his hands on her shoulders.

"When Everett left to come back here, even though I knew he had to, I resented him leaving. I couldn't decide what I wanted. One day, I'd tell him I was on my way, the next I'd change my mind and want to just do this on my own. I couldn't imagine a life here. I was going to do it myself if he was going to be in another country. Looking back, that was also stupid, inconsiderate. But at the time, I wanted to insulate myself until I figured it all out."

She continues. "It wasn't long until I missed him more than I could stand. I pled with him to come back. But I knew I should make plans to come here. I wasn't sure what his family—you—would think. Finally, he and I discussed me coming. I put things into motion for a timetable we agreed on—giving me time to make a smooth work transition and him time to tell all of you more about me and my pregnancy."

Everett interrupts her. "Mom, I wanted to do this right for everyone. I didn't want to spring it on Beth the minute I got back that I was in love with a woman from Italy, or that she was going to have a sibling. I wanted to find a place for us to live and not impose on you any more than I already had."

"Right, exactly." Gabby is nodding her head. "And that's what I wanted, too. Who wants to meet a new family halfway across the world when they are not prepared? Heck, you'd just gotten Everett back from a long absence, in the middle of the world being upside down."

Gabby stops and takes a deep breath, rubbing her middle as if she's already calming the little one, or ones.

"I went to my doctor and he sat me down to—what do you say—'knock some sense into me'? He'd told me there were two babies earlier. I didn't believe him. I told him it was not possible. I'd been taught to trust what your body tells you. Wouldn't I know, wouldn't I feel them both? This time he said that whether I believed him or not, it would be unsafe to travel after a certain point. The doctor's declaration changed the timetable, but I didn't tell Everett why. I wanted to tell him the news about twins in person."

She drops her head at her admission, and Everett steps in. "She just got her ticket and came. I didn't know about the twins until after she got here, after you were all back from your trip to see the butterflies. That's why it was so hard to tell you the whole story. I was basically torn. Part of me was mad at Gabby for holding back the truth, the other part was just happy she got here."

"Larissa, I need to say this. We were both being dumb. My grandmother once told me there are two ways to live your life: with your heart as a sponge or with your heart as a clam. If it's as a sponge, you'll have many joys by opening up and allowing others in, but there will be hurts that come with being open. Or you can have a closed heart, tight as a clam. You might not get hurt as often, but you will miss love and companionship, and all that comes with those. So, for a long time, I did as she suggested and lived like the sponge. But, then, I was hurt by someone a few years ago and closed up like the clam."

Nodding his head in agreement, Everett offers, "Yeah, and I started out more like a clam. I'd been trying to open up more with you, Beth, and Gabby, but it doesn't come easily for me. So, when she closed up about the details, so did I. She's right, we were both missing too much that way. It was dumb, and lonely, to close up."

While they're explaining, I'm marveling. I'd never heard Gabby's grandmother's saying, but only moments ago during the brothers' sparring, I'd thought of Everett's personality as closed like a clam.

Eric has been listening quietly in the background as they share what's been going on. Having held himself back as long as he could, he walks over to the two of them and proclaims, "Let me give you some advice from someone who's been in this family since day one. If you close up like a clam, Mom's just going to keep trying to pry you open—sometimes gently, sometimes with the force of a crowbar. My suggestion—you can't fight a crowbar—be the sponge, open up, and soak in all the love you possibly can. It's worth it."

There is absolutely nothing for me to add. I could protest the crowbar analogy, but why bother? The important stuff has been said and Beth is expected home any minute.

Clearing my throat, I offer, "Thank you for sharing, you guys. Now my head is spinning. Like I said the other night, none of this is easy stuff."

The need to veer away from the intimacies of Everett and Gabby's last few months motivate me to talk about more practical things.

"In the end, these details that got you to this point are irrelevant compared to what needs to happen next. We were talking yesterday, or whenever—I'm kinda losing track of the days—about living arrangements. It occurred to me, with a suggestion from a certain someone close to us, that we could make some changes and figure out a way for this new, growing family to have some time to themselves without needing to spend precious time right now looking for something to rent or buy. Steven offered his house as an option."

I explain the conversation and options. Before anyone has the chance to respond, Beth comes to the door yelling, "Gamma, Isabel is out in the car and wants to say hi—can you come out here?"

Isabel rolls the car window down and says, "She was great, as usual. They had snacks about an hour ago. What's going on over here? All good?"

"It's a little hard to capture succinctly, but I can honestly say things are fine. Lots of new developments. I guess that's natural with so many people under this roof now, right? I'd love to catch up with you sometime soon." We hug, she backs out of the driveway, and I watch her for a minute. It strikes me yet again how blessed I am to have kind, ever-present friends in my life. Whether it was holding me as I sobbed over my daughter or taking my granddaughter home after school for a snack and playtime, Isabel and Renee have my back. And Steven, well, he has risen to the late-life discovery of Eric as his son, and now he's offering to help when my other son is in need. The housing offer speaks to the wonderful man that he is.

I walk into yet another precious scene. Gabby and Everett are showing an ultrasound image to Eric and Beth, pointing out to Beth how they know that there are two babies. She looks up at me with eyes so wide, it looks like they could pop right out of her head.

"Gamma, did you see this? Them?"

She soaks up every detail that they share with her. Eric comes over to where I'm standing to speak with me privately.

With one arm around my neck, he puts a finger under my chin and teases, "So, Dad offered for you to go live with him? What's up with you two? Ever since you got back from Callaway Gardens, when he's around, you get a look on your face I've never seen before. Is there something you need to tell me?"

I wrestle myself away from his embrace, then shake my head.

"Don't go letting your imagination run away. I'm not going to live with him, Eric. He offered to help out with a crowded household until they can figure things out. I don't think that's how it's going to go, but it made me realize there may be other options than them rushing to find a place. Heck, I could come stay with you, or go to Renee's, right? I've got options."

With that, he backs away further, wrinkles his brow and starts to laugh.

"Yeah, I guess you do. Can't blame a guy for trying, right?"

Returning his banter, I add, "Which guy? Your dad for coming up with the idea, or you for promoting it?"

34

Hilary and I accelerate the baby shower planning. We alter the title of the electronic invite to "Welcome to Double Trouble" and include some other cute rhymes to let the guests know there will be two. The shower will be at Hilary and Eric's house. There's too little time to secure a venue elsewhere and my house is quickly feeling less spacious than ever before.

I've included Beth in the planning as much as possible because she is so excited. She loves that it is all girls planning and attending. She whispers about the details whenever Gabby is around. She tells everyone, everywhere we go, that she's going to have two babies in her house—a brother and a sister. Her pure joy is contagious, and serves to get me through the far too many what-ifs that race through my mind daily.

I'm waiting in the school parking lot for her. We're meeting Hilary and Benjamin (Beth agrees that he can come along, in spite of being a boy, because he's so little) at the party store to pick out all the decorations. The second I spot her, I can tell that something is wrong. Her steps, that are always spring-loaded with energy, are slow, with her feet barely leaving the ground. I jump out of my car to see what's going on. As I get closer, I see the tell-tale white, salty streaks of tears crusted on her face.

"Hey, little sunshine girl, what's the matter?"

She stops in her tracks, looks up at me, shakes her head side to side and continues walking toward the car.

This time, I kneel down in front of her and pull her into my arms. After a minute or two she answers, "A boy said a mean thing again."

"Oh no, were they teasing Brittany?" I thought we had put all of that behind us.

"No, they were mean to me. At sharing time, I told my teacher and class that I'm going to have a baby brother and sister. The teacher said congratulations and the kids all clapped."

"That sounds nice, I bet you felt good."

"Yeah, but then at recess, one kid's big brother came over and said, 'You can't have a brother and sister cuz your mom's dead, stupid. They're only gonna be half, and you'll just be a half-sister.'"

My stomach is immediately in knots and my fists are clenched. Where in the world do these kids come up with these hurtful things?

"Oh, honey, that is mean. But it only shows he doesn't know what he's talking about."

"My mamma is dead, but why does that make the babies and me only half?"

"It's hard to explain, but you know that sometimes brothers and sisters share the same mama and the same daddy. When they only share one parent, some people call that *half*. But a lot of us never think that way or use those words. Your daddy and Eric do not have the same daddy, but they're both my sons. We always say they're brothers, not half."

"Half makes it sound like the person isn't as good as a whole. I don't like it."

"I don't like it either, honey. I guess sometimes words make things harder to understand rather than easier. It's an important lesson to learn to use our words carefully. Maybe the boy didn't realize saying that could be hurtful."

"Yeah, maybe. Except he laughed. The same way he laughed when he told Louis that Renee isn't his real mommy. That made Louis cry too."

"I can see why." I wonder if Renee knows about that? Do we need to go back to the school principal?

"Is Gabby going to be my mommy?"

Caught off guard, I offer, "I think that's up to you, your daddy, and Gabby. There's been a lot of changes the last few weeks, huh? Too many decisions to make at once. I can tell you one thing from watching you and Gabby together. It's clear to me that you like each other very much. You may even be starting to love each other. That's what's really important. The rest will figure itself out, give it time."

"I do like her. Gabby listens to me."

Such a simple, yet profound comment. Tells me everything I need to know for now in only four words.

Beth's smile returns. She grabs my hand and drags me toward the car.

"Let's go find Aunt Hilary and Benjamin. I want to see the party store and the pretty stuff they have."

Shopping is quite the project with Hilary pushing the stroller and Beth wanting to push the shopping cart. Hilary packs the bags of pink, blue, and lavender paper products in her car. Beth and I agree to be at her house a few hours before the guests to set everything up. Hilary thanks us and adds that Eric, Benjamin, and Everett are going to lunch and the zoo, to give the ladies the run of the house for the shower.

After she goes to bed, I tell Everett and Gabby about how Beth was feeling when I picked her up after school.

Predictably, Everett is indignant. "What the heck? Isn't that just weird for a kid to say?"

Gabby puts her hand on Everett's elbow and says, "It is. But maybe he has been in a situation where he or someone he cared about was called a half-sibling and it hurt him. Many people hurt others when they've been hurt themselves."

"Oh, babe, you're so kind. I remember when someone told me that Kristy wasn't really my sister because I was adopted. I threw the first punch and blackened that kid's eye. My mom, Harriett, made me apologize, but I didn't really mean it. I thought the guy was a jerk the rest of the time we were in school together."

"Well then, I guess the kid is lucky Beth told Larissa instead of you. Could have been a nasty scene."

The image of that scene relieves the tension. He clarifies, "Oh, come on, I wouldn't have gone after the kid. I guess you're right, though. Once a kid is hurt, they sometimes hurt others."

"You both might also want to know that she asked me something else. I told her it's something that's between the three of you, not me. Anyway, she asked if Gabby is going to be her mother. You may want to be prepared for that one—if you can be."

They look at one another and Everett answers, "Thanks for the heads-up. These kids don't let anything go, do they?"

The house is loud and chaotic the next morning as Beth and I prepare to go to Hilary's early, and Everett and Gabby work out the rest of the schedule. With hugs all around, we hustle out the door to pick up the cake and take care of party preparations.

Three hours later, the house is fully adorned with yesterday's purchases. Snacks, beverages, and extra chairs are carefully arranged throughout the great room. We pick a comfy chair to put right in the middle of the space for Gabby, so that she can rest and see everyone at the same time.

All of the guests have arrived, but still no Gabby. I text Everett to check on them, but a minute or so later, they walk in the door. I notice she has one arm on Everett's and her other is at the small of her back. I lead them straight to the designated chair and she settles in.

Almost immediately, Beth starts squealing, "When can she open the presents? There's lots of big ones! Take a picture of the packages, Gamma. Then can she open them? They're so pretty!"

I take the photo as suggested and ask Gabby if I can get her anything before we start.

She starts to shake her head, but then says, "Yes, actually, I think I need more water." She grimaces and shifts her body around in the chair before smiling up at me.

Poor thing. She's at that stage where she never looks fully comfortable.

About halfway through the enormous pile of carefully wrapped boxes and gift bags, Gabby stands and leaves the room, I assume to use the restroom.

After several minutes, I notice that it's been a rather long time since she left. Not wanting to intrude on her privacy, but concerned, I quietly go after her and knock on the door. There is no response except a long, low groan.

"Gabby, are you all right? Do you need anything?"

Silence, then another groan.

I open the door to find her sitting on the floor, head leaning against the vanity and more of the same noises coming from her. I squat down and take her hand in mine.

"Larissa, there are pains. I think something is happening. It's too early, the doctor said five more weeks. My back hurts. Can you call Everett? I'm scared, Larissa."

"Don't be scared, I'm here and we will help you."

By this time, Hilary and Isabel are at the door as well.

"Hilary, maybe you and Is can take Gabby into the den to lie down. She'd like me to call Everett. Then, can you give me the doctor's number? I think we need to call him as well."

They do as suggested and slowly help Gabby into the other room. I make the calls, then text Renee rather than announcing the new development to the roomful of ladies. I suggest she lets Beth open a few of the presents to keep things rolling.

Everett answers immediately, "Geez—yes, call the doctor. Eric and I are on the way."

The receptionist at the answering center says they will have the doctor call me. I pick up the call before the first ring is even complete and describe Gabby's current status to the doctor.

He replies, "Yes, she might be early, but some of the records from her previous doctor are not so clear. With twins, you never know. Take her to the hospital and I'll meet her there."

I meet my sons in the driveway with the news that Everett needs to get Gabby to the hospital. Visibly concerned, he leads her to the front entrance slowly, with her groaning and moaning the whole way. The whole houseful of women holler goodbye as he helps her toward the car. Eric leaves Benjamin with us and does the driving so that Everett can sit with Gabby.

We all stare at one another for a few minutes as the plans for finishing the presents, playing games, and eating now seem unimportant. Yet, what can we really do? Looking around, I finally say, "How about we eat while we wait to hear from Everett or Eric? It could be awhile, and you must be hungry. We'll finish heating the casseroles and call you to the buffet in a few minutes."

Once dinner is finished, several people prepare to leave. As they head out the door, each one says some variation of "Keep us posted." I make the appropriate assurances with no idea when or what that might entail. After finishing kitchen cleanup, Beth and I stack the presents to take them back to the house.

Thanking Hilary one more time for all she did, we figure it's time to go home. We'd all hoped to hear by now, but my phone has been silent.

There are headlights in the driveway and Eric comes running up the sidewalk. "They're admitting her. Guess it might be time for our newest family members to make their appearance!"

35

December, 2020

*This happiness consisted of nothing else
but the harmony of the few things
around me with my own existence,
a feeling of contentment and well-being
that needed no changes and no intensification.*
HERMANN HESSE

Amazing—another Christmas is about to roll around. Another year without Emma. Another year to learn the lesson that time goes on, and life must go on, regardless of those who will not be with us. Where did the year go? Last year, Beth and Everett spent their first Christmas with us. Last year, we heard Monica sing "Smiles from Her Heart" for the first time. Last year, there was no little Benjamin, and no twins.

Yes, amazing, but right now, there's no more time for musing. I've got to get this house back in order—it's been weeks since I was alone in my own space. I have to admit, as happy as I was to let Everett and his family take over, there is an immeasurable sense of comfort from the familiar, surrounding walls beginning to settle over me.

Steven yells to me from the front door. "Here's your last box and tote bag. I guess I never noticed how much of your stuff migrated over to my place. Sure is going to feel empty now." His voice lowers and slows with the last five words.

As much as I've been ready to get back into my house, he's not been looking forward to it. He's dropped hints about our close proximity being "just like it used to be" almost since the day I moved some of my things over. Like it used to be? Over thirty years ago? I argued that point the first few times, then let it go. Too much energy wasted with explanations that clearly did not resonate with him. I care too much about him to continue that battle.

As it turned out, the best solution to the housing dilemma was for me to move over to Steven's. We shared some wonderful moments. But, my plans had never been anything but to return home when the time came, and leave him to his own home.

"Guess that does it, Larissa."

He heads toward the door at nothing faster than a snail's pace, seeming to wait for me to catch up. I reach my arms out to hug him.

"I appreciate everything you've done—more than words can say. Opening up your house to me so that Everett, Gabby, and the kids could have their privacy, was, as I said when you first offered, far too generous. You gave them the gift of getting to know one another as a family before thinking about moving. It worked and I thank you. I know in my heart that they are ever so grateful as well. I'll call tomorrow with the details for Christmas dinner."

Steven kisses my cheek and walks to his car.

It takes me a few hours to put my things away and restore my kitchen to its previous arrangement. The counter that was strewn with bottles and bibs the last time I was over to visit the babies looks empty now.

I pour a glass of wine and plop into my favorite chair. Swirling it around in my glass, a thought interrupts before the first sip. I jump back up and scramble in my tote bag for the journal. This is the time. Time to honor the pledge I made over a year ago, and re-pledged before the twins arrived. No more empty intentions. Sipping wine and pouring out thoughts.

Dear Diary:

What a grand scheme of contradictions has unfolded in the recent past. No, actually, over the course of my life. There was a time when I felt I was either happy or sad, lonely or in a crowd, grateful or resentful. One or the other. One extreme end of the spectrum seemingly eliminated the other end. Now I realize that the ends are not disconnected. They are a continuum, there's a bridge between seemingly opposite emotions.

I may feel one way or the other, but at the same time, know with certainty that the extremes are short-lived. I may be heart-broken, overcome with grief, but at some point, the constant energy drain instigates an almost imperceptible change. I gently nudge myself back to existing without such gut-wrenching pain. Other times, like when Beth came for Christmas, or with the twins' birth, I will revel in boundless joy, feel an emotional high that elevates my spirit, but then the everyday demands pull me back. Back to the middle, to contentment.

I've learned that content is good enough. Content means I'm in some kind of equilibrium that is not exhausting, that allows an appreciation of the world around me. It's a decent place to settle in and live. Being content is my choice. It doesn't always come easily, but it is a way to survive.

Like when the twins were born. A little early, but healthy. Reason to be happy and grateful. Tears of joy streamed down my face when Everett and Gabby introduced me to Natalie Emma. Joy that they cared enough to honor Emma, joy in remembering how I felt when I first laid my eyes on her. Moments later, tears of regret for Emma's far-too-short life. I needed to settle in the middle of joy and regret. Then, the introduction of her twin brother, Emery. I was ecstatic they gave him the name that Everett received from dear Harriett, a loving tribute. Then, dragged down when I heard his middle name, Joseph. Make the choice to be content. The child is a blessing. A name must not bring on sadness that overshadows the happy introductions of my newest grandchildren. Life is too short to choose anything but the middle ground between tugging emotions.

It's not only surviving, sometimes it's actually thriving. Never thought I'd be able to say that a few years ago. I was so totally alone—had my friends, of course, but none of my children. Mother to three children, not one of them with me. Now, two of them are part of everyday life, and the four grandchildren besides. Every minute that Emma is not physically with us is a heartbreak, but I cherish her unmistakable presence. With that, I must be content.

And Steven? I don't know. We had the romance of a lifetime decades ago. Now, he's steadfast in his belief we can be that again. How can we? I'm not sure that's even anything that I want. Yet, I cherish his friendship and presence in my life, in Eric's life.

Regardless, my vow is to enjoy every moment of living while I can. Watching the children grow and discover is pure delight. I'm going to travel again and learn everything I possibly can about the world around me. I'm going to try to capture some of it in this journal, and maybe one of the four grandchildren will find it interesting someday. If not, just the act of writing brings me peace and time to be in touch with my soul. It's time now.

36

2021

Make no judgments where you have no compassion.
ANNE McCAFFREY

What was I thinking when I agreed to do this? The dampness under my arms feels like it's spreading to places I never knew I could sweat. I swore I'd never do it, never speak to total strangers about Emma, her death, or any other personal details about any of my children. No way I was going to let people grab on to the negative and close their hearts and minds to the rest. Yet, here I am.

A knock on the door is followed by a voice reciting in monotone, "Uh, Ms. Whitcomb, three minutes till you go on. Stand on this "X" on the floor until I give you the signal."

Does he have any awareness whatsoever that I am terrified, regret being here, and want to run?

Hardly any time lapses before the monotone voice announces, "You're on. Let's go."

My legs are wobbly, not totally sure how to get my body from back here to that arrangement of loveseat and two arm-chairs. Where the heck am I supposed to sit, exactly? My eyes are drawn to a giant image of Emma projected behind the seating arrangement. Emma in a yoga pose on the paddleboard. Emma, beautiful Emma.

Noise steals my attention from the image, what is that noise? Oh, my God, audience applause.

The familiar voice of the afternoon TV host breaks through my terror, "So, Larissa, welcome. Please join me. We've been talk-ing to Monica, here. She loved your daughter so much that she wrote a song about her. How does that feel?"

My mouth feels like I just finished chewing on dry toast. Somehow, I manage to croak out, "Amazing, terrifying, every-thing in between."

"Tell us about the amazing."

"I think it's amazing because Monica's song is beautiful. Amazing to me that a song can capture so much."

The audience startles me again with their enthusiastic applause.

"Wow—I guess most of you agree, or I, she, wouldn't be here." The applause continues and I don't know whether to wait or keep going. The noise fades quickly, so I don't have to be con-fused too long. They're waiting for me to fill the silence.

"The tribute to my daughter, Emma, is heartfelt and uplift-ing. It sends a message not only about her, but also about how a smile can change a moment, lift spirits, and build bridges between people. Yes, amazing."

The host smiles at the audience, then at me before continu-ing, "Tell us about terrifying."

"First, it's terrifying to talk about this to you, to anyone."

No applause. Now, I could definitely hear a pin drop.

"Secondly, because I'm terrified of the mean-spirited, judg-mental people in the world that seem to capture the public's attention, get the headlines. And when those people get ahold of the story of a young person whose life on this earth was over too soon, assumptions are made, judgments abound, and the person becomes *less than*. By that I mean, instead of the whole being more than the sum of its parts, the whole becomes less than its parts. All of the beautiful, endearing features that make up the whole person become forgotten; they're reduced to a cause of death. The circumstances of death replace the wonder of life. I find that terrifying, and well, despicable."

The host clears her throat, looks down at her notes, and asks, "That phrase—'wonder of life' would you please tell us about the wonder of Emma's life?"

The host makes the whole thing progressively more comfort-able. Before I know it, I've shared stories of Emma, talked about the signs I see that tell me she's nearby, even recognized Monica's monetary contributions to the special charities in Emma's honor. With that, she's introduces Monica to sing. As the words and mel-ody resonate throughout every corner of the studio, I'm taken back to the time that Monica performed it for the family on Christmas. The pure magic that surrounded us that day returns, and I savor every beat of the three minutes and thirty-three seconds.

Monica comes off the platform, embraces me, and we return backstage. *What just happened?* I look at the clock and see that twenty minutes have passed since I went out there, dreading the whole thing. Twenty minutes to describe precious Emma, the love of our family and friends that carried us when our knees hit the ground, and to show gratitude for the blessings in my life, despite the tragedies. It was nothing like I expected those minutes to be.

I hear pings on my phone across the room. The first message warms my heart, "Gamma, you rocked it! Love, Beth."

The second and third messages are from Eric and Steven telling me that our charities are being overwhelmed with online donations. The information had gone up on the screen at the conclusion of the broadcast, and people responded. The result of speaking was none of the negatives I'd feared. The song and its story resonated with kind, generous people, and they showed me the good in the world.

37

Beth: 12 years old; Summer, 2025

Those who dwell among the beauties
and mysteries of the earth
are never alone or weary of life.
RACHEL CARSON

She did it. She kept her promise. It took a few years, but it
happened. Lisa, Bobby, Louis, and I are all strapped in the
back; Gamma, Isabel, and Renee in front of us. We're one hour
away from being back home after more than five thousand miles
in this RV and twelve new states added to the list that I started
five years ago. To say nothing of all places we saw, people we met,
postcards we sent, and historical stories she read to us. While the
goal was to visit the places we'd researched and pitched way back
during that crazy year of COVID, the itinerary expanded more
than a little. Any time we were thinking about an unplanned stop,
one of the three adults would respond, "What's stopping us? It'd
be a shame not to see it while we're here!"

As he catches the outline of Atlanta's buildings ahead of us, Bobby mumbles, "Do we really have to go back? Being on the road is better than being home."

Of course, he'd say that. He hates school and doesn't really have anyone at home he misses. I mean, I've had a ball, but I miss the rest of my family. It was weird to be away from everyone. Weird, but fun. And, I'm ready to go back to school in a couple of weeks. I can't wait to tell Brittany and my other friends about the trip. They'll be jealous for sure.

My phone dings and I see a text from Dad. He wants to know my ETA. After I answer, he says Grandpa Joe is with him? What? Oh man, it didn't go so great last time Grandpa Joe visited the U.S. He's cool to me and Dad, but Gamma got pretty weird. I don't really get the whole deal. They told me the story of how, well, they sorta liked each other once a long time ago, but they acted like they were speaking in like secret code. Whatever. Not my problem.

As we pull in to the driveway with this giant RV, there's about a dozen people in the driveway. Holy shit! (I only swear to myself, in my head. Dad and Gamma say swearing makes me sound ignorant. Though once in awhile they let it slide.) It's almost like when we got back the day after I sprained my ankle on a trip to see butterflies.

Uncle Eric and Benjamin walk over to Gamma as soon as she's out of the driver's seat, and she bursts out crying.

Benjamin startles and looks up at his dad.

"It's okay, buddy, she's not sad. Those are happy tears—she missed you." Uncle Eric puts his arms around both Benjamin and Gamma and gives them one of his awesome bear hugs.

Running toward them, I make myself heard, "Hey, I want in!"

Then, Dad comes over with Emery and joins the pack. Before I can let go of Benjamin, I see Gabby carrying my little sister. Natalie practically jumps out of her mama's arms while she calls out, "Beth, sissy, you're here!" Hell, Bobby, you may like the road life, but I'm happy to be here.

Aunt Hilary comes over to join the welcome-back crowd. She offers, "Bet you guys are starving. Dinner is set up out on the porch, let's go get some." Yup—exactly like when we got back from that other trip.

Lastly, Steven walks over to the friend trio, first hugging Gamma, then Renee and Isabel, and says, "Hey, you three—you survived!"

Gamma smiles up at him and answers, "Better than survived. Other than being road weary, it was an amazing trip. Bobby and Louis didn't want to come back. They are true explorers. And Beth and Lisa? They read us interesting trivia about our stops, wrote in their journals almost every night. Maybe there will be a book about this road trip, huh, girls?"

Lisa rolls her eyes—that's how she reacts to pretty much everything now. I nod my head and secretly think writing a book would be amazing. It's kinda my dream. I just haven't told anybody yet. Sounds too crazy to even think about, but who knows? I hear Gamma's voice echoing in my head with one of her sayings about doing anything you put your mind to.

I lag behind the group to talk to my dad. "I thought you said Grandpa Joe was going to be here. What's going on?"

Dad puts his arm around me and says, "He did fly in, but he's staying at a hotel. Gabby and I went with the twins to visit him today, but he needed to get to bed early. He's in the U.S. to visit an old friend for a few days, and then he'll come back and stay at our house, when he can spend time with you. I didn't think it was wise for him to be part of the welcome-home thing today."

"Yeah, good idea. Gamma's tired and maybe not up for him visiting. I wish she'd get over whatever that is, but not my problem, I guess."

"Exactly. There are some things we just can't get involved in. It's weird for me sometimes too, but nothing I can do that will change it."

During dinner, it's Aunt Hilary who tells us we each need to say something about our favorite place on the trip. This time, all of us kids roll our eyes, but once Isabel starts with, "Gotta say, surprised the heck out of me, but those cliff dwellings in Mesa Verde were my favorite. The way they set up the displays, I felt like I could picture people right there having their dinner looking out over the valley. And the stars at night—stunning."

That got everyone into it, each spilling out details of their favorite sight.

"Now, last one. Beth—what was your favorite?"

"It's going to sound weird, but everyplace and no place were my favorites."

Gamma has a smile on her face and encourages me. "Tell us what you mean, Beth."

They might think I'm avoiding the question, but here goes. "Every single place we went was special for a different reason. Like Isabel said, for just a few moments, I imagined life in those cliffs. At Dinosaur Monument, the size of the dinosaur footprint made me realize how small we humans really are. Or in Colorado, when we saw the whole group of butterflies land in the wildflowers in front of us, I could hear their wings all flapping—like a hum. And there were hummingbirds everywhere as well. The day after that huge rainstorm in, I think it was Utah, the most gorgeous double rainbow came out. It absolutely glowed. It felt like my mother and Auntie Emma letting us know they were watching over us, protecting us on the trip. Telling us to enjoy every minute.

We also saw Natural Bridges National Park in Utah—Gamma and I have a thing for bridges, so seeing ones that were formed by water just blew my mind. I never thought about the power of water before, then Gamma read me something she once wrote about the resilience of water. Oh! And collecting our own crystals in Herkimer? I made earrings that I can wear to always remind myself of the trip. It's like Gamma told me a long time ago about why she likes to travel. I learned so much and loved being with you guys." I stop because I feel my throat tightening and I don't want to cry in front of everyone.

Everyone is quiet for a minute. Then, Dad breaks the silence. "Thank you to the ladies who took these kids on this adventure. You rock. I know I was the one who wasn't sure about the whole idea of you taking off by yourselves. I spent way too much time worrying about what could go wrong. The tires blowing out, or someone robbing you at a gas station, or who knows what the hell else. But, man, now I wish I'd been there. Next time, okay? Count me in."

He points at Emery and then Natalie snoozing in Gabby's lap, ruffling her hair while he continues on.

"Yeah, not so sure there's a vehicle big enough, but I'd like these little ones to someday have a great trip, like you just did. Gabby and I need to see some of the West—never been. What about your crew, Eric? We'll need to form a caravan to include the whole family."

Uncle Eric nods and I look over at Gamma. Her eyes look droopy and tired, but she's grinning like a Halloween pumpkin. She chuckles. "Well, if we're going to do that, better start the planning now for next summer. But, don't forget, Everett, I promised Beth that when she turns thirteen, she and I are going to start going farther—we're going to be international travel buddies."

He half-smiles. I know he's covering up. He gets so nervous whenever Gamma starts talking about these longer trips. It's a miracle that he ever went to Italy, especially back then, but if he hadn't, wow! Things would have been way different. No Gabriella, no little brother and sister, probably no Grandpa Joe.

But ever since he married Gabriella (I think that name is way prettier than Gabby), she tells Dad over and over that he should never keep me from traveling. Then she launches into a lecture about learning when you travel, different cultures, that kind of stuff. He usually shuts up because Gamma loves that lecture and joins in. When Gabriella first showed up, it was obvious Gamma didn't really know what to think of her. But I think her view on travel is one of the things that eventually won Gamma over. Daddy started being outnumbered when the two of them ganged up on him. I don't even have to pout or whine about wanting him to let me go along with Gamma any more, because the two of them wear him down.

Gamma also softened toward Gabriella quite a bit when Natalie and Emery arrived. We all did. Gamma says Emery is a little bit of Uncle Eric, and Dad, yet totally himself. Uncle Eric goes on and on about Natalie looking like Aunt Emma did as a little girl. I only know Aunt Emma from pictures, but it kinda seems like they're right. Gamma told me that a few times when I was younger, but now, my looks have changed, so not much any longer. I think that I look like my mamma's pictures—I barely remember seeing her in person, but I have lots of photos to remind me.

Daddy and Gamma are still talking, and I realize it's about this travel thing when I turn thirteen. It's a couple of months away, but judging by the details she's going into, I guess Gamma's been thinking about this for a long time!

"Yeah, so, on her birthday, I'm going to give Beth a travel tote. In the tote, there will be slips of paper, one with each letter of the alphabet on it. Beth is going to pick a letter. A few days later, after I do some research, I'm going to put five places that start with the letter she chose in the bag. Whatever place she picks from those five—eyes closed of course—that's where we're going as soon as she gets out of school for the year. How does that sound?"

Dad seems to be speechless at the methodology she's laid out. Just plain amazing. "I think it sounds great, Gamma. Makes the idea of turning thirteen even better."

Uncle Eric chimes in, "I can't believe you're not going to make Beth research the places that start with the letter. Not like you to take the research out of the picture. You always used to say that it's part of the learning."

"First—this is a birthday present, Eric. It's not like when I was her teacher back during COVID. Now, I'm the fun grandma. Second—I'm not removing research. I'm focusing her research efforts on the fun, yet essential details. Once Beth has the location, then her research starts. What hotels, what sites, all that kind of stuff."

"Know what I'd really like to research? The things that mean a lot to us together. Like finding bridges or places to be by the water or more butterfly parks!"

Gamma reaches for my hand and squeezes three times—her silent sign for saying "I love you." To the others she says, "Great idea, right?"

Eric's not ready to let it go yet. "How come I didn't get birthday presents like this? Picking countries out of a hat, or a bag, or whatever? I remember getting school clothes, or maybe a bike on a special birthday, like ten years. Surprise trips—none for me!"

Gamma laughs but kinda sounds like she's defending herself at the same time, "You had your share of opportunities. Then, when you got to be about fifteen, you started saying they were boring. Washington, DC? San Francisco? Pittsburgh? Sparking any memories in that brain of yours?"

"Yeah, okay. But weren't those all cities where you had conventions and Emma and I got dragged along?"

"Wow—how many kids would have loved being 'dragged along'? Seeing professional baseball games and amazing zoos and iconic sites?"

Uncle Eric walks over close to Gamma, wraps his arms around her, and says, "I wasn't exactly grateful was I? Emma was a way better companion, and I'm guessing Beth will be as well. You go, my favorite ladies on the planet!"

As soon as Uncle Eric backs off, Dad gets into the fray as well. "I think I'd like to stuff that bag with the places I approve of—reduce my stress over where you two are going to explore. Like if the letter is 'I,' maybe I'd just put Italy or Indiana in there five times so I'm sure you're going someplace that makes me comfortable."

Gamma starts to laugh, but her face shows that she's perfectly serious, "Your comfort, my darling Everett, is not the primary consideration here."

They go back and forth for quite some time while my mind wanders. Are there really places on this earth for every letter of the alphabet? And what *will* she put in for a letter like "I" or "A" when there are so many possibilities? Is it going to be states or countries or both?

"Hey, Earth to Beth! What do you think of this hullabaloo around your birthday gift? You in, or you want me to talk her into something a little less controversial?" Ever since Steven went along on our trip to Callaway several years ago, Gamma listens to what he has to say—well, at least as much as she ever listens to anyone; actually, maybe a little more than anyone else. She talks and lets out her own thoughts with her friends Renee and Isabel, but she listens to Steven. Point it out to her and she denies it, but it's true.

"I want to do whatever Gamma wants on this. She always says that a gift is something that comes from the heart—so if her heart wants to give me a trip, then that's what I want."

38

Beth: 22 years old; 2035

All journeys have secret destinations of which the
traveler is unaware.
MARTIN BUBER

*A*nd so it went. For the last ten years, Gamma did the destination-in-a-bag thing for each birthday. As the Dr. Seuss book says, "Oh, the places you'll go." We've been to India, Belgium, Sweden, Quebec (she cheated and added a city with the letter 'Q' so it wouldn't automatically be Qatar), Japan, Aruba, Peru, Cuba, France, and Malta.

In every one of those places, we found bridges and spent time by the water. All along the way, we had signs from Emma, my mamma, Gamma's parents—all assuring us our angels were watching over us. We saw the tallest bridge in the world in France, the longest suspension bridge in Japan, and some places had too many small, picturesque bridges over rivers to even count. And water, oh my heavens, did we see stunning bodies of water. The orange-gold sand of Malta was a magnificent place to relax at the end of our last trip and simply stare at the Mediterranean.

Got to hand it to her for putting Malta in there. The whole thing with her and Grandpa Joe was touch and go over the years. He kept trying to find a way into her heart, or at least a smidgen of warmth. But she wanted no part of it. She was civil and didn't ever stop Daddy and Grandpa Joe from their relationship, she just kept her distance. She confided in me that she felt 'morally obligated' to put Malta in the bag when it was the 'M' year. When I asked her what she meant by that, she explained, "Honey, he's your Grandpa and his country is part of who you are. I'd never deny you that. Plus, truth be told, I always wanted to visit Malta's historic sites. I also love going places that not many people think about going. We gotta check off some things on my own bucket list before I get too old to travel. Decided to leave it up to fate, and your hand, to decide!"

I hate when she mentions things like being too old. I just turned twenty-two and she's turning seventy this year. I want our trips together to continue forever. Maybe it's selfish, but I love our time alone together. Sure, she has taken the younger kids on trips all over the U.S., but she has always reserved the "birthday in a tote bag" for me. It's been that way so long, no one has ever questioned it. Each trip brings us closer together, if that's even possible to imagine. There's something different about Gamma when we travel. She's lighter, happier. She's game for anything, has endless energy, and infinite curiosity.

39

Beth: 32 years old; 2045

There is a land of the living
and a land of the dead
and the bridge is love,
the only survival, the only meaning.
THORNTON WILDER

What a shock. What a secret Gamma kept. When she called us all together two months ago to tell us she had arranged for her own hospice care, I couldn't breathe. Now it feels like I held my breath from that moment on. That is, until she took *her* last one a week ago. I thought my world would stop with her breath, but then I knew. I knew I had to keep going. I knew exactly what Gamma would say. Sad or not, tired or not, my kids need me—all of me.

Before her planned admission to the care home, she called and asked me to come over to the house. Not Dad, not Uncle Eric. She even kicked Steven out for the day. Just me. What a day that was.

Knocking on Gamma's door, I can't help but wonder why the sudden invite to her house? I saw her two days ago. But, when Gamma beckons, I come. It's always been that way, from the moment I met her so long ago. She reached her hand out for mine and we were bound.

Gamma throws open the door. She looks radiant. Better than she's looked in months. She's wearing layers of flowing fabrics in blues, violets, and moss green, her long, silvery hair drawn back on top, with tendrils spilling down her back. Did I totally miss a special date on the calendar? A day we're supposed to be recognizing or celebrating someone?

"Oh, Beth, come in my sunshine girl. Thank you for dropping everything and coming over. I sent Steven out on a phony errand just so he'd stop hovering over me and we can talk."

I shake my head at her reference to Steven. That guy has adored her for more than fifty years. Last year, when she got so rundown from being ill that she couldn't do everything to keep up the house, she finally let him move in. Of course, he practically had to sign a contract with her about the terms of living under the same roof, but he did it and has been around to help however she needs. Some days, she's a total whirlwind and refuses help, other days, she has to admit defeat and slow down.

"Let's go sit on the porch. My wildflowers are in full bloom and three hummingbirds have been appearing every morning, maybe you'll catch a glimpse."

"Gamma, want your walker? It's a bit of a hike out there." Some days she uses it, others not so much.

She looks at the apparatus with disdain. "Yes, I'd better. I hate that damn thing, but this week has been tiring."

She tells me to make tea while she makes her way to the chair where she watches for her beloved signs. Her bird/butterfly/

flower/stargazing sanctuary is her favorite place. We may have traveled the world, but she always craves her return home to this spot. Hutchinson Island was a close second until a year ago when the travel became too much of a chore. Even with Steven or Uncle Eric along to help her, the trip was no longer doable.

"Sit down, Beth. How are my greatest grandchildren?"

The greatest is of course, a joke. Neither my cousin nor the twins are even close to settling down with a family yet, so my three—Jeremy, Kevin, and Grace are the only greats.

"Good, crazy, fun, and exhausting. I dropped them off at Gregory's mother's house. She has a friend over, so they figure the two of them can handle the little trio." My mother-in-law is absolutely the best. Between her and Gabby, I have plenty of help.

"So, Gamma, what's all this about? By the way, you look amazing today."

"Thank you, dear. I look amazing because a weight has been lifted from my shoulders. I made a decision and I feel terrific about it. I'm telling you first because the others get a little weird when I tell them what I want. I know that you'll listen."

Her voice drops away as she stares at the tea bag hanging from her mug. "Really, how's this for a sign that I made the right decision? This tea bag says, 'Life is either a daring adventure, or nothing.' What do you think of that?"

"You told me that a long time ago, Gamma. Actually, you told Dad when you were convincing him to let me travel with you. You told him, and Gabby said it to him almost every day after. I know that it was Helen Keller who said it. But since I don't know what this momentous decision is, I don't know if it's a sign or not. Help me."

"Exactly why we're here. Just please, listen to me and don't react right away. It's the right thing, trust me."

Whenever someone asks you to trust them, it means the next sentences are going to be rough, but I had no clue how tough this was going to be.

"It's no secret that I love an adventure. Whether it's to the park down the street that you used to call the 'magic butterfly garden,' or a journey across an ocean, making every day an adventure is what has kept me going. Finding adventure and wonderment has made for a life of love and fulfillment. But, this blasted illness has made it harder and harder to find adventure, to have the energy to wonder at the marvels along the way. I'm tired, Beth."

I reach for her hands. The hands that reached for mine when I was six. The hands that took me to school, the hands that lifted me up when I hurt my ankle, the hands that led me through airport after airport, the hands that lovingly cradled each of my babies' heads. Her skin is thin and bluish, but she grasps at mine fiercely.

"So, the decision. I went to my lawyer this week and made sure everything is just the way I want it to be. I don't know if it will be four years or four months or four weeks, but when I get too tired, I want to go to a hospice facility. I don't want Steven—or you or your parents or Uncle Eric—to turn into day-to-day care providers. None of you needs to give me a bath or change my sheets when the time comes. I want you to visit with me, to look at photos, to play music, to tell stories, but not do the other stuff."

No, no, this can't be happening. "Gamma, what are you talking about? Big families take care of one another. I'm not going to let--"

She pulls her hands away and interrupts me. "No, my love, I'm not going to let your final memories of me be scrubbing my backside. My decision is made, papers are signed. I'm getting ready for embarking on my next adventure my own way."

And she did do things her way. After she gave me a few more details, she told me about journals and notes hidden in books and jewelry boxes that she wants me to look for and share with the others after she's gone. She says she wants us to think of looking for those as one more adventure that she is leading. A way for her to hang around awhile, after her spirit soars to be with the loved ones on the other side.

And oh, my gosh, the day she called the rest of them together? Thankfully, she and Steven had their own private discussion the night before, so he wasn't blind-sided, but Uncle Eric and Dad almost lost their shit. Each in their own way, of course. Uncle Eric screaming, "No way this is happening," and Dad wringing his hands and pacing, but ultimately, they had no choice but to go along with it.

Last week, I walked out to get something out of my car just as the sun was rising. It had been raining during my quiet hour—the hour when the kids are still asleep—and Gregory had left early for work, and I was sipping my coffee. Looking for yesterday's to-do list and not finding it, I went out to grab my tote bag. As I turned back toward the house, a rainbow appeared over the trees behind my house, and a pink glow emanated from the clouds bordering the spot where the rainbow met the tree line. I stopped and stared at the majestic display. No wonder Gamma always says rainbows are bridges from beyond. Bridges linking us to those who moved on before us.

Ten minutes later, Steven called me.

His raspy voice alerted me to what was coming. "Beth, I'm so sorry to tell you that your Gamma decided the adventure is done. I just got a call from the hospice house. They said she put down her cup of tea, smiled, closed her eyes, and that was it."

"Was it about ten minutes ago?"

"Yes, honey, I called you right away."

I knew the minute I saw that rainbow that Gamma was connecting with Auntie Emma. Whether Emma reached down from wherever she is, or Gamma reached for her, they connected, and the sky celebrated their reunion with its splendor.

And now, I'm over here every day, searching for those notes and journals. When I'd visited her the night before she passed on, she gave me more details. She told me that there were notes—one for each grandchild (except me)—and three journals. The journals are for Dad, Uncle Eric, and me. So far, I've found all but the one for me. Everyone else says they can't stand to look through her things long enough to search, but I'll be damned if that stops me. She took the time to write these things, I'll find them all.

I've got one room left before I either go through each room again or give up. That's not happening.

Then, I remember. One day a long time ago, I came home from school and looked all over the house for Gamma. I didn't see her anywhere. That scared me, but Dad came home and found her in the attic. He said the ladder was rickety and I should never go up. So, I never did. But, I bet Gamma did.

There's an old looking trunk—red with metal hinges—faded, but not at all dusty. Looks like it has been used more recently than most everything else up here. It's next to a window and a semi-comfortable looking chair.

My heartbeat picks up as I sit down to open it. It's mostly full of clothing—looks like stuff from the '70s—envelopes bound together with rubber bands, and right in the center are two journals. There are sticky notes on each in Gamma's writing. The one with butterflies on the cover says, "1981—I'll tell you about it in the other one." Okay, interesting. The other says, "To

Beth—always my sunshine girl." Once I told her that my mamma called me that, Gamma always used the term of affection at just the right times.

A folded note falls out from inside the cover of the one addressed to me. On the outside of the fold, another sticky instructs, "Read this first." Still doing things her way, from wherever she is!

Dearest Beth–

I'm guessing you found the other notes and journals already and are cursing me for making you wait until last. No, I just didn't want to take the chance that anyone else would find yours. I would never want any of them to misunderstand.

I love every one of you dearly. The reason that you are different to me is hope. You brought me hope when I needed it desperately.

In the journal labelled 1981, you'll read of my feelings after I lost my first baby during pregnancy with Steven. I'd had to give your daddy away several years before, so already felt like a failure as a mother. When another child couldn't be held in my arms, hope became elusive. Gradually, over the following years, I had more happy times—when Eric and Emma were born, I was elated and for quite some time, my life rolled along as I'd always thought it would. Hope was restored.

Then came the years of my mother, my father, then younger brother passing. If not for Eric and Emma, I would have been alone, given up. But, I kept going for them. I wanted their years to be joy-filled, not dragged down by a mom who could only think of her loss.

Emma passing and Eric leaving home stripped away that carefully built-up belief in hope. I recall several times becoming angry when people mentioned hope as the thing that makes us human, keeps us alive. I had none.

Those months felt like decades. Then, slowly, I found the resilience to try to live in the moment, not dwell on the past or worry about the future. Uncle Eric returned, Steven came back into our lives, then the miracle of reconnecting with your dad. With your dad, came you. With each reconnection and new connection, hope was creeping back into my life. Hope for the future with all of you seemed reachable.

Since that time, we have each made new connections, built bridges and found hope in unexpected places. The time of the pandemic was tough, yet without it, our lives and the people in it may have been very different. Would I have found out about the utter splendor of blue morpho butterflies? Would Gabby and the twins be with us? Would Monica's amazing song have brought us another connection to Emma?

I've shared more with you over your life than with your cousin or your siblings, not because of more or less love, but because of the way and when we became connected. You had lost your mamma, I had lost my daughter, and your dad needed help. You and I built a different kind of relationship.

I have no profound parting message besides a thank you. Thank you for all you brought to my life. Thank you for sharing the adventures. Thank you for listening to my philosophy, reading the tea bags, and believing in the signs. Thank you for being kind to your friends, loving with your family, and for bringing those beautiful greats into my life. They are the next beacons of hope.

Actually, yes, I do have parting thoughts. You know how I like to have little mottos to live by. Here's a few for you:

Find a reason to HOPE—*let it carry you through rough times*

Watch for the SIGNS—*they're waiting for you to see them*

Cross the BRIDGES—*you never know what the new connection will bring*

And, always, know that my LOVE *for you will not die.*

Gamma

My eyes catch movement at the window next to me. Of course, there's a bird feeder mounted on the ledge. Three cardinals are sharing the feeder's perch and looking in the window. Of course, they are.

I smile, close the journal and stroke the cover. Signs, connections, hope, and love. All the things she taught me and showed us her whole life. She captured it in four words.

Acknowledgments

I continue to be moved by the love and support of my dear family and friends every single day. Writing the books in this trilogy have allowed me to honor those loved ones, to discover new paths, and to live by the mantras that inspire me. Along the way, I have fallen in love with the characters and what they bring to Larissa's journey, much like what my loved ones bring to my own. *Bridges Between Our Hearts* is an ode to the deep, unconditional love between generations, a nod to the importance of connections, and a pledge to myself to live all my days with as much grace as possible.

I also wish to acknowledge the people who have helped me see myself as an artist. This role, or identity, is one I've only experienced recently. My education and career were science-based. I regarded art as something that others shared with me. Being regarded as an artist by fellow authors, visual artists, and organizations advancing the arts is a new identity and brings me great joy.

This book features three organizations whose missions speak to Larissa. It is no secret that while the story of Larissa is fictional, I often draw upon my own life experiences for inspiration. Over the last few years, finding organizations to support, in honor of loved ones, has been rewarding to me personally, and hopefully, is a way to enrich the lives of others. The organizations in *Bridges Between Our Hearts* are not fictional and speak to me, to my soul. Each of them, in their own unique way, honor the importance of the healing power of water and its integral role in the human experience, the quality of life. Take a moment to investigate them and see if they speak to you as well.

One Last Wave Project
https://onelastwaveproject.com/

> Our mission is to harness the healing power of the ocean to help grieving families coping with the loss of a loved one who had a deep connection to the ocean or nature. We memorialize your loved ones by carefully etching their names onto surfboards that are hand-shaped locally and then carrying them out into the ocean to catch a symbolic one, last wave as an active way to honor them in a place they loved.

Florida Oceanographic Society
https://www.floridaocean.org/

> Florida Oceanographic Society is a non-profit organization founded in 1964 with the mission to inspire environmental stewardship of Florida's coastal ecosystems through education, research, and advocacy.

Saunders Finger Lakes Museum
https://www.fingerlakesmuseum.org/

> Our mission is to inspire appreciation and celebrate the cultures and ecology of the vast Finger Lakes Region.

Finally, thank you to Mary Neighbour of MediaNeighbours and Sarah Maxwell of BlueViewsStudio. You add all of the elements that I cannot. I'm deeply grateful.

Questions for Discussion

1. Larissa is conflicted when she first finds out about the song written in honor of Emma. Why do you think that is so? Have you experienced something that most people consider to be good, but have felt conflicted about it?

2. Everett reveals information about what is happening in Italy that makes Larissa wonder if he is being truthful with her. Do you think she deals with that effectively? Why or why not?

3. What are some of the good consequences of the COVID pandemic for Larissa and her family?

4. Renee and Isabel are both long-time, special friends of Larissa's. Compare and contrast their personalities and the ways in which they support Larissa.

5. Eric and Everett have only known one another as brothers for a few years. What events indicate the ways in which they are growing closer?

6. How does the circumstance of Everett being an adoptee influence his decisions and his relationships? Do you think that he and Larissa have acknowledged the impact on his choices?

7. Over the span of twenty years, Larissa and Beth become very close. What are examples of the shared experiences that bring them together?

8. Besides the physical bridges that are crossed in this book (George Washington Bridge and others), what other kinds of bridges are important to the story?

9. What do you think of the visit between Larissa and Beth in Chapter 39? Have you or your loved ones made decisions about the final stages of life that cause mixed reactions within your family?

About the Author

Jennifer Collins began writing novels in 2020. A retired physical therapist and college professor, she became inspired to write after experiencing the loss of several loved ones. Her debut novel, *Comfort in the Wings*, and its sequel, *Wonders in the Waves*, are now joined by *Bridges Between Our Hearts*. These emotionally satisfying books tell the story of Larissa and her family as they navigate the joys and tragedies of life.

A testimony to the poignant works she has created, Collins recently won the MartinArts Council 2023 Award in the Literary Arts. Next on her writing docket is a non-fiction study of people who have discovered rewarding life paths in spite of predictions they would never succeed. *Funny Thing About Luck* (working title) is a tribute to the author's father and others like him—people with drive and commitment, who strive for accomplishment against the odds.

Collins spends her time writing and running a family business alongside her eldest son. She does both from two residences—her long-time family home in upstate New York and Hutchinson Island in Florida.

Printed in the USA
CPSIA information can be obtained
at www.ICGtesting.com
JSHW010816170124
55526JS00007B/44